*She was hunting a master of death . . .
and running for her life.*

DR. KURT WALLNER

**The S. S. Doctor of Auschwitz.
One child had escaped his atrocities.
Now she's a lovely woman
soon to meet him again.**

JUDITH WEBER

**A beautiful, talented young pianist.
When her father was murdered she knew she was
the last person alive who could take revenge on the
medical butcher of Auschwitz—the last person
Wallner would now have to kill. Vowing to
get Wallner before his henchmen get her, Judith
runs headlong into an icy tangle of love and intrigue
spanning two continents—and into a chilling encounter with her own past. She knew the man
she hunted, but she didn't know
how well . . .**

MORTAL ENCOUNTER

*The final act in an inhuman tragedy
spawned by the Nazi terror!*

MORTAL ENCOUNTER

PATRICIA SARGENT

AVON
PUBLISHERS OF BARD, CAMELOT AND DISCUS BOOKS

To Caroline and Daniel

The characters in this book are
imagined; the historical background
is authentic.

MORTAL ENCOUNTER is an original publication of Avon
Books. This work has never before appeared in book form.

AVON BOOKS
A division of
The Hearst Corporation
959 Eighth Avenue
New York, New York 10019
Copyright © 1979 by Patricia Sargent Zegart
Published by arrangement with the author.
Library of Congress Catalog Card Number: 78-62040
ISBN: 0-380-41509-7

First Avon Printing, March, 1979

AVON TRADEMARK REG. U.S. PAT. OFF. AND IN OTHER
COUNTRIES, MARCA REGISTRADA, HECHO EN U.S.A.

Printed in the U.S.A.

MORTAL ENCOUNTER

One

In a public phone booth on Eightieth Street and Lexington Avenue a man spoke with controlled savagery into the phone.

"They went all the way, the goddamn barbarians. . . . Yes, he's dead. They finally killed him—the poor bastard. Damned Neanderthals. No brains, only brawn. If they'd let him alone, he'd have led us to it. . . . Christ, we all ask for it one way or another. . . . You're damned right, I'm complaining—sloppy, inefficient, unprofessional idiots. . . . Only that it will take some doing to clean up the mess they left. . . . I've got someone working on it. . . . Yes, she'll be easier, all right. She's there now. . . . Don't worry about that. I'll be in touch."

The man dropped the receiver onto its hook and stepped outside into the cold rain of the December night. Across the street on the fifth floor of the twenty-story apartment building he could make out a dim shadow outlined against bare windows. He didn't have to see more than that to know what the apartment looked like. He didn't have to see the woman to know what she looked like.

Hunching deeper into his coat against the icy rain, he pulled a flask out of his pocket and with a quick, practiced hand twisted the lid off and tipped it to his mouth, recapped it, and slid it back into his pocket. Then he leaned against the booth and waited motionless in the shadows.

Two

Motionless, the woman waited too, head bowed, arms wrapped tightly across her chest as though containing a force inside herself that might explode, while the ghosts of the dead man's nightmare, silent and unseen, moved from their concealing shadows to stand beside her, binding the living to the dead, directing her feet along his dark path in search of justice. Or vengeance.

She was a tall woman, large-boned but slender, and under ordinary circumstances, remarkably beautiful, with eyes that would have been quick and intelligent and full of humor. But these were not ordinary circumstances at all and the beauty and intelligence were hidden under the white mask of shock which pulled the translucent skin taut across the slender, high-bridged nose and broad cheekbones. The wide, full lips were pressed together, bloodless. Around her face fell the heavy black hair, and through it, large, dark eyes stared blankly at the brutalized body of the man where he lay at her feet. He was sprawled on his back, his battered face twisted sideways on the corded neck, and his eyes were fixed in that blind stare of the dead on an empty chair in a dark corner of the room.

Who had sat there, asking questions between the beatings?

Blood mixed with spittle on the rug beneath his mouth gave evidence of the internal injuries he had received and his swollen hands with their broken fingers lay palms up in an attitude of supplication.

2

Deep round wounds covered the bare soles of his feet and the acrid smell of burned flesh haunted the room. The spittle and blood were still wet. He had not been dead long, and considering the apparent strength of the man's big body, it must have taken him a long time to die.

The room in which he lay had received the same brutal treatment—a place torn loose from tranquil moorings and cast into a violent sea. Desk drawers tilted at crazy angles, papers spilled over and littered the floor. Upholstered chairs, turned upside down, had been slashed and torn. Books from the bookcases had been flung to the floor; records and stereo equipment smashed. Even the window drapes had been pulled from their hangings and lay on the floor in crumpled, pathetic heaps.

The city's normal sounds drifted alien and unheeded into the room. Traffic noises from the street below blended with voices from a nearby apartment singing in slightly drunken joy, "God rest ye merrie, gentlemen, let nothing you dismay . . ."

Judith, my darling, remember what I've told you. If it happens, and no matter how it happens, don't waste time mourning for me. You must hang on to all the control you have and you must move fast.

The voice in her ear, as clear as though the dead man had spoken aloud and brought her a message she had been waiting for, broke through her trancelike state and sent her quickly to one of the piles of books. She knelt down and looked through them, selected one, moved on to another scattered pile, and then another, seeking and selecting. Once she paused to straighten a worn, leather-bound book, her large, square hands caressing it as she placed it on the bare shelf.

Though she breathed with rapid, shallow breaths, drawing the air in through half-open bloodless lips,

3

though her face was still white and drawn with shock, every movement was without panic, governed by a kind of mechanical assurance, as though she had rehearsed this a hundred times before.

When she had finished her search, she held six books in her arms. These she carried to a small suitcase that stood by the door and dropped them on top of a few articles of clothing. She snapped it shut, pulled on a heavily-lined raincoat that had been tossed over one of the torn chairs, took a broadbrimmed rain hat from the coat pocket, and put it on.

Suitcase in hand, handbag over shoulder, ready to leave—to leave him like that, the exposed savaged body in the savaged room . . .

She swayed away from the door, dropping the suitcase and purse, and with a kind of drunken gait disappeared into the bedroom to return immediately carrying a blanket. Kneeling down, she began to cover the body with great gentleness as though he might still be able to feel pain. Her own hands began to shake as she pulled the blanket over one of the man's hands. The shaking grew, convulsing her body. She closed her eyes and moaned, unable to hold it off —the storm of emotion that seized her, tossing her helpless, like a leaf in a whirlwind, leaving her blind and shattered for a seemingly endless time, until somewhere in the apartment, a clock chimed one musical note. Like a signal. The shaking eased, she opened her eyes. The storm was over.

"You can let go now, Father," she whispered, raising the cold hand to her lips. "I promised to finish it, and I will."

She left then, closing the door behind her with a final firm click.

She hurried along the empty corridor past the elevator, making for the stairway—walking seemed safer somehow—while the slurred voices of the revelers from the next apartment swung into a version of "Silent Night, Holy Night."

Stumbling once or twice she made her way down the five flights of stairs and pushed through the heavy firedoor into the lobby. After the dimly lit stairway, the glittering, glaring splendor of the big Christmas tree in the center of the room assaulted her. Flinching, she half-ran past its relentless cheer to the outside door. It was after one in the morning. The lobby was empty except for the elderly doorman in his chair tilted back against the wall, dozing, making soft, snuffling sounds through his nose. She opened the door, and the rasping of the hinges woke him. He jumped up guiltily, sending the chair clattering against the stone floor.

"Miss Weber—good evening. Let me get that for you, please. Miserable out there tonight, isn't it? Pity you have to go out in it."

More clatter while he straightened the chair and reached for the door, moving as fast as his old bones would allow, chattering at her all the while to cover the fact that he had been asleep at his post. He should have been awake, he knew that, but he was an old man . . . "Not like Christmas, is it? A little snow would be better than this cold rain. Everyone likes to see a little snow at Christmastime."

They stepped out together into the raw night.

"You'll want a taxi, of course. You don't want to be walking at this hour." He blew a shrill blast on his whistle. "How's your father, Miss Weber?"

"My father . . ." Brooding dark eyes stared at him vacantly.

"Everything all right with him? He doesn't seem to go out as much as he used to."

In a bleak voice, Judith said, "He's fine," and wondered how the two words could pass her lips without choking her. If she were to explain what lay in that fifth-floor apartment . . .

"Of course, he's getting older like the rest of us, isn't he? Slowing down a bit, as we all have to."

. . . Police would come swarming over the place, asking questions that called for answers. Her search slowed, deflected, perhaps stopped altogether. "Fine," she whispered again, feeling pain at the thought that he must lie there under the blanket waiting for strangers to find him.

"A real gentleman of the old school, Professor Weber is." The wrinkled eyes scanned the street for an empty cab and he blew another blast on his whistle. "That's what I was saying earlier tonight to his friends," he went on.

"His friends?"

"Old friends. Hadn't seen him for years, they said. Wanted to know if he had changed. I said gentlemen like that don't change."

"These friends—how many were there, Pete?"

"Three."

"What did they look like?"

"Nothing unusual about them. One was small, one was big—well, maybe *he* was a little out of the ordinary. Real big, he was. Hefty, you know? Looked like a wrestler. He didn't talk much. Fact is, he didn't talk at all. The third one did all the talking—a very pleasant-spoken gentleman. But there was nothing unusual . . ." Uneasiness showed in the old eyes. Something in her manner . . . "Is there anything wrong, Miss Weber?"

It seemed logical that the big one, the silent one, had performed that long, slow torture. And the pleasant-spoken gentleman? Had he sat in the chair asking the questions?

White-faced, she began to shake her head, she began to form the words of the monstrous lie that nothing, nothing was wrong, but the old man had already turned away and was blowing his whistle at an empty cab pulling around the corner. He chuckled as he helped her in, his uneasiness quickly forgotten.

"Didn't want me to announce them. Said they'd like to surprise him. Nice to see old friends, particularly at Christmastime."

Judith stared at him as he placed the suitcase on the floor at her feet. An old ruse and it still worked. Chat with a lonely, garrulous old man; get friendly, confidential . . .

"Shall I tell the driver where to go?"

Pete was the enemy. He didn't know it, but he was the enemy.

"Where would you like to go, Miss Weber?"

"Where?" Sudden panic clutched at her throat. Where to go? She had to have time to think, to plan. She felt off-balance, disoriented, thrust into a gray area where friends became enemies and familiar places strange and dangerous country. For her father it was the end of a six-month nightmare, for her, the beginning. Fear numbed her mind but the fiercely demanded pledge bound her to him and not for a moment did she consider breaking the promise.

"The Plaza," she said without conscious thought.

Pete instructed the driver and was about to close the door when Judith reached out and pressed a bill into his hand.

"Good-bye, Pete," she said, and added mechanically, "Merry Christmas." And God forgive you, it wasn't your fault.

"Thank you, Miss Weber." The old man looked in surprise from the bill in his hand to the woman, but she didn't answer. She had turned her face away and no longer seemed aware of him. There was nothing for her here any longer.

Three

The cab followed so closely behind hers it had to be more than a coincidence. Through the rain-misted rear window she peered at it. It must have joined hers the moment she left the apartment building, and yet if someone were following her, would they make it so obvious? She had no way of knowing what to expect. It was like being in a different world where they played by different rules. I'll study them, she thought grimly, and learn them.

Paranoid, her father had said. *Every time you look over your shoulder, you'll see an enemy. You'll become paranoid.* And with a terrible bitterness he had added, *Like me. At least everyone tells me I am, and perhaps they're right. I'm no longer sure.*

And now we know that you weren't paranoid, Father—and at what a cost. Judith twisted away from the window and huddled in a corner of the seat until the cab pulled up in front of the hotel.

She paid the driver, picked up her suitcase, and moved quickly up the broad stone steps. At the entrance she paused for a brief, furtive glance over her shoulder. The other cab had also stopped in front of the hotel and the passenger lurched out onto the sidewalk, saying something to the driver in a thick, slurred voice as he fumbled in his pocket. He dropped a bill and picked it up, swaying clumsily. A drunk? Perhaps. . . . If not, he was giving a very convincing performance. For her benefit?

8

She turned her back on him and entered the hotel, shaking her head firmly at the porter who came forward to take her bag. He was wearing a Christmas smile on his face, a sprig of holly, jaunty, in his button hole. Returning his smile with a stiff, meaningless one of her own, she hesitated a moment, gazing over his shoulder at the elegant Palm Court, at the little tables occupied by the elegant people. The string trio was playing a medley from Franz Lehar's *Merry Widow*— gay, lilting melodies. A carefree scene that she had once been a part of—sitting at one of the little tables with Max, soft lights gleaming on white skin, on his blond head bent toward her. . . .

Suddenly she became aware of the curious glances directed at her as she stood there tall and white-faced in the drab raincoat and wrinkled hat. She took a few tentative steps toward the reception desk, then stopped, brushing a vague hand across her face as though waking from a dream. What was she doing here? Had she come to say good-bye? Foolish. She had to learn to live all over again in another and darker world.

A quiet, safe place where she could think, plan— that's what she needed. But not here. Like her father's apartment, there was nothing for her here anymore. Abruptly she swung around and headed in the opposite direction toward the public telephone booths.

"Miss Weber!"

The voice came from some yards behind her but Judith didn't pause. Perhaps they would think they had made a mistake. The voice called again and this time it was closer. She turned unwillingly.

"What a pleasant surprise, Miss Weber. I knew I couldn't be wrong. Even from the back it's hard to mistake you."

"Mr. Babcock."

"Max isn't with you, of course," he said, making it

9

a statement. "He's in Washington, slaving over hot cables, hmm?"

He smiled up at her. She was almost a head taller than he was. Judith forced an answering smile and held out her hand without enthusiasm. He took it and held it in his soft, small one.

She had never liked this man for no reason that she could explain. Though he was Max's superior in the State Department as well as an old friend of her father's, she never called him by his first name. Something about him forbade intimacy.

He was a short, slender man, a well-preserved fifty-seven, with a round, bland face and smoothly tanned skin that spoke of sunlamps rather than Caribbean sunshine. Always meticulous in dress. Too meticulous, perhaps, as though he were trying to prove a point. Babcock was a bachelor, a man who seemed singularly alone, and he poured all his energy into his work. There had been some unsavory gossip a few years ago concerning his relationship with another man but there had been no proof and the gossip died for want of anything to feed on. If his taste in sexual matters wasn't socially acceptable, he concealed it with great care. Altogether a cold and careful man.

Judith could offer nothing to the conversation except a nod and a stiff smile from time to time. She scarcely heard what he was saying as she watched his lips form words which made no sense to her in the world she now inhabited. He was talking of how much he depended on Max, of how on the rare times when he took time off to be a little frivolous here in New York, Max had to be at his post in Washington.

"We can't both be away from the office. There's no getting away from the harsh realities of our times. The Middle East has become a bad habit—been with us so long we'll never be rid of it. But never mind about all that." He put a hand on her arm. "You must join me and my friends for a nightcap."

Judith shook her head wordlessly. She must get away. How helpless she felt without some reasonable explanation of why she was here at this hour, alone. She gestured to the suitcase on the floor and said, "I really can't. I'm on my way to visit a friend and I'm very late. You'll have to forgive me."

He accepted her lame excuse with a suitable sound of regret but she wasn't to be let go that easily. "Then you must let me get you a taxi. Max would never forgive me if I let you go off alone."

He reached for the suitcase and Judith, in a panic, almost grabbed it from his hand, saying, "No!" so sharply that the man froze for a moment in his half-bent position and stared up at her in amazement.

"I'm sorry," she apologized. "Sorry." And she seized on the first excuse that came to mind. "I've been preparing for a concert, and, as always, it exhausts me, makes me feel I'm strung on a wire."

She tried to smile without much success while Babcock straightened up, his face rather flushed.

"Of course," he said rather stiffly. "I should have realized. I saw your father in Washington a few days ago and he told me. How is he, by the way?"

The string quartet was playing a Strauss waltz, the violins singing in frantic three-quarter time. The room, the people, the music seemed suddenly to press in on her, suffocating her.

"How is your father, Miss Weber?" he asked again from what seemed a great distance. "He didn't look at all well when I saw him. Thin and pale. I was quite concerned."

Had her father told her he had seen Babcock last week? She couldn't remember. It seemed terribly important for her to know, but she couldn't remember anything. She was confused and frightened and the brown eyes were watching her, very guarded. Or did she only think they were?

11

"I suppose he's just been working too hard. Leo always did overwork himself. I hope he isn't really ill."

"Ill? No!" Was she shouting? "No, he's not ill. I'm very late, Mr. Babcock. Please excuse me." And she added the small social lie with as much grace as she could muster, "It's been very nice to see you."

She left him abruptly, her movements more awkward than graceful as she hurried to get away. The man's eyes followed her until she passed out of sight, turning down the side corridor which led to the public phone booths. Finally, with a vague frown on his face, he returned to his guests in the Palm Court.

Four

She could feel Babcock's eyes on her back as she walked away, and the cold that gripped her was too deep to be dispelled by the warmth of the lobby. It pressed achingly against her heart. She had become an alien in her own familiar land, isolated from it by that tortured body, by the burden in the suitcase, by the wasted, beckoning fingers of a thirty-year-old ghost.

If she could wish it all away . . . ! Wipe out the past six months, erase the story in the *New York Times* that had plunged her father back into the old nightmare. If she could have him back with her in that peaceful, booklined apartment, his eyes not haunted and remote, but reflecting his gentle smile. A fire in the fireplace, sending cheery warmth into the room; Max there, perhaps, and talk of ordinary things. . . .

Suddenly, angrily, Judith shook her head and pushed the thoughts away. She couldn't afford them. They would inform against her, make her weak and vulnerable, expose her to failure.

At the phone booth, coin in hand, she hesitated. For the moment Max was out of reach. Even at this hour he might be at his office, or if not there, than at some official function, and how would she be able to find the cruel words to explain? She would see him tomorrow. Making a quick decision, she dialed a New York number, had a brief conversation, and hung up. As she reached for her suitcase, the man in the next booth turned toward her with a slow, deliberate move-

13

ment and looked at her. He was a big man with broad, powerful shoulders and a square, solid face that was devoid of expression. He no longer seemed drunk. The man from the taxi was quite sober and in full possession of his wits. From under the low hat brim, his cold, gray eyes stared steadily into hers.

Suitcase heavy in her numb hand, Judith ran. Clumsily, she ran from the phone booth to the side exit of the hotel, pushed through the door, stumbled down the rain-slicked stone steps. The suitcase banged against her legs and threw her off balance. A voice said, "Steady there." A hand on her arm. She jerked away and darted across the street through the rain and the traffic. There was a screech of brakes, an angry voice shouting, "Where the hell do you think you're going?" Heedless, she ran on toward her destination— a cab just dropping a fare. She climbed in, ignoring its Off Duty sign, slammed the door, and pushed the button down to lock it. She leaned back, gasping for breath, and closed her eyes.

"You blind, lady? I got my Off Duty sign on."

She opened her eyes and looked into the dark, hostile face of the driver. "I know, but—"

"I'm finished for the night. You'll have to get another cab."

"No, please—"

"You heard me, lady. It ain't fair. My sign was on before you climbed in. We're not taxi drivers all the time, ya know. We're human beings, just like you. We got homes and families, we get tired and hungry just like everyone else!"

She leaned forward and spoke urgently. "I know you're tired, but couldn't you please—just as a favor. It isn't far."

She reached into her purse and took the first bill that came to hand. It was a twenty. She held it up for him to see.

"You in trouble—the cops?"

"No, no, nothing like that. It's only to Central Park West. You don't have to pull your flag."

"You wanna get *me* in trouble with the cops, is that it?" He pulled the flag with an angry jerk and reached for the bill.

"When we get there. I'll give it to you when we get there," she said, and sat back, shocked by the distrust she already felt for everyone who crossed her path.

"You're actin' pretty peculiar for someone who's not in trouble," the driver was saying sullenly. "What number do ya want?"

She told him and he headed for the Park entrance, turning up his radio volume until a chorus of sweet voices singing "Deck the halls with boughs of holly . . ." filled the cab and drowned the city noises.

Judith huddled into a corner of the seat, twisting once to look out of the rear window. If he was following, he wasn't making it obvious this time.

She heard her father's voice, a whisper in her ear: *They are professionals, not supermen, no, but very skillful. Good at staying close to you without your being aware of them.* (But this man was making no attempt to conceal himself. How, then, could she be so sure he was her enemy?) *Don't make it easy for them, but don't worry about it any more than you can help. Chances are they won't take any positive action until you have the letter and the photo in your hands to complete the manuscript.*

And then . . . ? When she had the whole indictment in her hands . . . ?

She met the driver's eyes briefly in his rearview mirror. Ridiculous. She would question every strange face she saw. Who was he? A black man who drove a taxi and didn't like white people. His face had relaxed a little, she noticed. It had lost some of its rigid lines of hostility, perhaps because of the Christmas music and the thought of the gifts the extra twenty dollars would buy for his children.

He traveled at top speed through the park and hit a red light at the exit onto Central Park West.

"Not much like Christmas," he said in an almost friendly tone. "Don't really want snow, but it would be better than this freezing rain, and the kids like a white Christmas. Ain't Christmas otherwise."

Judith didn't answer. She probably hadn't heard him. She was gazing out of the window, arms crossed, hugging herself tightly, her face white and tense under the broad-brimmed hat.

He shrugged and swung onto Central Park West and a block later pulled to a stop in front of an old gray stone building. With a soft "Thank you," Judith handed him the twenty and climbed out of the cab. She glanced quickly up and down the street before she disappeared through the arched entrance.

Five

Shadows in the courtyard took sinister shapes as Judith walked swiftly to one of the half dozen entrances that circled the yard. She hadn't seen anyone on the street, yet now footsteps sounded loud and menacing on the sidewalk. Her trembling fingers reached into her bag for a key ring. She fumbled a key into the lock. After what seemed an incredibly long time she was able to turn it. She flung the door open, stepped inside, and slammed it shut behind her.

The footsteps moved softly outside, then silence. She thought she could hear someone breathing on the other side of the door, or was it her own breath gasping in her throat? This wouldn't do. For the second time in a short while she had been panicked by fear. If this continued, she would never be able to finish what he began, and that, she realized with sudden shock, is exactly what they want. A campaign of terror to force her to drop the search, let the letter rot where it is, no one the wiser.

"I will not stop," she said in a loud voice. "I will not."

Feeling better somehow for the foolish words, she pushed away from the door and headed for the stairs, ignoring the elevator.

Yes, all right, she thought, they know where I am. That shouldn't be a surprise. This would be the first place they would look when they found she wasn't at her own apartment. And if fear was going to be her constant companion, she would have to learn to live

17

with it as Leah had learned all those years ago, alone and running, playing her deadly game of hide-and-seek until the final betrayal and the midnight pounding on the door and the brutal hands of the Gestapo.

That's what had haunted her father, waking him in the night, moaning sometimes with a pain no drug could ease.

She had reached the fourth floor and she rapped softly on the apartment door. After a moment of watchful waiting, she saw an eye appear at the little peephole, a disembodied eye, bulging through the small, round glass. It disappeared, a lock was turned, a chain released, the door was opened, and a woman took her hand and drew her in. She was a small, fragile woman with large blue eyes in a young-old face; her hair, ash-blond, was kept so by skillful artifice.

Before she spoke, Judith replaced the chain and turned the lock. Then she leaned down and kissed the woman on the cheek.

"I'm sorry it's so late, Mother."

"It doesn't matter, my dear. I don't sleep well, as you know."

"I had nowhere else to go."

"Nowhere. . . ? Your own place? Your father's? I don't understand . . ." The woman's thin, sweet voice faltered as she looked from Judith's grim, white face to the suitcase she carried. She drew in her breath with a sharp hiss and though she repeated in a whisper, "I don't understand," there was fearful understanding in her eyes.

Judith murmured, "I think you do, Mother," and walked away from the woman into the living room. There was no way she knew to soften the blow but she could postpone it for a moment for both their sakes.

Her hand was stiff from holding the suitcase. Dropping it beside the brocade-upholstered sofa, she flexed her fingers and looked around, accepting now without question the unfamiliarity of a familiar place—this room, like a painting she loved but hadn't seen for a long time. It was all soft shades of blue and gray with touches of pale yellow. Like her mother, beautiful and expensive, everything in harmony. A small Christmas tree, still bare of decoration, stood in the corner where it had stood every year for as long as she could remember, just beside the fireplace where the dying embers of a fire sent the right kind of warm glow into the room. In an opposite corner in an alcove the gleam and polish of the old Steinway seemed to beckon to her seductively. A serene and orderly haven with the dirt and frantic noises of the city held at bay by sealed windows and heavy draperies.

What was here that could possibly have any connection with the vicious assault on her father and his apartment? Nothing. Perhaps least of all this porcelain-delicate woman who stood in the entrance hallway watching her, the blue eyes wide and dark with fear, the fine, frail hands fluttering in front of her in a vain effort to ward off the blow she knew was coming.

"Your face—it's like his when he saw that picture—so hard, angry—"

"He's dead," Judith said in a flat voice.

The woman bent forward, half collapsing, let out a low moan, and stumbled toward Judith for sympathy and support, but there was none in her daughter's cold face.

"He's dead," Judith went on relentlessly. "In a horrible way—oh my God, how they must have hurt him! Burned and beaten, his fingers—"

"Don't, Judith, for pity's sake, don't!"

"—every one broken. Three of them—Pete said there were three of them—"

"Don't, Judith, I can't bear it—"

"*You* can't bear it!" Judith's voice was harsh and

19

ugly. She ignored her mother's out-thrust, appealing hands, uncaring or unaware of the other woman's pain, so great was her own. Again, as in her father's apartment, the trembling seized her, shook her, broke her control, and, like water rushing through a broken dam, the harsh voice rushed on and on, piling word on word, image on image, as though she were under some terrible compulsion to hurt this woman and at the same time to rid herself of an intolerable burden.

Her hands to her ears, her eyes half-closed, Sheila Weber backed away until she tripped and fell against the piano bench, her outflung hand crashing against the keys, sending loud discord echoing through the room. It died away, leaving the room filled with a deathly stillness.

Exhausted by her outburst and ashamed of it, Judith stood motionless by the sofa, her arms hanging limply at her sides, her head bowed, while the woman remained half-crouched on the bench, an expression of both fear and compassion on her face.

Finally in a thin, exhausted whisper, Judith said, "I'm sorry, Mother, I'm sorry. This—isn't what I came for—at all. I needed a refuge. Forgive me, please, I didn't mean to hurt you like that."

"I know. It's a bad dream, my poor darling, a bad dream."

"Yes."

"And you'll carry it with you wherever you go."

"I'll have to."

"*You'll have to.* My poor Leo—how could he do this to you?" Her voice rose. "You'll have to go on with this thing that he started—though he's dead—though they killed him?"

In the same tired whisper, Judith said, "Because he's dead. Don't you see? There are two to avenge now—his death and hers."

"No, I don't see at all. After—have you thought of

what comes after? If you're not destroyed in the process, what will you have accomplished? It won't bring Leo back to life. It certainly won't bring *her* back. It's nineteen seventy-four—she's been dead for thirty years!"

"I know all that, Mother. This is the way it is," Judith said mechanically, as though repeating a lesson learned by rote. "We make certain choices, take certain steps—"

"And fulfill our destinies. I've heard all that."

"One must do what has to be done. I promised Father."

The woman sprang from the piano bench, flinging an accusing hand at her daughter, her voice rising thin with hysteria. "How like him you are! God help you, how like him you are." She paced the room with quick, angry steps that were soundless on the thick pile of the blue carpet. "Six months ago he stood there where you're standing, told me he had to leave, he had to find some way to bring this man to justice— a hard and lonely way, he said. Something has to be done, do it. No thought to other people, to conse- quences." She halted abruptly in front of Judith. "Now you're his instrument of justice, is that it? He's handed you the flaming sword. Even your name—*Judith, we'll call her Judith.* My God, he couldn't have planned that! He didn't know the man was alive then. Oh— what can I say . . . ?" She broke off suddenly, expelling her breath with a long sigh. All spirit seemed to leave her. The blue eyes filled with tears as she stared helplessly at the tall woman who stood pale and silent under the attack, her eyes unnaturally bright.

Softly she said, "Sit down, Judith." She put her hands on her daughter's shoulders and with gentle pressure forced her down onto the sofa. Sitting close beside her, she clasped Judith's hands tightly in hers and said, "I don't want you to do this."

21

"Mother—"

"No, wait, listen to me. I'll try to be calm, really I will. What's done is done. It's you I'm concerned about. Think about this—until six months ago, Leo and I had a good marriage. He was—content, I suppose, is the word I want—perhaps even happy sometimes. Oh, I don't mean he didn't think of Leah. She was there— always, I'm sure—in the background. You don't forget people you've loved. You don't forget what's happened to them, but—life has to be lived. He was able to keep it in the background where it belonged—no, let me finish—where it belonged. He had built a good life. His work at the university was important, satisfying to him. His family—I don't have to tell you how much he loved you and Andrew—and me. I helped him— not enough, perhaps—but I tried. And then—that picture in the paper . . ."

"You're saying," Judith said with a brief tortured smile, "that if Father hadn't seen the picture it wouldn't have existed, the man wouldn't have existed."

"For Leo—yes, why not!"

"But he did see it."

"And all the horror came to life for him again. It was destroyed—suddenly, overnight—everything that meant anything to him, to me, was swept away."

"How clever they were," Judith whispered. "How clever. For twenty-six years Father thought he was dead and all the time he was living in comfort some- where—working—respected—Doctor Karl Klausing, medical scientist—Doctor Kurt Wallner, medical sadist."

"Ah, why can't I make you see!" Sheila Weber said, staring helplessly into her daughter's face, which had grown remote and withdrawn. She had a sudden urge to seize her by the shoulders and shake her until she had severed this bond between Judith and the dead man and dead woman. Hopeless, she thought. It wouldn't do any good. "I can't make you see, can I?" she said. "Or you don't want to see. I'm not thinking of that awful man. Let God demand payment from him—if there is a God. But suppose Leo hadn't seen the picture—he had many more years of life ahead of him. Now it's finished—"

The woman's thin shoulders began to shake under the elegant blue velvet robe and tears spilled down her cheeks. "My poor Leo. Everything changed for him. He was a different person, a stranger. I tried to understand, to go along with it, but there was no living with him after that. There was no room in his life for me any longer. He was living with ghosts—with Franz, with Leah, with her murderer—"

"Her murderer isn't a ghost. He's very much alive."

"He didn't want me with him, Judith. I made him uncomfortable in some way. There was only one thing left for him—his implacable hatred, his implacable drive for revenge."

She paused a moment, seeming to gather her forces for the next question. She twisted her delicate hands into a tight knot and whispered, "Who did this to him, Judith?"

"Ah . . . who? I don't know." The words came out haltingly over the image they could both see of the tortured body. "Someone—some organization—protecting the doctor—protecting the people who brought him here. Foreign-born or home grown—I don't know. Father never really said, only hinted. I must find out—"

"Find out!" Sheila Weber cried wildly. "Let it alone, Judith, let it alone. If they did this to him, what will they do to you?"

"I made him a promise." It was all there in those words. Better than that she couldn't explain. *If I can't finish it,* her father had said, *I entrust it to you. I have no right to do that, but I have no right not to either.*

"You can forget it. Leo would forgive you."

23

With sudden, savage passion, Judith half-shouted, "Would you have him live—this monster!"

Unable to sit still, she rose and paced the room with long, rapid strides, hugging her arms to her chest, her eyes almost feverish in the pale face, her voice harsh with emotion.

Pursued by demons, Sheila Weber thought as she watched her. Like Leo. She shivered. The warm room seemed suddenly cold.

"Father might forgive me, yes," Judith was saying, "but how could I forgive myself? Now that I know what he felt for so long—that these people—these— monsters like Wallner and those who helped them, knowing what their crimes were, should not be allowed to go free of punishment no matter how many years it takes to find them in their comfortable hiding places. No statute of limitations for these criminals— ever. Father believed that—was obsessed with it. It wasn't just vengeance for Leah. That was part of it, but if that had been all, he could simply have taken a gun and shot the man. He wanted to do it legally on sound evidence. Have Wallner indicted and brought to trial. Everything out in the open. These —the greatest crimes against humanity—not to be forgotten—ever. I know why he felt like that now. When I found him dead—like that. You don't know— you didn't see him. . . ." Her voice faltered, faded to a tired whisper as she finished. "Knowing they could kill him—the way they did. My father—a man without fault—a man—" Judith stopped speaking abruptly, leaned her arms on the mantel over the fireplace, and bowed her head over them.

"Oh God, it's hopeless," Sheila Weber said. "Is there nothing I can say to make you change your mind? You've inherited his disease. I saw it in his eyes. I see it in yours."

Both women had exhausted themselves and silence

lay heavy in the room. A log in the fire split and fell from the grate. Mechanically, Judith leaned down and adjusted it with the poker. As she straightened, she heard her mother's light step behind her and felt her hand touch her shoulder gently.

"Come into the kitchen. I'll make you something hot to eat. You need it, I'm sure. And take off that wet raincoat. You'll catch cold." Her voice was almost as light as her step had been.

She's put away the horrors for a while, sealed them up, and now it's time to pay attention to normal things, Judith thought, everyday things like food and drink and wet raincoats. How could she expect her mother to cope with this dark, brutal thing? Sheila Weber's father had protected her from anything unpleasant, kept her in the finest cocoon money could buy. And when she had married, Leo Weber had taken over the protector role. Even the smallest things. . . . *Let's not tell your mother just yet. We don't want to upset her.* That's why he had moved out of the apartment six months ago—so as not to upset Sheila.

I came for a few hours of rest, for time to plan. Surely I didn't expect anything else? Judith asked herself as she followed her mother into the white-tiled kitchen.

There she found her busy with eggs and a stainless steel bowl and wire whisk. On her lips was a small, fixed smile and in her eyes a silent pleading: Don't let's talk about it anymore.

"I'll make you some scrambled eggs. That's the quickest and most nourishing thing I can think of and then you must get some sleep."

Scrambled eggs and sleep—was that the cure for her disease?

Butter was sizzling in the frying pan when the phone rang and Judith reached out automatically to the instrument on the wall. Then she jerked her hand back.

25

It was after two in the morning. Who would call at this hour? Her mother had put the bowl down beside the sink and was again twisting her hands together, watching Judith and waiting, like a child, to be told what to do. The horror had returned.

Whoever it was persisted. The phone rang and rang. "You'd better answer it, Mother," Judith whispered. "Pretend you've just come awake. I'm not here." She added urgently, "Under *no* circumstances am I here."

Sheila Weber nodded and picked up the receiver and said, "Hello," tremulously. "This is Mrs. Weber speaking." Then she was silent, listening. Judith could hear only enough to make out that it was a man's voice and that he was speaking in a flat, calm tone, but whatever he was saying had no calming effect on Sheila Weber. Her face paled and she turned wide eyes in strained appeal to Judith.

"I don't understand—I thought—no, are you sure? . . . Yes, of course you are. . . . Tonight? It has to be tonight? . . . Yes, you'll want to do that. I'll—I'll be waiting then. . . That's very kind of you.

"It was the police," she said, almost before she had hung up. "The police. They want me to—they found Leo's body. They want me to—"

Judith said it for her. "Identify it."

"Identify it, yes."

The butter in the pan on the stove was hissing and spitting and Sheila Weber turned the gas off.

"They said there was a fire—his pipe, perhaps. Leo died because of the fire. He made no mention of—of torture."

"A fire . . .?"

The smell of burned butter lingered in the room and Sheila Weber opened the window wide and stood there staring down into the dark, wet street. A horn honked, a voice shouted something. She shivered and closed the window.

26

"They knew you had been there," she said vaguely.

Deep in thought, Judith answered with equal vagueness, "Pete, of course."

"They had already called your apartment. They said if I heard from you, I should ask you to get in touch with them. A Lieutenant—or was it a Sergeant —Bloomfield? I don't understand. I can't seem to put it together somehow."

"I can," Judith said. "It's all very clear." She rose and with the same savage energy that had possessed her before, she paced the kitchen floor, hugging herself, looking too big for the little room. The bright light threw a huge, grotesque shadow of her on the wall and her mother thought again of the pursuing demons.

"How clever they are! They wanted me to find him —a warning, a threat, the beginning of a campaign to frighten me off. They waited, hidden in the apartment somewhere—or in the hall, perhaps. Well, I'll not be frightened off!"

"How did they know you would come?"

"I had been staying with Father. He was not well these past weeks—not eating, not sleeping. He needed me. They knew that, of course, and tonight after I left the apartment—a fire—enough to destroy the evidence of torture and search."

"I don't know. How could that be?"

"How could what be?"

"How could they set a fire and destroy just enough?"

Fiercely Judith said, "Why not? They're experts. They must have experts in that field as well as others. One of them called Pete in time to tell him about the fire, of course. I don't know *how* they did it. I only know they *did* it. My God, what kind of people—" She broke off at the look of horror on her mother's face and something else as well—a shadowed doubt.

"No!" Judith whispered hoarsely as she stared into

the other woman's eyes. "You don't think—you can't think that I imagined this, dreamed it, somehow? The picture is all here in my mind, indelible—"

"No, no, of course you didn't imagine it." The answer came too quickly. "I—I just don't know what to think." She walked toward the door, avoiding Judith's eyes. "I have to change," she said in a low voice. "They'll be here soon."

"Then I must go. They can't find me here. They'll have questions and there's nothing I can tell them. It will only mean a delay." She moved toward the door where her mother stood, then back again to the center of the room. Suddenly unsure and frightened, she slumped into a chair at the kitchen table and put her face in her hands. Go? Go where at this hour? She had counted on staying here until morning.

"There's nowhere you can go at this hour," her mother said with surprising firmness. "You stay here. I'll go down to the lobby and wait for them there so they won't have to come up here at all."

"Yes, all right," Judith said in a muffled voice, without looking up. She felt her mother's hand on her shoulder briefly before she left the room.

Not long after, she reappeared in the doorway, dressed now to go out in slacks and sweater over which she had pulled a mink coat. Judith remembered when her father had given it to her for a Christmas present. She had grown thinner since then, smaller somehow, and she looked like a child wearing her mother's coat.

Judith went to her and put her arms around her. "Only answer the questions they ask you and don't worry. Don't tell them what I've told you. There's time enough for that after I've found the letter. And don't tell them you've seen me."

"That's a lot of 'don'ts.'" She put a hand to Judith's cheek and smiled unsteadily. There were tears in her

28

eyes. "I wish I were a stronger person. You look so tired. Rest. I won't be long, I hope, and I'll—" She glanced over Judith's shoulder at the stainless-steel bowl with the two eggs floating in it. "I'll make the eggs for you when I come back."

She turned and left and Judith heard the door of the apartment click softly shut behind her.

Six

The apartment seemed unnaturally still after her mother left. The sounds in the street had diminished. Only the rain could be heard hissing against the window.

In the dead of night . . .

Judith stared down at the littered table in front of her, at the circle of white styrofoam, the evergreen branches, the broad red velvet ribbon, glittering ornaments, and gilt angels. They waited for her mother to fashion them into a wreath. She frowned at them as though she were trying to place them in some context that had meaning for her.

"God rest ye merrie, gentlemen . . ."

In the dead of night on another Christmas they had come for Leah to set her on the sure, slow descent into hell. The long journey in the boxcar to that unique and terrible railroad station that was for arrivals only. . . .

Leo Weber had been haunted by that memory for thirty years and in the dead of night they had come to him. Now it was up to her.

She left the kitchen, went to the living room, opened the suitcase, and took out the six books she had brought from her father's apartment. She placed them in a neat pile on the sofa and sat down beside them.

Six books. *The Maltese Falcon* by Dashiell Hammett, a collection of short stories by Frank O'Connor, *Sea and Sardinia* by D. H. Lawrence, *Seven Gothic Tales* by Isak Dinesen, *The Centaur* by John Updike, and *The Stranger* by Albert Camus.

Memorize them, her father had instructed her. Hammett, O'Connor, Lawrence, Dinesen, Updike, and Camus. *Memorize them.* And she would repeat over again the titles and authors, like a child learning a lesson at school, to please him, to take away the driven, desperate look from his face. *If you have to find them, it won't take long. It will be automatic.* And it had been.

He hadn't known, had he, that his books, a collection of a lifetime, would lie in torn and scattered piles on the floor?

Into each of these six books Leo Weber had inserted a chapter of his own, properly printed at the university press. Had he done the actual printing himself? He had been almost fanatically secretive those last few weeks. It was easy to believe he would have distrusted all eyes except his own and she could picture him working feverishly at night under a dim light, his eyes burning in a white face, the tall, bony body bent forward in concentration.

As head of the history department it would have been easy enough for him to do it and only keen eyes and long searching would have spotted the insertions. *They* hadn't found them, had they?

Why six books? And why *these* six out of the hundreds in her father's library? Had it been a random selection or had there been a reason for it?

They were questions that would come back to trouble Judith but for now she pushed them away and concentrated on the first part of her father's story that she found in the Hammett book.

Essentially it was material she already knew. It described how her father had first met Leah when she came to Heidelberg early in 1939 to give a concert. Leo Weber was a student at the university and living with Franz Halman, a young instructor in the philosophy department. Halman, who was married to an

American journalist, was Leah's cousin and her only close living relative.

That is, Franz Halman *had* been on the staff of the university until the Nuremberg Laws had decreed that Jews must not be allowed to "pollute" pure German culture. After he was fired, he and his wife, Mary, lived on her earnings and what little Franz could eke out in private tutoring jobs.

Her father wrote:

It was love at first sight and I don't apologize for the cliché. I can still remember that passionate excitement when I saw her for the first time in Franz Halman's living room, seated in her natural place beside the piano, one hand resting on the keys. She was a small, dark-haired girl with glowing ivory skin, a vivid, shining kind of person, half-girl, half-woman. She was only seventeen then but a proud and assured seventeen. She had already been a concert artist for three years when we met.

To discover that she loved me as well . . . How all-generous fate seemed to me then. For a few short weeks we walked together in that separate and radiant world that only two young people in love can inhabit.

Though we must have seemed very young to my dear friend, Franz, he made no objection to our marriage. On the contrary he was delighted. Not just for the usual reason—that he loved us both—but because in that strange and terrible Purgatory that was Nazi Germany he thought that his talented young cousin's marriage to an American, and one who was not a Jew, would protect her. And she was after all, he also reasoned, only half-Jewish. How little all that mattered later! Defined by the dictionary of the Third Reich,

Leah was a *Mischlinge*, a mongrel. And for these, the Nazi medical scientists had special plans.

Our marriage ceremony was a small, almost secret affair in the Halmans' home and after the briefest of honeymoons, Leah went off to finish her tour which would end in Prague in March and I was to meet her there.

I have never forgiven myself for not going with her. Do I even remember why I didn't? Vaguely. I had my studies, this would be just a brief separation, then we'd be together for the rest of our lives. None of it makes sense now! Franz and I agreed, too, I recall, that Prague seemed a safe place for her to go. We were wrong but how could we have known?

It was March, 1939, and a few days after she arrived there with the orchestra, we were cut off from each other and I never saw her again. On the Ides of March in the early morning hours, Hitler's troops marched across the border into a betrayed and passive Czechoslovakia.

My last message from her was a hurried note smuggled out to me which told me not to worry, that she was all right, safely hidden with friends. "We'll be together again soon—soon! I love you, my dear Leo, my dear husband. I love you!"

Like a man on a rack, Leo Weber had written Leah's story. Judith had watched him helplessly as each day passed and his face grew thinner, his body more gaunt. Obsessed . . . Her mother was right. He had been obsessed. He ate little, slept less. After he and her mother separated and he had moved to another apartment, Judith had taken to spending nights with him whenever possible and she would hear him tossing in his bed, moaning and muttering. In the morning his face would be ashen, the skin drawn taut over the big bones, the blue eyes shadowed and remote, focused on some desolate landscape only he could see.

He would talk to her, or she would make him talk, about the guilt that rode him like a demon, the guilt and hatred that were destroying him. In the end, perhaps, might he not even have welcomed his torturers, welcomed the pain to purge him of his guilt, knowing he was suffering, if only in small part, as Leah had suffered?

"I'm not personally responsible for her death. My reason tells me that. Emotionally, never in all these years have I been able to come to grips with it. I could have tried harder to find her—"

"How? How could you? You were hundreds of miles away, cut off from her by an army. You were an American in a country already hostile to Americans. You had no way of knowing where to go, what to do."

He had waited as long as possible at Heidelberg, hoping for word from his young wife, writing frantic letters to German and American officials. Laying siege, practically, to the offices of those he thought could help. Nothing. The Americans were kind but powerless; the Germans, correct, cold, and as uncommunicative as a stone wall. He lived in a vacuum. The intellectual community of the university had already been decimated and the place was sterile and empty.

Franz Halman had sent his wife, now pregnant, to Switzerland to wait for him while he prepared to leave the country. A Jew, an outspoken Socialist and anti-Nazi, Halman had made many dangerous enemies, and when he said good-bye to Leo Weber one dark night, he walked out of the house and into the waiting arms of the Gestapo. Dachau and Treblinka, way-stations to Auschwitz. It was only one small human betrayal added to the millions being committed throughout Germany.

When Judith played for her father, his eyes would

rest on her face, but the agony in them told her he was seeing Leah, small, exquisite Leah with her long black hair curling softly over her shoulders; large, dark eyes in the small oval face intent on the keyboard. Leah's first concert in Paris at fourteen had sent audience and critics alike into raptures. "Who would think that one so small could draw such sounds from the piano!" wrote one critic. "A female Mozart," raved another.

"Poets and peasants, rich men and poor men, the talented and untalented alike—all went into the mass graves and furnaces," her father had said, his blue eyes burning in his white face, and he had asked for her promise then—that if he couldn't finish his task, she would do it for him.

"A person's mind can't encompass *all* the horror. One can't mourn statistics. I mourn for one. Never mind how many years have gone by, it's only yesterday. Now that I know he's alive, I can avenge her."

It was the first time he had demanded her spoken promise. Until then there had been a subtle, unspoken agreement between them, but, driven by some premonition, he had told her, "You will finish it. You will bring the evidence together and see that this man is put into the dock. You must do it for me and for her."

The shadow of something sinister had come into the room as she gave him her promise, her face as tense and ashen as his own. Now he was dead. You couldn't break a pact with a dead man and how could she have broken it under any circumstances? Through the years, for as long as she could remember, her father had brought the dead girl alive for her—how she had loved caviar and walks in the rain and Bach, the perfect composer, how she held her head and gestured with those long, slim, beautiful hands—until Judith felt as close to her as to anyone living, even Max. Max . . .

The thought of Max lifted her spirits a little and she rose and paced the room, her body awkward and stiff with fatigue, telling herself that she must concentrate on today and tomorrow, not yesterday, get the job done as fast as possible. Tomorrow she would see Max and the burden would be shared. He would surely have information for her about her father's research trips to Washington and something of what he found.

She paused at the window and pushed aside the heavy drape, peering at the apartment house across the street where some lights still showed. She glanced down at the cold, wet street, almost deserted, then started to turn away when she saw the glow of a cigarette. She wouldn't have noticed him otherwise. Through the thick curtain of mist it was difficult to make him out but she thought she saw his head jerk up toward the window. He was in the dark doorway of the fine-foods shop her mother liked to patronize, and she stood framed in the light of the room. She stepped away quickly and pulled the drape closed with a trembling hand.

Don't worry about them until you have the letter and photo in your hands. They'll be watching and waiting for that.

"You keep talking about *they!*" Judith's fear made her voice shrill. "You must tell me who *they* are."

"I'm not sure."

"These are people who would protect the doctor's identity and past, is that right?"

"Of course."

"But why now—so many years later? What difference does it make? Most people are tired of the whole business, bored with it. Those who had anything to do with the Nazi brutality, on the receiving or the giving end, want to forget it."

He had almost shouted at her, "Not all!"

"Not you, Father," she answered softly, "and a few like you, but there's a grown generation and a growing one who don't know and don't care. It's history, turn the pages. Perhaps they don't even believe it. So why now should anyone be so concerned with protecting the doctor?"

"Some out of fanatical devotion to a cause. There's an American Nazi party—you know that. Others worry because they have names and careers to protect. It still carries a stench—thank God—to have had anything to do with those monsters."

"You suspect who they are?"

"I'm not sure."

He had been holding something back, but though she pressed him, he would only say stubbornly, "When I'm sure, I will tell you."

A few days later Leo Weber had made a final trip to Washington and when he returned he had seemed to be in a state of shock, stunned, moving like a sleepwalker. He had mumbled something about telling her as soon as he put some pieces together but they had silenced him before he could do that, and, more important, before he could tell her where the letter was. Now she must put the pieces of the puzzle together, with only hints of where they belonged.

Drawn back to the window against her will, she peeked through a narrow opening in the drapes and saw the lighted butt of a cigarette arch through the air into the wet street where it flickered and went out. It had been a casual, arrogant gesture as though the watcher didn't care if he were watched.

There's no point in worrying about the man in the doorway. There's nothing I can do about him, Judith told herself as she returned to the couch. And perhaps he has nothing to do with me. But she didn't believe that. It was like throwing a dog a bone to quiet him— she was quieting her fears. Who in the world would keep a harmless rendezvous out there in this weather? Perhaps, she thought, he'll catch pneumonia, and she was immediately shocked at the satisfaction the idea gave her.

She picked up the O'Connor book which held the second part of her father's story.

Neatly folded and stapled to the first page she found the news article and accompanying photo that had appeared six months ago in the *Times*. The photo was small and old, not very clear, of a younger man who would be in his sixties now. The story was full of "it is alleged" phrases about the doctor and certain sterilization experiments in the Nazi death camps many years ago. It was by-lined by a reporter named Theodore Rosen. Ultimately, Judith knew, her father had planned to give his story to this reporter if he could find no other way of handling it.

I accuse this man, Doctor Karl Klausing, whose real name is Kurt Wallner, of the murder of my wife, Leah Weber, née Halman, by performing the most brutal kind of medical experiments on her which resulted in her death. Others had a hand in her murder but he's the one I want brought to justice. Justice . . . Is there any system man could invent to cope with the crimes of monsters like this?

I had believed, I had hoped, he had died at war's end as painfully and as alone as she did, or if not, then my prayer was that I would find him one day and be the instrument for bringing him to justice. In 1948, however, I was told by a State Department official that he had died of natural causes. I believed him at the time and only recently have I learned that it was simply a matter of his family having him declared legally dead, thus closing his file officially. You can't prosecute a dead man.

Someone had given him a new set of papers, a new identity, so he could emerge from his underground hideout, a man without a past and whose present was manufactured innocence. I believe

I know who these people were. They helped him immigrate to this country, knowing what he was. I shall deal with them later.

Do not be deceived. These are not the ravings of a madman. I have documented proof—a letter written by my wife along with a photograph of the man. They are safely concealed and I will produce them if I live long enough to do so. I have already been warned off this exposure. Never mind. If I can't see it through to the end, someone else will.

When Franz Halman reached me after traveling hundreds of miles across Germany to Holland in the winter of 1945, he was more dead than alive but he had accomplished something that amounted to a miracle. What he brought me gave me more pain than I have ever known. How could it help but do so? I had little time to think of it then because Franz was very ill, dying, though I didn't know it at the time, and I had to see that he was cared for. During the few days he spent in the army hospital near Maastricht, he told me about Leah's death.

I had never stopped looking for her. When I finally was forced to return to the States after the fall of France, my reason told me that she must be dead but my heart clung to the hope that she could have remained hidden and safe with her friends in Czechoslovakia.

I kept in touch with Mary Halman, who had returned from Switzerland with her small son, Max, at the same time I had. Together we haunted the State Department but there was no information they could give us about Leah and Franz. The two might as well not have existed—or have existed only in our desperate imaginations.

After Pearl Harbor I joined the army, exploited a few of the right friends in Washington and with my knowledge of Germany and its language, I had no trouble being assigned to G-2, army intelligence, and I was off to England and the long years of the war. More and more information filtered back from the continent of the horrors of the death camps. In my agony it became my war, a private one, for one purpose only—to find Leah if she were still alive, to avenge her if she were dead.

D-Day. The continent. I moved as our armies moved until after the Battle of the Bulge I found myself in a small town in Holland on the German border where I had remained to tidy up before moving my office and staff into Germany. The war was almost over. Many of us knew that.

It was there that Mary Halman's letter reached me, hysterical with joy. Franz was alive. Somehow he had stumbled into a British refugee camp. I contacted my opposite number in British intelligence, asking him to give all aid and comfort to Franz Halman and help him on his way.

It's true, I could have gone myself, but fear held me back, fear of what Franz might have to tell me. Perhaps if I had gone. . . ? But conjecturing about the *what ifs* of something that's past is a trap. There's no point to it.

I was due for some leave so I sent my staff on ahead to set up quarters in Germany with Bob in charge and I waited.

Judith closed the book at the end of this second part and placed it in the suitcase.

Here at least was a place to begin—at the small town in Holland where Franz Halman had come to her father. Is that, perhaps, where the letter was hidden? She felt a surge of excitement, of confidence, but it was lost almost immediately as the question came to her: how many small towns in Holland were on or near the German border?

She sighed and reached for the third book but a light step in the hall outside stopped her and the sound of a key in the lock told her her mother had returned. At the same time the phone began to ring.

Seven

"Don't answer it!"

Sheila Weber swung the door closed and leaned against it, wild-eyed, gasping for breath.

The phone rang and rang while Judith stared from the instrument to her mother, bewildered.

"Don't answer it," her mother repeated in a hoarse whisper as she whirled around to the door and locked it, pushing the chain into place with stiff fingers, muttering frantically, "It's him, I know it." Then she ran to the window with crooked, unbalanced steps and pushed the drape aside as Judith had done a short while ago. She was looking not at the shadowed doorway of the shop directly beneath, but at the lighted phone booth on the corner where a man stood holding the receiver to his ear. Through the rain from that distance it was impossible to tell whether he was talking to someone or just waiting. Both women stood in tense silence and watched and waited while the man in the booth waited and the phone shrilled angrily.

They saw the man replace the receiver and the phone stopped ringing.

Delicate fingers gripped Judith's wrist with surprising strength and Sheila Weber pulled her away from the window, closing the drape so no crack of light showed through.

Still gripping Judith's arm with fingers that were so cold Judith felt it through the sleeve of her sweater, she went on, "Yes, I knew it! When they brought me home—the police—just now—*he* was coming out of the courtyard lighting a cigarette. He didn't say anything, of course. The policemen were with me. He only looked at me from under the brim of his hat. The light of the match was on his eyes. They were cold and hard and, Judith, I knew—my God, what are we going to do?"

"How do you know that's the same man?" Judith asked, gesturing toward the window, knowing as she asked that it was a foolish question. The phone business was too much to be a coincidence.

"I know it is! What are we going to do?"

Judith removed the hand from her arm, saying gently, "You're not going to do anything, Mother. I'll rest for a while; then I'll leave. No one will bother you once I'm gone."

"No, don't leave me alone!" Shudders ran through her body like convulsions, so violent she could scarcely stand.

Judith, instead of removing the mink coat as she had started to do, wrapped it tightly around her mother, half-dragged the woman to the sofa, and then hurried to the small bar in the corner of the room and poured a large brandy into a glass. Sheila Weber, face in hands, rocked back and forth, gasping out words between sobs.

"I'm not brave. I didn't want to look. I didn't want to know. I'd never seen anyone—burned, tortured. It wasn't Leo, I kept telling myself. I didn't want it to be. But it was. The ring—the one I gave him for his birthday—you remember?"

"I remember." A small ruby set in heavy gold, elegant and expensive on a swollen, broken finger. "Drink this." Judith held the glass to her mother's lips, half-forcing the brandy down her throat. Some of it dribbled down her chin onto the soft fur and she wiped it away with her hand.

"They said they'll have to double check with dental records—that sort of thing—to be sure. But it doesn't matter. It was Leo. They found him on the couch. His pipe—they said he must have fallen asleep. . . ." A long, drawn-out shudder passed through her body and she fell silent.

"Yes," Judith murmured, stroking her mother's head lightly—it was wet with rain—while she thought with pain of someone, one of *them*, picking up her father's body without gentleness, dragging it to the couch . . .

"Pete—you were right—someone called Pete and said they saw smoke." Sheila Weber's voice was less convulsive, the shivering had eased, the brandy had done its job. She looked up at Judith. Her face was ravaged and tear-stained, but her eyes had lost their wild look. "The police can't figure it out. They couldn't find anyone who said they'd called. Even the people next door . . . But it was noisy there. They'd been drinking a lot."

"Silent night, holy night . . ." Judith said, hearing the drunken voices in her mind.

"It's finished," Sheila Weber said, her voice thin and drawn out with fatigue. "It's finished." She rose, staggering slightly, and walked toward her bedroom, the mink coat slipping from her shoulders and trailing on the floor. "There's no help for him now, my poor Leo. You get some rest, Judith." She closed the door behind her.

You're wrong, you're wrong! Judith thought angrily, staring at the closed door. To finish what he began— that's the help he needs and I'll give it to him.

Leave your mother out of it, her father had told her. She's a kind and loving person, but weak, and I've made her unhappy enough. Leave her out of it.

Leave her to heaven. . . . But no, Judith thought, her anger draining away. She has no thorns *to prick and sting her.* Her lack of strength is her only sin, and

44

anyway, what could she have done against her father's morbid drive?

She went to the sofa and packed the books into the suitcase. A few hours' rest now. The remainder of the manuscript she would read with Max or on the plane. At least she had a starting point—a small town in Holland. Near Maastricht! Of course. Her father had taken Franz Halman to a hospital near Maastricht. That narrowed it down a little. Could *they* know about the small town on the German border? Had her father talked about it to anyone who might betray him? Drawn back to the window against her will, she parted the drapes and looked down into the misty street. It was empty now and the phone booth on the corner was dark. No watcher there.

No watcher at her father's apartment either. No mysterious good Samaritan with X-ray vision happening by at just the right time to make the phone call about a fire set with such malicious care. That part of it was finished for everyone.

Eight

After four hours of rest, Judith rose, her movements slow and drugged with fatigue. Call it rest, she thought, for want of a better word. She had lain, wide-eyed, in the dark, alert to every sound in the street, unnerved by every knock of the radiator. Once she had dozed and dreamed, quickly and dreadfully, of soft footsteps, of a broad-shouldered, cold-eyed man standing over her and saying, "It's finished, don't you know that? There's no help for anyone now. You'd better just answer the telephone, answer the telephone. . . ."

She had awakened, bolt upright in bed, her body cold with sweat and like the child she had once been in this room, afraid of the shadows in the dark, she had switched on the bed lamp and left it on for the remainder of the night.

She showered, letting the water steam hot over her body, shocking it into wakefulness. Then she put on the black knit slack suit again with the white turtleneck sweater. Not the smartest costume in the world, she thought, but that was all to the good. With the drab raincoat and hat there was an anonymity about it and except for her height . . . Well . . . She shrugged that away as there was nothing she could do about it.

She checked her purse. It held a large sum of travelers' checks and her passport, which was up-to-date, something her father had insisted on. *I don't know what might happen, when they might make a move. Best to be prepared.* She was as prepared as she ever would be.

At the door, suitcase in hand, raincoat flung over shoulder, she cast a swift good-bye look around the bedroom. Her youth was here. The double bed with its chenille bedspread had seemed so huge when she was small. There she had sprawled on her stomach to read Dickens and weep over the death of little Paul Dombey as his creator had done. The door with its small ink lines . . . "She's growing tall and strong and beautiful—my girl," Leo Weber would say as he made the mark each birthday to record the inches she had grown.

She closed the door on the childhood sanctuary and went into the living room. The heavy drapes kept out even the hint of dawn. One would have thought the whole world was sleeping but almost immediately she saw the slit of light under the kitchen door and then it opened and her mother stood there, small and thin, her face drawn with fatigue, the blue eyes smudged black with shadows. She was still wearing the slacks and sweater.

"I heard you taking a shower so I made you some breakfast." She scraped soft yellow eggs onto a plate beside a piece of buttered toast.

Judith's throat closed at the thought of food. "Coffee. I'll just have some coffee. Have you slept at all?"

Defensively, Sheila Weber said, "I'll sleep later. Where will you go now?"

Judith sat down at the table, cradling the cup of coffee in her hands. *Where will I go now? I'll follow the path he laid out for himself—to Europe, to the letter's hiding place—but I'll have to become as secretive as he was, tell no one—except Max—to protect myself, my mission.*

The plate clattering from her mother's hand to the table brought her sharply to attention and she looked up to see Sheila Weber staring at her, eyes wide with shock.

"Judith. . . !"

"No—don't you see, Mother—"

"You don't think that I—"

"—it's better."

"—would betray you? My God!"

"It's better if you don't know."

"Give me something to tell them!"

"They won't bother you when I've gone."

"*If* they do. Don't you see?" She added quite simply, "I'm afraid."

"I know, I know." Judith paused, looking down at the Christmas-littered table, creasing and uncreasing the red velvet ribbon, assuring herself that they wouldn't, couldn't, concern themselves with her mother, and yet . . . "Tell them—tell them the truth. Tell them you're not sure where I've gone, that you think perhaps I've gone to Washington to see Max. That's logical. They'll believe that," she said, trying to sound convincing, but to live constantly with distrust as these people did, she thought, it must be impossible for them to believe others didn't do the same. Distrust was a sickness in her too, now—of everyone—of Pete, the doorman, of strangers on the street, of her own mother. And that thought didn't even horrify her.

She finished her coffee and rose, saying with the finality of good-bye, "Once I'm gone, Mother, there won't be any more phone calls or strangers in dark doorways. I'm sure of it." She pulled on her raincoat and hat.

"But there will be for you—no, no, I shouldn't have said that. I just—I can't let you go like this. You haven't eaten. You'll be ill if you don't eat."

"I'm sorry," was all Judith said as she picked up the suitcase and her purse and left the room while Sheila Weber followed behind, already feeling a great distance between them. She made a last try, saying in a bleak whisper, "If you stayed—told the police—they could help you."

"No." Judith turned at the door and explained slowly and carefully, wanting her mother to understand. "They would only delay me and I can't afford that. I want you to know, Mother, that I'm not willing to let his murderers go free. Never. They'll be taken care of after this is over. Make no mistake about that. I promise you. But now, as far as the police know, he died in a fire. It must rest like that for the time being. One other thing—" She changed the subject abruptly. "Did Father ever mention anything to you about his meeting with Franz Halman—before Franz died—anything they might have talked about?"

Sheila Weber stopped twisting her hands and became suddenly very still. A strange expression came over her face, a stubborn, closed-off look. After a moment of silence, she shook her head.

"Nothing? Nothing at all?"

Sheila Weber again shook her head silently.

There was no reason why Judith should have felt disappointed, knowing her father hadn't confided in her mother about this matter, yet she knew that her mother was holding something back. Sheila Weber had never been very good at dissembling, but Judith also knew that when she looked like this nothing could force her mother to change her mind.

"You wouldn't tell me, then, if you did know something?" Judith asked softly.

"Yes—no—I don't know. I don't want to help you do this. I don't want you to go." She threw her arms around Judith, saying, "You've gone so far away from me already. It's hard to remember what you were like when you were small—so sweet, so beloved—" Her arms tightened convulsively and a sob shook her.

"No—now, Mother . . . Don't. Please don't. It only makes it harder." Judith pushed the small woman away from her gently and tried to smile. "I'm twenty-eight years old and look what a big girl I am." She bent down and kissed the soft cheek. "Are Andrew and Betty coming for Christmas?"

"They'll be here tomorrow."

"That's good. Do you have any cash you could let me have?"

"Certainly." Her mother disappeared quickly into the bedroom and returned with bills in her hand. "It's only sixty dollars."

"It won't make you short, will it?"

"No, not at all. I'm sorry I have no more."

"I have travelers' checks. I'll go to the bank."

They were talking as casual acquaintances do about a shopping trip or the weather.

"Is there anything else you need?"

"No."

They had run out of things to say and in the brief silence that followed, Sheila Weber gazed at Judith, her eyes very large with something almost predatory in them, as though she would devour her face with them.

"Take care," she whispered as Judith opened the door.

Judith simply nodded, stepped out into the hall, closing the door tightly behind her. The swinging chain made hard, clacking sounds against the wood. With tears streaming down her face, Sheila Weber fumbled the chain back into place.

"I'll call Max," she said aloud as she walked blindly back to the kitchen and sat down at the table. "He'll tell me what to do." Her fingers absently plucked dead needles from the evergreen branch and she stared at the eggs congealing on the plate without seeing them.

"How could you do this to her, Leo?" she whispered into the silence. "You knew what she would be going to." Then she remembered the smell and sight of the blackened corpse and she gasped, "Forgive me, forgive me. I should have been there with you. No, no, no, that's a lie. What good would I have done? I'm a coward. Forgive me." And she dropped her head into her hands and her shoulders shook with soundless sobs. It would have been hard for her to explain at that moment whether she was weeping for herself, for Judith, or for Leo Weber.

Nine

He dropped the dime and dialed the unfamiliar number and while he waited he brought out the flask and deftly unscrewed the cap with one hand while holding the receiver with the other. A long drink, a long expelled breath, and he screwed the cap on again and was slipping the flask back into his pocket when he heard a voice say, "Hello," cautiously.

He said, "Smith here. . . . A phone booth—Christ, at my age, to spend my life in a phone booth! . . . It's important, or I wouldn't be calling. I have some things to say and not much time to say them. She's still there, but she'll be leaving soon. . . . I'm sure, that's all. She's got places to go. Now listen to me: I don't want help from anyone. I'm going to do this my way. A leading-from-behind action. Make her move, think she has to get there ahead of us. . . . Of course, but she doesn't know that. . . . I can manage. I'll get help when I need it. . . . That's why you asked me to take this assignment, isn't it? Get the bully-boys off her back. I don't want another mess like the one I just had to clean up. Like hell it will! . . . You'll just have to try, won't you? Speak to your medical man and tell him. If he can't control them, who can? And if you want this letter, you'd better do it, because if she's dead or in a coma in the hospital, she won't be any good to us. It's time to move. I'll be in touch."

He hung up, pulled his hat low over his eyes, his coat collar well up around his ears, and watched Judith hurry out of the apartment house and hail a cab. "Penn Station" were the words her lips formed.

Nine

Ten

Though it was getting on to eight o'clock, the city was still in darkness and the cab had its headlights on. They beamed mistily through the cold rain that was still falling. A cold wind was rising. By nighttime it will be snowing, Judith thought. I want to be on a plane before then. I can book a flight out of Dulles from Max's apartment.

The cab pulled to a stop at the station. She counted out the fare, added a generous tip, and with a vague smile acknowledged his "Thank you" and "Merry Christmas," and climbed out, suitcase in hand. She wasn't really aware of the driver at all, only of the fact that the burden in the suitcase seemed so much heavier after the warmth and security of her mother's apartment.

She plunged through the crowds and headed down the long central passageway, flinching from the sudden onslaught of stimuli—the glaring lights, the noise, the smell of stale food, the hurrying crowds of damp-smelling people.

Anyone noticing her casually would have seen a tall, pale-faced woman walking with long, rapid strides toward her destination, having to do, they'd be sure, with Christmas. Everyone else was bent on holiday errands. But a keen observer would have been struck by the fixed, inward stare of the haggard eyes and would have seen no gleam at all of holiday joy.

In her haste Judith had walked past the bank of

54

lockers and she swung around and retraced her steps. When she found an empty one, she thrust the suitcase inside, inserted the coin, and locked it. Then, holding the key tightly in her hand, she went directly to the ladies' room. Inside the toilet cubicle she took off her raincoat and jacket, pulled up her sweater, and undid the strap of her bra. This she tied tightly around the key, reattached the strap, put her jacket and coat on, and left the rest room, feeling a little lightheaded. Safe, she thought, until I catch the train.

Walking slowly back the way she had come, she checked her watch. Eight o'clock. In half an hour she could go to the bank and cash the travelers' checks— cash would be simpler for her purposes—and she could get German marks at the same time.

And after that, Max . . . Perhaps the thought of Max accounted for her lightheadedness, or, more likely, she thought grimly, it's because I've had nothing to eat since yesterday afternoon.

She turned abruptly into a coffee shop and ordered coffee and a toasted corn muffin from the overworked counter man. His skin was gray, his eyes tired and resigned, and he was wearing an apron that was so soiled it was hard to believe it had ever been clean.

While she waited, she leaned her head against her hand and closed her eyes. Her throat felt hot and dry and her head was aching. Fatigue? A cold? There was a lot of flu around. She couldn't afford to be sick. Ignore it, she told herself, will it to go away.

Two sounds brought her sharply to attention. Neither should have had the power to startle her and send a cold shiver down her spine, but they did—the clatter of a plate on the counter and the creak of a stool as someone sat down beside her. In a second there was a third sound, a low murmur in her ear.

"All alone? Mind if I join you?"

A quick shudder ran through her and without looking up and almost without thinking, she said, "Yes, I do." Then she raised her head from her hand and saw without surprise the same gray eyes gazing at her as they had in the hotel phone booth and in the nightmare. She stared into them, hypnotized for a moment, feeling she could drown in their coldness. Hadn't she really been expecting some kind of confrontation as a logical move in their campaign of terror?

"Just a little talk, that's all." In a voice that was strangely soft and gentle, he broke the hypnotic silence and rose. He seemed very big and broad-shouldered standing close to her between the two stools. In one hand he held her plate with its corn muffin, the lumps of butter slowly melting into each half, and in his other he held her coffee. She noticed that the little finger of his left hand was missing and just a blunt, shiny stump was all that remained. At the same time she was thinking, I should run! Here is the enemy and I should run from him. She swung around on the stool to face the door but he had anticipated her and for all his size had moved around with astonishing agility to block her escape.

"We'll be more comfortable over there," he said and nodded toward an empty booth against the wall and stood quietly waiting for her to move.

For just a second more she poised on the stool and then with an obedience that surprised her, she got up and walked toward the booth. She could still run, couldn't she? Lose herself in the crowd outside. What could he do with his hands occupied with plate and cup and saucer? But fear made her docile just as fear had made them docile all those years ago—Leah and the millions who had walked unresistingly to the "showers." No, no, there must be more to it than that, she thought anxiously. There was the constant conditioning to expect the worst; there was abandonment by the world; there was despair, plus terrible fatigue and hunger. There was the whole brutal, grinding-down process to dehumanize that brought death at the end, perhaps, as a release.

By the time she reached the booth, Judith was aware of some relief through the fear and she was able to turn and face the man quite calmly. Wasn't it better, after all, to hear what the enemy had to say?

Their eyes were almost level and she saw that he was smiling. Then his gaze, provocative and insolent, moved from her face slowly down her body and then back to her face. "I've found me an Amazon. Please," he said, gesturing with a mocking bow to the seat.

His insolence brought a corresponding surge of anger in her and Julith thought, That's good, the anger is more useful to me than fear. As she pulled her coat close around her and slid into the booth, she said coldly, "There's no need to pretend that you're a lonely stranger from out of town looking for easy female companionship."

"Of course not, Miss Weber. You're much too intelligent for me to try such a sordid ploy and it wouldn't serve any useful purpose. We neither of us have time to waste, have we? It's just that I didn't realize, having seen you only from a distance, that close up you were so—" He searched for the right word. "—so formidably beautiful."

He smiled at her with deceptive gentleness as he set the corn muffin and coffee on the table in front of her and said, "That's not much of a breakfast. You'll need more than that for strength enough to keep going— where you're going."

Let him talk, Judith cautioned herself. Don't let him bait you. And she remained stubbornly silent as he sat down opposite her and removed his hat, dropping it on the seat. Judith, caught off guard, stared for a startled second at the scar that had been concealed under the hat's brim—a deep, angry-looking thing about an inch long that cut down through the left eyebrow, twisting it, and giving the eye below an unchanging, sardonic look. She averted her eyes, but he had seen her staring at it and he raised his left hand in a slow, deliberate gesture, bringing the two disfiguring scars together.

"Battle wounds. Would you like to hear how I got them? Very bloody, very dramatic, I assure you. There I was, surrounded and hopelessly outnumbered by a determined and vicious foe, but I fought courageously, nobly, for the honor of my country—and my life, I might add—until . . ." He broke off and made a swift, chopping motion through the air. It was graphic and horrible, made more so by the forced jocularity in the soft voice and the complete lack of expression in the eyes, as though they took no part in what was being said. "But that's a long time ago," he said, "and we're not here to give me medals, are we?"

His question didn't call for an answer and Judith wouldn't have had one in any case. She stared at the blank eyes, thinking with horror that this man believed in nothing, and how does one deal with someone like that? *Deal* with him. . . ? She was not about to. She looked down at the coffee and muffin in front of her, swallowed some of the coffee, found it lukewarm and tasteless, and pushed it away, saying, "You wanted to talk to me, so say what you have to say. I have work to do."

"And I would be the last one to keep you from your work, wouldn't I? It so closely coincides with mine as to be almost the same."

"I have no talent for cat-and-mouse games—"

"It does take a special talent. And you're right, you're out of your league." He leaned out of the booth and flagged a passing waiter. "Bring me a cup of coffee." Then he swung back to Judith, bringing his face close to hers as he did so. The strong whiskey fumes on his breath twisted her stomach with nausea and she pushed away from him. He acknowledged the movement with a slight smile and went on. "It's quite simple," he said. "We can avoid a lot of time and trouble if you'll give me the key to the locker where you put the suitcase, which must hold some information, I'm sure; tell me where the letter is, and then we can both go our respective ways, safely and peacefully."

"It's not that simple. . . ."

"Why not, Miss Weber?" He pulled back to give the waiter room to set his coffee on the table and went on talking. "You know I'll get it in the end. If I don't, someone else will. I'm stubborn. I want it to be me. So it's up to you whether it's to be hard or easy."

Judith was silent, looking down at the neglected corn muffin, crumbling it between her fingers. What he said bore out what her father had told her—that there were two groups interested in finding the letter.

"I'm only telling you something you already know," the soft voice said, as though he had been reading her mind. Then he slipped his hand into his pocket in a quick, almost furtive movement and for a wild, unreasoning moment Judith thought he was reaching for a gun. *He's going to shoot me, here, in front of all these people in this dirty little restaurant!*

The hand came out holding a whiskey flask, the shiny, scarred stump of a finger pressing ineffectually against it. Judith tried to quiet the gasping breath in her throat. She felt frightened and humiliated and she knew he knew what she felt. A thin smile taunted her as he uncapped the flask and poured a large measure of whiskey into his coffee.

He said, "Have some," and pushed the flask toward her. "You look like you need it. What did you think I was reaching for, Miss Weber?"

Another question that didn't call for an answer, and she simply shook her head silently. A part of the cat-and-mouse game. But she would like some of the false courage in that flask. She needed it and she let her eyes rest on it for a moment. He saw it and picked up the flask and poured whiskey into her cup.

She said, "I couldn't . . ."

"Couldn't drink with one of your father's murderers?" He asked it with blunt cruelty, making no pretense of not understanding her. "That was not in my department. Someone got carried away. Some damned fool. . . !" The narrowed gray eyes were like pieces of flint and the soft voice was hard with rage.

"Some. . . ?"

"You can drink my whiskey if that's what's bothering you."

Judith swallowed what was in the cup, hastily, guiltily, while the man went on in an angry undertone.

"Your father's blood isn't on my hands. I needed him alive. Damned blundering fools . . . Leaving their mess behind."

"Their mess?" Judith gasped. The whiskey had sent the blood pounding in her ears and she thought she hadn't understood. "It was you. . . ?"

"It hardly suited my purpose, Miss Weber," he said coldly, "to have the police find your father's body in the condition they had left it." The scarred, twisted eyebrow was red with his anger. "And I appreciate the fact that you didn't tell them about it—"

"You know that isn't why—"

"Of course I know. I still appreciate it. You see," he said, smiling, "you've done me a favor."

It was a nightmare, Judith thought, and the cold, empty man sitting across from her was a suitable inhabitant of the nightmare. He was drinking the liquor from his cup and for a fleeting moment Judith was astonished at the transformation in him. The heavy lids drooped over eyes turned inward, involved in some necessary and sensual ritual centering on the whiskey. He drank with barely concealed greed. When he finished, he refilled the cup and drank again, then wiped his mouth with his disfigured hand. His cheeks were flushed and his eyes glittered as he looked across the table at her.

His Achilles heel, Judith thought, and felt momentarily a lessening of fear. As though he read her thoughts, he flicked a finger at the flask and said, "Drunk or sober, Miss Weber, I'm an expert at the cat-and-mouse game. Make no mistake about it. I can play it until you get dizzy and run in circles. What did you think I was taking out of my pocket a moment ago? A gun? And you panicked. Your face went white, you could scarcely breathe, you were trapped. You tried to reassure yourself that I wouldn't do it here, in front of all these people. Well . . ." He settled his broad shoulders against the back of the booth and looked around the crowded restaurant and went on speaking in a cool, detached voice. "As a matter of fact, if I wanted to dispose of you, this would be a good place for it. One shot and I'm up and away, lost in the crowd outside before anyone realizes what has happened. There'd be two dozen different witnesses and two dozen different stories. Fear is a paralyzing emotion, Miss Weber. You'd be better off to quit now while you're still ahead." He lit a cigarette and watched her with narrowed eyes through the smoke.

Judith looked down at her cup, pressing her hands around it tightly to conceal their trembling and said in a low voice, "The advantage is all on your side, Mr. . . ."

"Smith."

"Smith. It would be something like that." She raised her haggard eyes to his face and continued speaking in a low, taut voice. "There isn't much point in prolonging this conversation because nothing you can say will stop me from finishing my father's mission. I'm not a fool. I understand what the odds are. I suspect you know a good deal about me. You must have known a good deal about my father—how he died, why he died, who caused his death—" Her voice trembled and she took a quick swallow of the whiskey.

"Your father was prepared for that." The voice was casually arrogant. "Perhaps he even wanted it."

"Expiation of guilt, you mean."

"Isn't that what you really think, Miss Weber? And didn't he perhaps have something to atone for?"

"He thought he had but that's not the same thing," Judith said in a scarcely audible whisper. And whether his guilt had been justified or not, Judith thought, he had paid a final and terrible retribution and thinking, surely, of his Leah in the end and only of her.

"It's not important anyway." The cold voice interrupted her thoughts. "I'm not here for that. I'm not prepared to discuss a man's guilt—"

"You're not prepared! You're not . . . !" A storm of rage, swift and terrible, swept through Judith. Her body shook with it, her voice rose, as she leaned across the table, heedless of the other people, heedless of any fear she had of this man. "Isn't that what this is all about? My father's guilt, if any, was small compared to the doctor's. His guilt is enormous—the basic guilt. Don't tell me he's an old man and what difference does it make now. Don't tell me it's thirty-year-old history. He's still the same man who planned and executed those torturous medical experiments in those camps of unnameable horrors and how can you—how can anyone—justify helping him? How can you stand in the way of justice—"

"I *have* found me an Amazon." The sardonic voice cut in. "Try not to get carried away, Miss Weber. There's a great deal more at stake here than you know about. I'm not concerned about the doctor. He's almost the least person involved."

"Those who brought him here after the war—someone had to help him. They're behind this, of course. Why? For personal reasons, or for gold, Mr. Smith?"

He didn't bother to answer, only gazed at her

silently, his gray eyes opaque and hooded, while Judith felt her rage seep slowly out of her, leaving her drained and vulnerable. What purpose, she thought hopelessly, had her impassioned rhetoric served? It wouldn't deflect him from his goal.

"Nor me from mine," she murmured and drained the last of the whiskey from her cup. A sudden, crooked smile appeared on her face. The whiskey was making her giddy and reckless. "Cat-and-mouse . . . I wonder if the mouse ever turned on the cat?"

"Possibly," he said icily. "But the mouse wouldn't have lived to tell about it." With a restless movement he stubbed out his cigarette and leaned toward her. "Where are the letter and the photograph, Miss Weber?"

"I don't know. I haven't—" She stopped abruptly.

"Haven't finished your father's manuscript. Of course," he said thoughtfully, "he would have been too careful to tell you outright. He'll tell you in the books, probably in some subtle way that only you can understand, guide you to it, to some small town in Holland, not far from Aachen—"

"If you know where the letter is, why are you wasting your time talking to me?"

"Because I don't know where it is precisely. There— you see how honest I'm being with you. We can take the suitcase any time. We could have had it last night, this morning. . . ." He tapped the table with one strong blunt finger, emphasizing each word. "If you insist on going after the letter, we'll do it the easy way and let you lead us to it. If you forget it, we will, too."

Forget it. The words are easily spoken. It's the memories that give the trouble. Forget her father's tortured body, Leah's agonizing journey to death, forget the man living in easy comfort who was responsible for both.

Some message of hate, of vengeance flashed from her eyes and Smith caught it and his face hardened.

"Avenging angels are out of fashion, Miss Weber. Don't be a fool. Drop it. If the letter hasn't come to light by now of itself, then it won't unless you bring it to light. There are important people involved in this who can't afford to forget it unless you do. Go back to your piano." On the last words his voice had changed subtly and his eyes fastened themselves on her hands where they were clasped around the coffee cup. "You're a concert pianist of some talent, I understand."

The words hung in the air between them. If he had struck her it couldn't have been more of a blow. Imagined, searing pain stabbed through her fingers and shot up her arms. She jerked her hands from the table and thrust them into the protection of the pockets of her coat, feeling suddenly cold and terribly alone in this hot, crowded coffee shop with its stale smell of food and musty odor of damp clothes. The whiskey she had drunk on an empty stomach had sickened her.

The soft, relentless voice went on. "Something else you should take into consideration: Has it occurred to you that your father might have broken in the end? One final, painful blow and he told them—*in extremis*, so to speak?"

"My God!" Beads of sweat dotted Judith's upper lip. "My God, how cruel ... !"

"Only to be kind. Or perhaps he simply changed his mind, like the suicide after swallowing the pills— decides too late that he wants to live. Your father had a great deal to live for."

"No," Judith whispered. "No."

"Then it would be too late for both of us."

In a kind of daze Judith started to pull her coat around her, fumbling with the buttons, watching for some move on his part to block her exit, and only half-aware of what he was saying.

"A word of advice. Don't find the secret of the

letter's hiding place too soon, because when you know it . . . It's easy to make you talk—anyone—and where a woman is concerned . . . The degradation of a certain kind of pain. Leah Weber knew it—and others . . ." The voice trailed off. His gray eyes were like glass.

As Judith stepped out of the booth, he made no move to stop her. "You're a very brave woman, Miss Weber," was all he said.

"No." She had to force the words out through stiff, white lips. "I'm frightened. Wouldn't you be in my place, Mr. Smith?"

She turned and started for the door.

"Miss Weber."

He surely wasn't going to stop her now! Judith looked back at him over her shoulder, her muscles tensing to run, but he hadn't moved. He sat with his head resting against the high back of the booth and he would have looked like any of the other businessmen in the place, having their coffee before starting the day's work, except that his eyes were too vague and his hand wasn't holding a cup. It was absently stroking the whiskey flask.

"Your friend, Max Halman . . . I'll save you a trip to Washington. He's here in New York. At the Plaza. Room five-two-one."

Eleven

Judith pushed through the crowds at the station's Seventh Avenue exit and swung north, abandoning any forlorn hope of finding an empty taxi in the area. She lengthened her stride to carry her away as fast as possible from the man with the twisted eyebrow and blank eyes. Was he still sitting in the stuffy coffee shop, stroking the whiskey flask? She wondered irrelevantly where he refilled it once it was empty.

He could, of course, be somewhere behind her, and she had to fight against the urge to look over her shoulder. You'll need all the control you have, her father had told her, and she was only beginning to understand what he meant.

Yet what would be the sense of his following her when he knew exactly where she was going, or did he expect her to think in their own twisted way and do the opposite of what was expected? I will be thinking their way soon, she thought sadly. It hadn't really surprised her, of course, that he knew where Max was. That was his job, and with a grim smile she muttered, "Thank you, Mr. Smith, for saving me a trip."

A fat man bundled in fake furs walking on the sidewalk beside her turned to stare at her and smiled expectantly. She stared back until she realized with a shock that she had spoken aloud. My God, be careful! She caught a green light and ran across the street heading east toward Fifth Avenue. She had been totally unaware of the crowds around her, so involved was she in her separate world, uninhabited by anyone but herself and ghosts and Mr. Smith.

She quickened her pace. The walking eased her tension, the nausea lessened, the rain cooled her hot face. She wasn't burdened by the clumsy suitcase. That was safe and the metal locker key was warm against her skin. She would pick that up before she went to the airport and . . . The bank! She had forgotten the bank, and no wonder. But never mind, that could be taken care of with the suitcase. –

An empty taxi was disgorging a tired mother and two whining children in front of a department store and Judith, with ill-concealed impatience, climbed in before the fare was paid and sank back against the seat, aware that the chilling rain had soaked through her coat and onto her jacket. By the time she reached the hotel, she was hot and cold by turns and trembling with fatigue. The warmth of the lobby emphasized the soreness of her aching muscles. Like a sleepwalker, she moved through the lounge, not noticing the short fat man slouched in the shadows, carefully reading the *New York Times*. He was a stranger to her, and she wouldn't have, in any event.

Peering over the edge of the paper, his eyes through dark-tinted glasses followed her progress to the desk where she said something to the clerk. Then she moved on, walking with that strange combination of grace and awkwardness, and disappeared into an elevator.

He folded the paper and tucked it neatly under his arm as he strolled off toward the public phones.

Max Halman was waiting in the open doorway of his suite when Judith stepped out of the elevator, his bright blond head catching the light and reflecting it. He started toward her, a tall, elegant man moving with the effortless grace that always made her feel gauche beside him. But that was of no concern to her now. She was only thinking that here was her beloved

Max and she hurried toward him, feeling that it was like coming home after being away, alone, in a strange land for a long time. Since last night Judith's strength had been nourished only by hatred for those who had killed her father. Now the sight of this man with the blue eyes and the gentle mouth unnerved her and she clung to him when they met, her hands pressing down hard on his shoulders, feeling the comforting flesh and bone beneath the cloth.

"He's dead, you know," she whispered against his shoulder.

"I know. Sheila called me. You spoke to her?"

"Not since last night."

"How did you know I was here? You phoned Washington?"

"No. Someone—someone told me."

"Someone . . . ?" He drew back and looked at her questioningly but the sight of the haggard eyes and white face shocked him beyond caring about the question. He put an arm around her waist, pushed the heavy mahogany door open, and led her into the gracefully furnished sitting room of his suite where he busied himself taking care of her as though she were a child. Removing her wet coat and her jacket which was damp as well, he hung them over a chair near the radiator. He tucked her gloves into the coat pocket and dropped her hat on the couch. He made her sit down and removed her wet shoes and placed them at a careful slant against the radiator.

Judith submitted silently to these ministrations, showing no overt signs of impatience, only her eyes, large and intense, remained fixed on his face. But when he said, "We'll have some breakfast," and pointed to the tray on the table in front of the couch which held juice and coffee and toast and two covered plates, she made a quick restless movement as though she would get up. Instead she reached over and grasped his hand tightly in hers and said, "Not now. We have too much to talk about."

Without looking at her, he said, "Some coffee then." And he filled two cups from the thermos. "For my sake." He smiled, caressed her cheek and abruptly left her, going into the bedroom. When he returned, he carried a blanket and a bottle of aspirin. Over Judith's protests, he tucked the blanket around her, shook out two aspirin and handed them to her along with a glass of orange juice.

"I'm not ill, Max," Judith assured him. "It's just fatigue. I had to walk a good distance before I found a cab and I got wet, but never mind, it's not important."

"While we talk, you'll rest," he said firmly, and stood over her until she had swallowed the tablets. Then before he could move away from her again, she seized his wrist in her strong fingers and said, "Father told me *Max is the only one*. Did you know that?"

Max sat down beside her, taking her hand from his wrist and holding it in his own. He turned to look directly into her face and said, "Did he, Judith?" in a voice that was strained and tired, but Judith scarcely noticed.

"Yes, but you know that, Max. Except for myself, you're the only one he placed his trust in."

"Tell me," he said gently, "about last night."

"I'd been to Lincoln Center with the Holcombs. It was a fine concert. Ashkenazy. He played . . . He played . . ." She broke off to stare at Max blindly and pressed a desperate hand to her forehead. "I—can't remember what he played!"

"It doesn't matter, darling."

"It's as though the concert were a year ago instead of last night. We had coffee afterward. I got to his apartment about twelve-thirty. You knew I'd been staying with him, of course. He had seemed more than usually disturbed lately. I think—he didn't say exactly—I think it was something he found out on that last trip to Washington. You saw him then, Max?"

Max nodded but didn't speak and Judith went on, her voice growing high and thin as she described how she had found Leo Weber, clinging all the while to Max's hand as though it were her lifeline. She finished, saying, "I had to leave him like that. I didn't want to. I covered him with a blanket." And as though it were somehow important that he know, she added in a bleak whisper, "When they started the fire they moved him to the couch."

She fell silent, staring vacantly into space and Max made another hurried trip to the bedroom, returning with a bottle of cognac. He poured generous amounts into both cups and offered one to Judith.

"No, no." She waved it away. "I can't. I've already had one morning drink and it didn't agree with me. A man named Smith. He's the one who set the fire to— my God!—to clean up the mess so the police wouldn't find Father the way *they* had left him. He said—"

"Smith?"

"He's the one who told me you were here."

"How did he know where I was?" Max set his cup down on the table with great care. "What did he look like?"

"You couldn't possibly confuse him with anyone else. A big, broad-shouldered man, cold gray eyes, a scar over one, a missing finger—"

That's as far as Judith got. Max swung away from her with an exclamation of rage so unusual that Judith forgot everything else for a moment and stared at him in shocked surprise. She had rarely seen him impatient, much less angry. He always held a firm rein on his emotions, having a reputation in the State Department for growing cooler and cooler as a crisis grew hotter. Now, though, he was pacing the room, every line of his body taut with anger, his face flushed, saying, "How dare they!" in a voice iced with fury.

"Max . . ." Judith called to him across the distance his anger had placed between them but he didn't answer. He may not have heard. Judith thrust aside the stifling blanket and sat up. "Who is he, Max? What has he to do with you?" What have you to do with him, he's the enemy, she thought, suddenly afraid to ask. She heard him whisper with terrible bitterness, "I loved him. They could do that to Leo . . . I loved him," while he remained with his back to her gazing out of the window with unseeing eyes at the wet street and the wet people struggling joylessly with Christmas and the weather.

Judith watched him and waited, not knowing what else to do, until finally he said, "He was someone I knew in Vietnam, a man I had to work with for a while."

He never talked about that brief stint in Vietnam. Judith knew nothing about it and it was easy for her to forget that it had ever happened.

"Forgive me, Judith," he said almost formally as he walked toward the couch. "It never does any good to explode like that."

His face was still cold and remote with his anger and Judith was aware for the first time how pale and tired he looked, how the tension had drawn fine lines around the blue eyes. I've been selfish, she thought. I've looked to him for strength and haven't given any thought to his sorrow.

"Sorry, my darling. I'm sorry," she said, reaching for his hand. "There isn't anything to say. The only way to bear it is to believe that he's at peace now and the one thing we can do for him is to find the letter and finish what he started."

Peace . . . Max looked down into Judith's gaunt face and haunted eyes. Leo had left no peace behind, he

71

thought, only a legacy of hate and vengeance. It was up to him to try to separate her from that legacy. He sat down beside her and raised her hand to his lips and kissed it.

"Tell me about Smith," he said. "Where did you see him? What did he say? Try not to leave anything out."

"I didn't know, of course, that you were in New York. I thought I would have to go to Washington and I put the suitcase into a locker at Penn Station and it was there that I saw him—or he saw me, rather. He was following me around last night as well—here, to this hotel, to mother's apartment. Babcock was here, too. Did you know? I saw him."

"I didn't know you saw him but I knew he was here. He had to see some people who were passing through, so to speak."

"I'm afraid I was rude to him."

"Go on about Smith."

She related slowly and in detail the conversation that had taken place in the coffee shop, not having to struggle with faulty memory because all the details were painfully clear. At the point where Smith had asked her if it wasn't possible that her father might have told his torturers where the letter was, her voice broke and she fought for control, while Max, his eyes hard, murmured helplessly, "Go on, my darling, don't dwell on it."

"You understand, Max. There's no doubt in my mind—Father could never have told them about the letter. It was just—the cruelty. . . ."

"Of course. He loves it—the cat-and-mouse game." Again fury edged his voice, anger sent him pacing the room. "The scare tactics. Hound you, frighten you off. Two groups, Smith said. We can trust him for the facts. Two groups, acting at cross purposes sometimes, perhaps—"

"Smith said there were people involved in this who are more important than the doctor."

"A domestic breed—those who helped Wallner come to this country under the innocent guise of Klausing. They must be protected, reputations not to be damaged. The others, bullies, self-styled protectors of men like the doctor, neofascists—you'll find them anywhere. They're the ones who got to Leo. They do the dirty work while Smith and his kind stand by and watch and wait and take advantage of the others' brutality. He's taking advantage of it now."

"He told me to forget it. If I forget about the letter, they will, too."

"You'll be opening up a whole keg of worms that someone's kept sealed all these years."

"Max—" Judith brushed the damp hair from her forehead. "I don't understand these people."

Almost savagely, Max said, "Why should you!" Seeing the startled look on her face, he softened his voice with some effort. "Sorry, Judith, but why should you have anything to do with people like this?"

The question itself was simple enough on the surface, but Judith, oversensitive to every inflection in his words, heard something underneath it. In a strained voice she said, "You aren't saying. . . ?"

He sat down close to her and took her hands in his. "Will you listen to me for a moment?"

Judith shook her head wordlessly and tried to pull her hands away but Max held them firmly.

"You haven't considered everything. You haven't got all the evidence—"

"What are you saying?"

"There's so much you don't understand—"

"There's only one thing I don't understand. Are you asking me not to go on? Is that it?"

"Yes, I am."

Judith jerked her hands free and twisted her head sideways as though she had been struck. The movement brought the heavy black hair swinging around her face, concealing from Max the rush of tears to her

73

eyes. She managed to say, "I understand Mother, poor, frightened Mother, but not you, Max. He loved you like a son."

"Don't do that, Judith. For God's sake, don't let's hurt each other. I don't want you to do this because I'm frightened for you. I want you to go to the police, tell them whatever seems reasonable—"

"There was never any question of that," Judith whispered, turning her face toward him. Her eyes seemed to have receded into her head, leaving only dark hollows looking out at him. Max rose, unable to bear looking into them, and walked away from her.

"Listen to me for a minute, Judith. If this is a betrayal, hate me for it if you have to, but listen to me. Have you ever considered the fact that there might not be a letter? When I saw Leo in Washington this last time, he looked so tired, so ill, so desperate, I wondered then if he might not have invented it. Something to give meaning to his guilt, something to hold on to."

"Why did they kill him, then?"

"Leo's secretiveness, his trips to Washington, his research at the department, the files I let him study— and shouldn't have. Easy for anyone interested to believe that he knew what he was doing, collecting evidence."

"I feel as though I were talking to a stranger. Things you should understand and don't. My father and yours went to a great deal of trouble to see that the letter and photograph would remain safe until they were needed—"

Angrily, Max broke in, "That was thirty years ago. Memory plays tricks on old people."

Looking not at Max but staring straight ahead of her, in a dead-calm voice Judith said, "Nothing you or Mother may say can convince me that Father was too ill to know what he was doing. He was tired, upset, driven, yes, but he remained the careful man he'd always been, meticulous about details. He must have been certain that the letter and photo were safe where he had hidden them, where he could lay his hands on them when he needed to, and I'm just as certain that he'll describe their hiding place in the manuscript." With a sudden decisive movement Judith got up and faced Max and said with a kind of pitiless simplicity, "I promised. It's for Father and Leah. There's no more to be said about it and there isn't much time."

Behind her words, Max could hear Leo Weber's voice as he sat across the table from him in the restaurant: *I have to work fast now, Max, because I don't know how much time I have.* Now Judith stood tall and gaunt in front of him, the dark-circled eyes challenging him fiercely. How like him she looked! At that last lunch, Max had been shocked at the change in him. The big, gentle man had grown thin, too thin. The mild blue eyes that used to be full of humor were hard and feverishly bright with a fanatic gleam. When they weren't on Max's face, they were looking around the room, searching for someone, something. He scarcely touched his lunch. As they parted, he put a trembling hand on Max's shoulder. "The past pursues me like a demon," he said. "I have all I can do to cope with it. I know I don't have to ask. . . . Judith—you'll take care of her."

How can I take care of her if you won't let her go, Leo? He stared across the room at the cold, beautiful face that was almost as white as the sweater she wore and a surge of emotion swept through him, leaving him shaking. He couldn't define what moved him. Fear, anger, sexual desire. What right had Leo Weber to do this to her? What right had Leo to do this to him, Max? He felt somehow involved in a battle with the dead for her soul. Like Sheila Weber before him, he wanted to seize her and shake her and shake her to break the connection with them. But he couldn't do that unless he wanted to lose her altogether.

As calmly as he could, he said, "Don't you see how fantastic it all is? To try to avenge a murder after thirty years—doesn't it go against all reason?"

Judith's face twisted with agony and she cried out, "You can't let him down, Max. He can't have died like that for nothing!"

In two swift strides Max was beside her, his arms around her, saying almost harshly, "Don't, don't. You break my heart talking like that. You know how much I loved him." The face he bent over her was as white and strained as her own. "He knew the chances, Judith, he was willing to take them. But you . . . I couldn't bear it if anything happened to you." He took one of her hands in his and looked down at it, a long-fingered, strong, square hand. "How long has it been since you've played?"

Go back to your piano, Smith said. Judith shuddered and pulled away from him.

"I'm thirty-six years old, Judith. You're twenty-eight."

Her lips moved in a faint, distant smile. "An old spinster."

"I want us to be together—you and me and Tommy. You've neglected your life for a long time. You have a concert coming up in a month—"

"I told Jeff to postpone it."

"How much longer are you going to sacrifice—"

"My talent? Lay it on a sacrificial altar to expiate guilt for the death of a woman—a girl, really—whom I've never seen? Until this is finished. Ah, Max, there's no point in our hammering at each other like this. We go back and forth and don't get anywhere. Just tell me what Father told you in Washington and I'll get on with it."

"Oh, Judith . . ." Max tried to smile but it was only a sad, strained kind of grimace. "My stubborn, stubborn Judith. Nothing I say makes any difference, does it? I'll tell you his exact words: 'Now that I'm sure of him I can go ahead with my plan.'"

Judith clasped her hands and waited for him to go on, but Max shook his head and said, "That's all he told me, Judith."

"That's all. . . !"

"I'm sorry."

He's lying, she thought, and bit back the sharp words 'I don't believe you.' What would be the point of it? The gulf between them was already too wide. She dropped her hands to her sides and shrugged. "I had hoped . . ." she said, "that—well, I don't know really what I had hoped. It means, of course, that he knew who was responsible for helping the doctor but I had suspected that already from something he said when he returned this last time from Washington."

She seemed to be speaking words to cover a gap, to fill an emptiness, to dispel the sense of death or dying that was all around.

Max had to make a last desperate effort to convince her. Trying to keep the harshness from his voice, he said, "Look at it this way, Judith. Suppose the letter does exist and is intact somewhere—somewhere in the area where my father met Leo. The war wasn't over yet. Leo was still in the army. He had to move on. Chances are he wouldn't carry it with him for fear it would get lost or destroyed and he had to take into account that he might not survive. So he hid it. Did he bury it in the ground? Did he give it to someone he trusted and is that someone still alive? If he is, where is he? Who is he? Is it moldering in a cavity behind a wall or under a floor?"

Max paused but Judith didn't speak. The lonely sound of the rain beating against the windows was all that broke the stillness.

Finally Max said, "I'll strike a bargain with you. Go back to Sheila's. Stay with her. Give me the books. If they hold a clue to the letter's hiding place, I'll find it."

"Even though you're sure the letter doesn't exist.

Even though you're convinced, like Mother, that Father was mad."

She had swung around to face him, flinging out a hand as though she were flinging down a gauntlet. The eyes deep in their sockets gleamed at him feverishly. She was only a few feet from him but it might have been miles. Dust and old ashes formed a bond he couldn't break. Max smiled bitterly at the sudden sting of jealousy he felt for two dead people.

In silence they faced each other like strangers without any of the inconsequential things strangers can say to each other.

"All right," Max said finally. "I give up." He walked to the couch and picked up Judith's purse. "At least give me the key to the locker. I can save you a trip in this weather." He handed her the purse. "I'll get the suitcase."

Judith took the purse and held it in both hands, making no move to open it. Her face was shadowed and remote.

"Judith . . . ?" His voice was husky. "My God, Judith!"

The phone rang in the bedroom. Max swung on his heel and went to answer it, saying coldly, "Never mind."

They had never quarreled before. The pain it left in her was deep and distant—and permanent, she had no doubt. A lovers' quarrel . . . Dark brows drew together in a frown as she considered, sadly, the wild irrelevance of the words. This was a schism, a clean and efficient break. She was committed to doing it alone. No loose ends of love dangling, only inherited hatred.

She reached for the bottle of cognac Max had left on the breakfast tray and poured some into the orange-juice glass, paused, then recklessly poured some more. It bit into her tongue and throat, but, she thought, it's the best courage money can buy. Through the window she could see the gray rain and felt its cold chill across her shoulders. She went to the chair by the radiator and slipped her jacket on, hearing Max through the open door saying, "I can't do anything with her. See if you can convince her."

He appeared in the doorway and said formally, "Your brother would like to speak to you."

"There's no point to it," Judith said just as formally, but she went to the phone.

"I can't, Andrew. . . . I know you don't understand and I can't explain." The young, impatient voice went on and on, following anxious instructions, certainly, from their mother. Judith listened without hearing while her eyes moved around the familiar bedroom. This was the suite Max usually had when he was in New York. Comfortable, expensive, first-class. Only part of it paid for by an expense account. The rest he willingly took from his own pocket.

Through the half-open door leading to the bathroom, she could see his shaving articles, arranged with his usual tidiness beside the washbowl. Draped across the foot of the bed was the blue silk robe she had given him for his birthday last September. His suitcase lay on the floor near her foot, some papers protruding from it. Without thinking, she raised the lid with her stockinged foot. A pair of socks, some underwear, on top of them two maps, newly purchased, from the look of them. Her exploring toe pushed them around so she could see them more clearly. A map of Holland and a map of Germany. She breathed the silent question, *Why, Max?* as she turned her head in the direction of the sitting room and saw Max, his back to her, fumbling in her handbag.

"No, Andrew!" She had almost forgotten the telephone and her brother who was saying that he would come to the hotel. "There's no point to that. You can't change my mind." Raising her voice she said, "I'll say good-bye now. Take care of Mother." And she hung up while he was still speaking. Her hand trembled only slightly as she replaced the receiver in its cradle.

Max stood waiting for her beside the couch, holding the blanket, his smile anxious and strained, his eyes impenetrable.

"There's no excuse for my getting angry," he said. "Forgive me. But if you're going to be stubborn enough to go out in this weather, at least take a nap before you go." He motioned toward the couch.

Judith hesitated.

"There's time," he said.

"All right." She lay down.

If her easy acquiescence surprised him, he didn't show it. He fussed over her silently, brought a pillow from the bedroom, placed it under her head, tucked the blanket around her very carefully as though he were performing a ritual. Then he bent over her and kissed her lightly. For a moment their faces were close. She felt his warm breath on her cheek and looked directly into the blue eyes, but they were clouded and she could read nothing in them.

"I love you, Judith. You know that, don't you?" His voice was stiff and uneven. "Sleep, then. I'll wake you in an hour."

He moved away from her and she closed her eyes. She wanted the release of tears but her eyelids were hot and dry and none came. She felt dead to all feeling.

Max, my elegant Max. How else, she had told him, can I describe the way you look. The long, fine bones, the slender grace. I fell in love with your temples and your wristbones, she told him, and you'll have to take special care of them. He had assured her gravely that he would. The gaiety of their love . . .

He's afraid for me, trying to protect me, she told herself without conviction. She twisted her head restlessly on the pillow and listened to his footsteps as he paced the room, moving quietly so as not to disturb her. Once they paused and she sensed he was standing over her, looking down at her for a long time. She feigned sleep and finally she heard his footsteps recede, heard the bedroom door close softly behind him. She raised her head and listened. Was that the sound of the telephone dial?

With a thief's stealthiness, she got up and went to the radiator. Her shoes were still damp but what did it matter? Swaying a bit from the effects of the cognac, she put them on, then her raincoat. She picked up her purse and walked to the door. There she paused with her hand on the knob, listening to the low murmur of Max's voice. Monstrous, to eavesdrop on Max, but it can't be helped. She tiptoed to the bedroom door, bent her head and listened.

"She's upset, you understand, and if she says a few wild things, don't pay any attention, Ted. You can imagine the kind of shock it's been. . . . I can't tell you how much I appreciate it. I'm desperate. . . . At this point I think you're the only one who can. I'll keep her here."

This is the way it is, then. She tasted a terrible bitterness, like salt on her tongue, as she moved swiftly from the suite and down the hall to the elevator.

Twelve

She turned south on Fifth Avenue, pushing grimly through the laughing children and smiling parents who crowded around the display windows at F. A. O. Schwarz.

I'll keep her here, I'll keep her here. The betraying words marched through her mind setting a kind of unsteady rhythm to her steps and echoing mockery in her ears.

Her father had loved Max Halman as though he were his own son, having for all practical purposes adopted him after Mary Halman's death, a rather lost youngster of eighteen, though not lost for long. Leo Weber's love and his careful investments of Mary Halman's money gave the boy both emotional and financial security. Harvard, government and law, and then the State Department after a few words in the right quarters from her father. A very bright young man, Max possessed a natural talent for moving easily through the intricacies of the Washington scene. He had made one mistake—a disastrous marriage at twenty-five—but he rectified it with a quiet divorce at thirty. Now he had a ten-year-old son in a boarding school in Massachusetts, the only positive result of the marriage.

Briefly in the cold rain her body played her false, flushing warm as she remembered the night two years ago when she and Max found themselves making love with passionate hunger. Afterward Max saying,

"It's delayed reaction. Why didn't we know eight years ago?"

Eight into two leaves nothing. The rain on her face mingled with the tears.

Behind her, unnoticed, followed the squat little man from the hotel lobby, breathing noisily through fleshy nostrils, moving with quick, jerky steps in his effort to keep up with the tall woman. A waddling duck following a swan.

She paused once during the long walk to glance into a department-store window which held a Christmas display of glittering, foot-high papier-mâché puppets. Puppet-women in spangled evening gowns attended by puppet-men in elegant evening clothes. Bait for the shopper. Why did it seem so obscene, this make-believe frivolous world? In one window a man-puppet sat at a scaled-to-size piano, the notes of a Strauss waltz tinkled like crystal drops through the window.

She was two. . . . Her father was playing Scarlatti. . . . A revelation of flashing sound and graceful movement. Then pillows on the piano bench, her father swinging her high and plumping her down, small fingers on the huge keyboard. It marked the beginning of her enduring and passionate love affair with the piano.

With a long sighing breath Judith turned blindly away from the window, bumping into an old man dressed in a worn red suit with dirty white cuffs and collar. He stood on the edge of the sidewalk, pumping his bell mechanically up and down, an old and hopeless smile fixed on his face. Santa Claus without jollity, with red-veined wrinkles and rheumy eyes. At his feet a large cassette tape recorder blared forth the hard voice of a woman singing a rock version of "Adeste Fidelis." "Oh, come all ye faithful," she shouted.

Judith hurried away, followed by the waddling

little man, who moved more easily now after the restful pause.

The edges of the steps of the big savings bank at Thirty-fourth and Fifth Avenue were icy. If this freezing rain turned to snow, how would that affect overseas flights?

"Are you *sure* you want all these cashed, Miss Weber?" the young teller asked.

"All of them," Judith said firmly and went on signing the checks.

With a sigh he counted the bills, peering from time to time over the glass at the grim white face of the woman, convinced she must be at least a little mad.

As she turned away from the disapproving teller and was stuffing the thick envelope into her purse, her eyes spotted the watcher. He stood in the glass-enclosed foyer, trying, though not very hard, to appear inconspicuous. With his hands stuffed into the pockets of his raincoat, with the pile-lined collar turned well up around his ears, and the brim of his hat pulled low over his forehead, he was gazing through dark sunglasses (sunglasses on a sunless winter day!) with self-conscious concentration at some spot on the ceiling. Knowing without concrete evidence of any kind that he was a member of the forces known as *they*, she made a quick decision to get the German marks at the airport. Then another decision. Though her hands were trembling and her heart pounding, she walked boldly up to him and looked directly into his face, trying to see the expression in his eyes. Cold and gray? She didn't think so. Close up, he didn't appear sinister at all, more like someone playing a child's game. All right, she could play it, too.

"I'm going to Penn Station now," she told him. "In case we get separated in the crowd, you'll know where to look for me."

The little man made queer ducking motions with

his head as though he were trying to make it disappear into his collar like a turtle's.

He said nothing and Judith walked away, admitting it was a childish thing to do even though it gave her some relief and a small sense of power to turn on these people with their cold eyes and ridiculous sunglasses.

At Penn Station she reversed her original procedure, going first to the rest room and untying the key, then to the locker. With suitcase in hand she walked slowly toward the taxi stand, her shoulders drooping with exhaustion, stepping aside at one point to let a group of young people pass her. They were full of shouting, boisterous spirits, close and conscious of one another, unaware of anyone else in the crowded station. Skis and poles were slung over shoulders, ski caps rode jauntily on top of heads, flopping with their movements.

She watched them go like ghosts of Christmas past. . . . Wide sweep of Swiss Alps. . . . Pure white powder snow, blinding under bright sunlight. Her father, happy and youthful, pulling her out of a drift on the learner's slope, laughing encouragement: "Let's try it again!" Only once near the German border had the laughter ceased and he had stood gazing bleakly across to the cold, windswept landscape.

He had learned to live with it, she realized, only by establishing rigid taboos. Itineraries in Europe carefully planned to avoid Germany and Holland; Heidelberg never spoken of; Czechoslovakia didn't exist. *After the Battle of the Bulge I found myself in a small town in Holland on the German border. . . .*

The letter *is* there, she told herself fiercely, waiting for me to find it. How could her mother and Max think it was the fantasy of a sick mind?

With her hand on the door of the taxi, she looked around almost automatically for her watcher. There he was, the round little man, not quite concealed by the three people in front of him. Impulsively she called out, "As we're both going in the same direction, we might as well share a cab."

Startled, he performed his little ducking routine, but as Judith continued to stand, glaring a challenge, and the waiting people made restive movements, he came forward and climbed into the cab. Silently and precisely, he took off his gloves and tucked them into his pockets, unbuttoned the top button of his coat, and placed his hat carefully on his lap.

Judith noticed he had small feet and small, rather delicate hands. She couldn't visualize them brutalizing another human being. But there was no assurance of that as there was no assurance of anything from now on.

She told the driver to take them to B. Altman's department store on Fifth Avenue. "You can do your Christmas shopping," she said to the man. And I can get lost in the crowds. She thought she detected a smile as he glanced sideways at her.

"How's your friend, Mr. Smith? I think I'd be a little lonely without him or you or whoever trailing along behind me. One gets accustomed to things, misses them when they're not there."

"You're a cool one, Miss Weber. I'll say that for you," he said primly. His voice had a flutey, musical quality that was completely at odds with his squat, ugly body.

"Yes," she agreed, but she had to say it through clenched teeth and still a harsh cough broke through.

"Sounds like a bad cold. You should have a hat on. A great deal of body heat is lost through the head, you know."

"No, I didn't know," she said, rather dazed at the turn of the conversation. She put her hand to her wet head, surprised, not at having forgotten it, but at having been unaware that she had. A small part of her still lay on the couch in Max's suite.

"There's a lot of flu around. You'll want to be careful."

Judith had pulled a handkerchief from her purse and was mopping her wet head. "You aren't really concerned about my health, are you? Better for your purposes if I'm ill and can't go on with this."

Again he glanced sideways at her, smiling slyly. Judith caught a flash of gold-capped teeth. "You *look* like you should be in bed," he said. "But, of course, that's up to you." His smile widened with a kind of vulgar suggestiveness, a look completely at odds with the melodious voice. "*In* bed or *out* of bed—everything about you concerns us, Miss Weber." He removed his sunglasses and looked from the handbag in her lap to the suitcase on the floor.

It was done quite deliberately, a casual reminder of their strength and her weakness. It's true, I'm too vulnerable to play these bravado tricks, Judith told herself harshly. If they change their minds and decide to stop me, how can I prevent them?

"What hold have you over Max Halman?" she asked, not caring that he thought it a naive question, only wanting to see what his reaction was.

He let her see his eyes widen with innocence before he covered them again with the sunglasses. "A hold?" he said. "He's a very independent man, your Max Halman. We have no connection with him at all— none other than the usual—one branch of intelligence with another. And as we're all pretty jealous of our secrets, it's not much of a connection. If he refused to help you, he must have had very good reasons."

She regretted having asked the question. His words had opened an immense, aching void inside her and she turned her face to the window to hide the pain.

"When did you start following me?" Not that it mattered. She simply had to change the subject.

"When you left the hotel," he answered agreeably.

Keeping her gaze on the window, Judith asked softly, "Are you married?"

A brief hesitation, then he said, "Yes."

"Do you have children?"

This time the little man beside her remained silent.

"Have you ever helped anyone cope with nightmares—night after night—tried to bring them out of it—soothe them—a child—an adult? Helpless—only able to watch them suffer?"

No answer again and Judith turned to look at the man. He was staring straight ahead of him, his face damp with perspiration. Why had she said these things? An arrow shot at random, hitting a mark?

The man remained stolidly silent and Judith had no more to say. The cab inched its way through the traffic and finally pulled up in front of the department store, by which time the little man had wiped his face dry with a pale blue handkerchief and had resumed again his noncommittal expression.

He climbed out to the sidewalk and buttoned his coat. "I appreciate the ride. It was thoughtful of you, but you'd better pay," he said coolly. "You have a great deal more money than I have." He pulled on his gloves and settled his hat firmly on his head.

"You would know that, wouldn't you?" Judith murmured.

She paid the driver and joined him on the sidewalk where they stood facing each other awkwardly in the cold, driving rain. What was the protocol here? Who left first, the followed or the follower?

Judith's purse, still open, dangled on her arm, exposing the thick bundle of bills in the envelope. She saw the direction of the man's eyes through the sunglasses, drawn to the magnet of the money. She put the suitcase down on the sidewalk and reached into her purse, pushing the envelope aside casually to take a Kleenex from a packet.

She asked, "What do you call yourself?" Not "What is your name?"

Half-smiling, he made the quick ducking motion with his head. *No names, please.*

"It's a stupid game," Judith said wearily. "Don't tell me it's Smith. That's already being used."

"How about Doe?"

She ignored the faint sarcasm that marred the musical voice. Seeing his eyes dart back to the money, she put her hand on the envelope. One learns the lessons one has to learn, she thought, fumbling with the bills.

"It must be very difficult to follow someone in these crowds, Mr. Doe. On an ordinary day New York is crowded enough but at Christmastime . . . It must be very easy to lose someone."

They leaned toward one another, this ill-matched pair, a buyer and a seller about to strike a bargain. Despite the cold wind whipping around the corner, small beads of perspiration began forming on the man's upper lip as Judith pulled some bills from the envelope, four fifties. Two hundred dollars was good pay for a day's work—or non-work. The man raised his arm and brushed his sleeve across his lip.

Speaking rapidly in a low voice, Judith said, "I can walk into that department store and leave at any of the other three exits, get into a cab, and be gone. No one will ever know you didn't really lose me. It could happen—it could happen to the best of them, couldn't it?"

She held the two hundred toward him and started to close her bag but his eyes remained fixed on the envelope.

"You've got a lot of money there. . . ." The musical voice hardened a little. This was bargaining time.

"How much then, how much?" Judith's voice was harsh. "Three hundred? Four?"

With a swift, furtive movement he held up the five gloved fingers of one hand and then shoved it into his pocket. Judith shrugged. He could have asked for more if he'd known. She counted the money with fingers grown numb with cold and handed it to him. He did a kind of sleight-of-hand disappearing trick with it and without another word Judith picked up the suitcase and turned to go, but he reached out and stopped her with a firm hand on her arm.

"It's a bargain!" Judith spun around toward him. "You agreed!"

"Oh, yes, it's a bargain. I only want to give you a bit of advice. It's included in the price." His lips twitched a little as he leaned toward her bringing the round, ugly face close to hers. The dark sunglasses glinted vacantly up at her and one drop of rain trembled on the tip of the bulbous nose. "You have some idea," he went on, "of what's at stake here. You must have after what happened to your father. My advice is that you would be smart to give the letter to Smith. I just wouldn't let anybody else get it if I were you."

"I haven't got it. Didn't Smith tell you that or do you keep secrets even from each other. As for 'anybody else'—I've no idea what you're talking about."

"Ah, you're not so naive as all that."

"Perhaps I am." She shook his arm off with a fierce movement and went on, "Do you sleep well in your bed, Mr. Doe? I don't understand you—any of you— being against this. Justice in abstract is meaningless. My father was trying to give it meaning—"

"Things aren't black and white, Miss Weber." The melodious voice was plaintive and a little angry as though she had no right to believe that they were.

"Sometimes they have to be."

"It's a pity you're so stubborn."

"Stubborn is just a word, Mr. Doe. I have something to do and I'll do it." She shivered in the chilling rain and started away from him up the steps.

His soft voice followed her. "You really should place a higher value on your life, Miss Weber, like Max Halman...."

She paused to look down at him where he stood smiling and nodding almost eagerly.

"You don't think Halman wants to end up the way your father did, do you? *He* knows what's involved. Why do you think he refused to help you?" He waved his hand at her as he turned away and added, "I'd buy a hat if I were you."

Divide and conquer.... An old technique....

She stumbled up the steps into the store. I can't believe the enemy propaganda. I won't believe it. She flinched away from her thoughts of Max. To think of him was to feel the emptiness, the final sorrow after the death of a loved one.

Without looking back, she hurried down the center aisle of the store toward the Madison Avenue exit. The ugly little man had greedily accepted the money and whether he would keep the bargain that went with it she couldn't know and she wouldn't worry about it.

The store was a sea of shoppers, moving in slow, engulfing waves from counter to counter, in rhythm, it seemed, to the melodies of Christmas that drifted through the store from some mysterious source. "On the first day of Christmas my true love . . ." Overhead, glittering gold and silver hangings festooned the ceiling and from nearby counters came the warm, sweet scent of expensive perfumes.

Something cold touched her heart and swept her, unresisting, back through the years to a dead holiday of long ago. The past drowned the present. No perfumed fragrance, she smelled, instead, as Leah had done, the foul smoke pouring from the tall chimneys of the furnaces, stoked with their terrible fuel, burning day and night but giving no heat. She heard the devil's mockery of an orchestra—pretty young girls dressed in clean white shirts and neat blue pleated skirts, reprieved for a brief while to play the lilting music of Strauss and Lehar that guided the thousands of naked shuffling feet to the shower of death. As they played, knowledge of their own deaths was reflected in their blank, hollow eyes.

Pale and hollow-eyed herself, Judith pushed through the exit into the street and as a cab pulled up, almost before it had dropped its fare, she had thrust her way in.

"What the hell . . . !" The passenger rounded on her but swallowed the rest of the expletive when he saw the gaunt-faced woman.

How rude she had become during this brief, fugitive existence.

"You know, lady there were lots of others ahead of you for this cab," said the driver, shaking his head. "People have been lynched for less in this city."

"Yes," said Judith vaguely. "Will you take me to Kennedy Airport, the Lufthansa building?" Then, withdrawing into her own private, lonely world, she leaned down and took from the suitcase the Lawrence book with the third installment of her father's story.

Thirteen

Sea and Sardinia . . . Sturm und Drang . . . A chapter
of man's dark sorrow . . .

"Hope springs enternal . . . " What a fool Pope
was! Oh, it's true that for a few brief days hope
gave me life but it vanished when Franz Halman
arrived, never to return. Despair has sat deep
inside me, giving me its constant and unrelieved
company, cutting me off from the ordinary pleasures others find in living. Had it not been for my
daughter, Judith, life would have been completely useless to me.

Dismayed, Judith looked up from the book. How
could he possibly mean that? Surely her mother and
Andrew and his friends had helped too. Why mention
only herself? The words were suddenly too heavy a
burden for her. She rejected them, feeling guilty as
she did so. Had she really known her father at all?
What other secrets had he kept hidden away from
his family all these years?

But I'm ahead of myself. After my staff left and I
waited for Franz there in that small corner of Holland, I relaxed as best I could, reading and taking
long walks through the town. A deathly kind of
quiet had settled over it, the kind of quiet that
comes only after the savage sounds of war have

passed on. The Dutch inhabitants—what a wonderful people!—were already hard at work repairing the destruction.

My walks led me out of town into the country. On a hill overlooking the German border, I could see Aachen lying below in its pleasant valley. Aix-la-Chapelle, birthplace of Charlemagne. In his time a center of Western culture. How the mighty had fallen! For ten long days in October the battle for this city raged, the first major German city to fall to our forces, and when it fell, it lay in ruins. The twelfth-century cathedral, Saint Foillan's, destroyed; the fourteenth-century Saint Nicholas, destroyed; fifteenth-century Saint Paul's, gone. Their magnificence nothing but rubble heaps in the dust. Only Charlemagne's own cathedral remained standing through some strange decision of fate, and from my vantage point on the hill I could see its spire reaching for the bare sky. I could see some of the people, too, who still inhabited that dismal place, scurrying in and out of holes under the rubble. They seemed bent over and always in a hurry, like nocturnal animals who must scuttle back to the dark hiding places. "O poor mortals, how ye make this earth bitter for each other."

Of course the Germans have rebuilt it all now into a bigger and better industrial center and who really cares what happened there in 1944 and '45. The blood that soaked the earth has been absorbed by the earth, the rubble and battle-scarred buildings have vanished from sight as though they never existed—except in "that great dust heap called history."

Bob came back to report on how things were going in our new headquarters and to fill me in on the war. Shameful, I'd almost forgotten about it, so involved was I in my own private war. He sported new captain's bars with great pride. Poor Bob! His sense of security and self-respect had always been very tenuous. The captain's bars helped, I guess. He stayed on and on. I wanted him to go but he told me he thought I needed company to keep my mind off the bad thoughts that obsessed me. I didn't particularly believe him. He had never been a very generous or sensitive person and I thought at the time that he was simply "goofing off." It had been a long war and a lot of men, otherwise responsible, were doing it.

The only times I could really escape from the numbing fear of what Franz might tell me were those I spent at the organ—a magnificent instrument, quite hidden away—that I discovered almost by chance. I would trick myself, imagining that Leah was beside me, her soft hair falling around her face as she bent over the keyboard, and it seemed that her long, slender fingers guided mine. Bach has never sounded like that again! It was my friend, Cornelius Steen, whose guest I was, who led me to it. I wonder if he or my brothers, my dear, dear friends, ever realized how much that music meant to me? Those few days represented the one bright time between endless periods of darkness—darkness that was soon to close over me for good.

Franz arrived, looking like the walking dead, emaciated and hollow-eyed, alive and on his feet only because he willed himself to be.

"Leah!" Her name was torn from me, a cry of anguish that was question and answer at the same time. Franz said nothing. Poor ghost of a man, he had no strength to speak. He looked at me with those terrifying eyes and shook his head.

He needn't have done even that. I knew the answer. I had really known it all the time.

That was the end of the third chapter and Judith let the book rest in her lap and turned her pale face to the window, watching the endless flow of traffic, her thoughts harsh and unyielding.

You're wrong, Max, and I think you know you're wrong. Perhaps Father did bury it in the ground, perhaps he gave it to someone who has since died, but somewhere over there justice is waiting. Somewhere there's an organ and a friend named Cornelius Steen—and the letter.

The organ . . . Something special. That would mean a cathedral. In a small town in Holland? Maastricht? No. *Quite hidden away*. The organ in the ancient cathedral in Maastricht could hardly be described as hidden away.

Cornelius Steen? How old had he been during the war? Was he still alive? If he was, she would find him. If he had died, he must have family, friends who would know about his wartime life.

She had a few facts to go on now and she felt more confidant and also suddenly very tired. She put her head back and closed her eyes. She would read the rest on the plane.

Fourteen

"What's important, Sheila, is that I find her and that's really all that's important. I'd hoped you might have just a small hint, but if you don't, never mind, I'll be on my way. I'll have to find her somehow." It was hopeless, Max realized, to have come at all. A waste of time and he had none to waste. But he had to try. "What makes it difficult is that I'm sure Leo prepared her for this. He had months—"

"Months! How little you know of it, Max. Years— in slow and subtle doses. Oh, I don't mean this mad search she's on now. That's of recent vintage. But since she was a child—long before Leo knew the doctor was alive—he was telling her about Leah— how beautiful she was, her exceptional talent, their separation, Prague, her arrest—the whole ghastly story—"

"Sheila, I understand all that—"

"No, you don't, not really. I was here. I lived with it."

And Sheila Weber went on talking like a small, compulsive machine, restlessly pacing the room, flinging out her arms from time to time, then clasping and twisting the small hands together.

Max stood beside the fireplace, watching her but scarcely listening, feeling transient and disoriented in this familiar room. Once before, in Vietnam, he had

97

felt this sense of moving between two worlds, unrelated to either, in a kind of no man's land.

He hadn't removed his coat. It felt cold and damp across his shoulders. His eyes were shadowed with fatigue, the lines around his mouth were hard. His fingers toyed with an unlighted, frayed cigarette.

On the sofa beside him, shoulders touching, hands clasped, sat Andrew Weber and his wife, Betty—two young innocents, watching the older people in bewildered silence. Max wished they weren't here or that Sheila would stop talking. How much did they know of the details of Leo Weber's death? The surface story only, he hoped. Death by fire. With Sheila's talent for avoiding unpleasantness, he didn't think she would have told them the truth.

For the thousandth time he asked himself how he could have left Judith alone while he made the phone call. How could he have been stupid enough to assume that she would rest peacefully on the couch when he knew she was infected with the same disease that Leo had, that sickness that pulled the skin taut over the bones of the face and drove life and gaiety from the eyes?

"I argued with him," the thin, plaintive voice was saying. "I told him it wasn't good to burden a child with such horrors—that she couldn't understand, that it would make her ill. But Leo couldn't help himself. The pressure of his guilt, or whatever it was, seemed to build up inside him until he had to talk, had to get it out. Andrew was too young. I wasn't much help. I think—no," she said with sudden sharp honesty, "I know I was jealous. But normally I'm not good at that sort of thing anyway. I told him to forget it, put it away. What good was he doing? So he turned to Judith. He would have anyway, of course. They were so close, so alike. . . ." She paused a moment, then she resumed in a low voice. "I don't mean it was all bad. We had good times—more good than bad— it wasn't always there between us. But why—why must one always remember the bad!" Her voice faltered, a sob broke out, and young Andrew leaped from the couch and threw a protective arm around her shoulders.

"We don't have to go on and on like this, do we?" His round blue eyes flashed angrily at Max. "The police are taking care of whatever has to be done. Father is—" His voice broke but with a quick indrawn breath he recovered himself. "This is painful for all of us. I spoke to Judith. I gave her a chance to change her mind, but she's always been stubborn, so—all right—if she wants to run off on some fool mission— let her. She can make her own decisions."

Max rounded on him with sudden, uncontrolled fury. "Don't talk about something you don't understand!"

The boy, shocked into silence, stared at him white-faced, while Sheila Weber in an anguished tone said, "Oh, Max ... Andrew ..."

Still in the grip of anger, Max nodded and said curtly, "Sorry, Andrew," and Andrew nodded back, saying sullenly that it was his fault.

Andrew Weber was a young, male edition of his mother, slender and delicate, like her, with the same soft eyes and the same facility for turning off unpleasant things as you would turn off a faucet. Max had often thought how curious it was that Judith should so closely resemble Leo in both looks and temperament and not the son. A pity, he thought, then quickly, no, I wouldn't have her any other way.

"I think," Betty, the young wife, was saying, "that we should all carry on as normally as possible. It would be better for Sheila, better for all of us."

99

Her voice was sweet and pompous and it grated on Max's nerves. *Better for Sheila* . . . He lit the cigarette he had been holding and then promptly and savagely threw it into the fireplace and moved toward the door, silently, because he didn't trust himself to speak. Since yesterday, his movements had been dictated by some unseen force over which he had no control. It was entirely contrary to his nature and he hated it but he followed the dictates all the same because he had to—for Judith's sake.

"Max, wait, please," Sheila called. "Andrew, do me a favor—you and Betty. Make some sandwiches and good strong coffee. We can all use it, I'm sure. You'll find the makings in the refrigerator—ham, beef, and whatever else."

"That's a great idea!" Betty, relieved at the thought of something to do, leaped to her feet, grabbed Andrew by the hand, and pulled him into the kitchen before he had a chance to agree or disagree.

As soon as the door closed behind them, Sheila moved swiftly to Max, holding out a hand. Max took it. It was cold but quite steady.

"Max, my dear, don't be angry with us. We are all under such terrible strain. You most of all, I think. I'm not used to seeing you like this—so hard and angry. I understand, of course." She touched his cheek gently. "You're trembling," she said in surprise. "I'll let you go. I know you have things to do. If that letter exists, she mustn't get it, must she? You don't want her to, surely?"

"How can you ask me that? I've been trying to find her since she left the hotel this morning—phoning everywhere I could think of. No luck. It's almost as though she had rehearsed this disappearance, planned it step by step—"

"You think that's not possible?" Sheila asked bitterly. "That Leo might not have gone over all this in case . . . ?" She shook her head and stared vacantly out of the window for a moment at the ugly patch of gray sky. Finally she said in a low, sad voice, "I told her I was a coward. I was thinking only of myself. I didn't even want her here. She knew it. She went away knowing it."

"She understands, Sheila." My God, he was thinking, what a sense of betrayal she carries with her. Sheila . . . Myself . . .

"I know she understands. That's what makes it so unbearable. Leo understood, too, when we separated. But he had to do what he had to do. And now Judith, like him, obsessed. "Whom the gods would destroy . . . !"

"Don't be melodramatic, Sheila; for God's sake, we haven't time for that. If Leo was a little unstable toward the end, that's understandable. He'd lived with it for so many years and the shock of finding Wallner still alive . . . But Judith hasn't lost her grip on reality—"

As though she hadn't heard him, Sheila Weber, in a voice lost in memory, said, "Brainwashed . . . Judith loved him so much she would accept anything from him, do anything for him."

He saw her standing in the hotel room, tall and white-faced, saying, "I promised," and a sudden, shocking thought struck Max. He felt it like a physical blow. A sacrifice . . . ? Could it be possible, unconsciously perhaps, that that's what Leo had been preparing Judith for? He recoiled from the thought, thrust it aside in horror. *Now* who's being melodramatic? he asked himself. If only he hadn't let her get away. If only . . . He looked down at the lovely woman in front of him and anger and disgust flared in him. This passive, helpless woman living in her beautiful safe haven. If she had been a little more aggressive, she might have . . . What? Held Judith here? Deflected Leo from his course and perhaps saved his life? How could he expect this porcelain-delicate woman to do what he, Max, had been unable to do? The anger passed and he put his arms around her in a kind of despairing tenderness. We are what we are, he thought, and how could Sheila help being what she was? She had been protected all her life, first by her father and his wealth and then by Leo, over-protective. Was he compensating for not having been able to protect Leah? When Sheila was stepping out of her father's Cadillac to enter an exclusive girl's school in Connecticut, Leah was stumbling from the cattle car onto the platform at Auschwitz to begin the long, slow descent into hell. At the same time his own father had already been brutalized by years in the slave camps. Accidents of birth in different worlds. The worlds meeting now, thirty years later. . . .

"I'll go now." He kissed the soft cheek.

She clung to him. "Where will you go?"

"I don't know," he said evasively. "It's probably better if you don't know anyway."

"That's what Leo said the last time I spoke to him —as though I were a child—"

"When was that?"

"When he asked me to find his passport and I asked him where he was going. To Europe, of course, or he wouldn't have needed the passport, but where in Europe? He didn't trust me enough to tell me. He didn't trust anyone in the end—except Judith."

"If you hear from her—"

"I won't. Somehow I know I won't."

Max knew she was right. Judith was gone.

"I'll be in touch," he said as abruptly he released himself from Sheila's hand and left.

Sheila stared at the closed door for a moment, motionless, her eyes shining with tears and a kind of anger as well. Then she shrugged slightly. "If there

102

were something I could do, I would do it," she whispered, as she secured the chain on the door. "But there isn't and it's Christmas after all." She walked toward the kitchen, calling, "Where are those sandwiches, children? Don't make too many. Max had to go."

"I've been hoping we'd meet, too." The thin lips twisted into a tight smile.
"You call ... picked up a phone."
"Well ...
"Wha...
"If you ...
"No ...
The ... Max notice ...
he was ... brief

Fifteen

From the warmth and light of the apartment house, Max stepped into the cold, gloomy courtyard, pausing to turn up his coat collar and pull on his gloves. As he did so, a figure detached itself from the shadowed entranceway and moved toward him. A cigarette flashed briefly through the air and hissed out on the wet pavement.

"Halman."

A familiar voice spoke his name. A familiar, broad-shouldered figure walked toward him in that lumbering way he knew so well. Max waited, smoothing one gloved finger against the other, uneasy again with that sense of transiency, of being caught between two worlds.

They stood face to face in the shadows, studying each other in silence, like two fighters calculating the opponent's strength—the one, tall and slim and hatless, looking cool and remote, his blond hair the only brightness in the dim light; the other, shorter by a few inches but strong and broadly built, his dark hair hidden under the hat that was pulled low over the forehead. Max didn't have to see the eyes to know what they looked like, with the old scar lifting the left eyebrow in its permanent look of mockery.

"I've been hoping we'd meet," Max said. "I called your office. They told me you were away on an assignment."

"I've been hoping we'd meet, too." The thin lips twisted into a cynical smile.

"You only had to pick up a phone."

"Well, now that we have met, can we talk?"

"Why not? It's a free country."

"If you say so. Where would you like to go?"

"Right here is good enough for our purposes."

The man looked tired, Max noticed. His face was pale and pinched and he was hunching his broad shoulders forward as though he were cold. He had probably been waiting down here for the better part of an hour in the cold rain. Long enough to be chilled through, but Max couldn't feel any sympathy for him. He knew how deceptive it was—that look of fatigue and dissipation. A dangerous man—he had always been able to use his weaknesses to throw the enemy off guard. And the drinking . . . Max watched him bring the familiar flask out of his pocket. Another deception. Not that he didn't need it. Max had often wondered in the past if the flask had some magical properties. It was always full.

"No, thanks," he said, as the man offered the flask to him.

Smith shrugged and raised it in toast. "To old times, then." He tipped his head back and took a long drink.

"You look a little ragged around the edges, Smith, like you've spent a few sleepless nights. Or are they signs of a developing conscience or growing too old for the racket?"

"Wrong on both counts. I'll die in the harness."

"I'm sure you will."

A brief silence, then Smith said in a quiet voice, "There's nothing to be gained by baiting me, Halman."

Max gazed into the man's eyes, which were just as blank and cold as Judith had described them, more so than he had remembered. He's right, damn him. Slow down, Max cautioned himself. I'm losing my temper and my objectivity because I'm too emotionally involved. He asked, "What did you want to talk about?"

"Isn't it the other way around? Or have you been able to find the answers you wanted?"

"I have some answers, but they're not the ones I want."

"Pity." Smith shrugged.

"Let's not waste time with question-and-answer games. We both know what this is all about. Where is she?"

Smith shrugged his broad shoulders again but this time there was something in his manner, something evasive and wary, an old and familiar smell of defeat. Max felt his pulse leap with excitement.

He said carefully, "You figured I'd want to talk to you. It's the other way around, isn't it? You've lost her."

"Temporarily. We'll find her." He added in a hard voice, "It's not easy for *her* to get lost in a crowd."

The deliberate stress on *her* was meant to give Max pain and it did. There was no way he could avoid its sharp stab as he thought of Judith moving through some crowded street alone, made outcast by her terrible search. He steadied himself, lighting a cigarette, and asked his next question with no hope of an answer. "Who killed Leo Weber?"

"Now, Halman . . ."

"Come on, it's too late for games, Smith. I know you know. I don't think you did it. I don't think your dirty tricks go that far, not in this country, not yet, but you know him—name, country of birth, place of employment. Place of employment—those are the key words."

"I'd like to tell you, Halman, believe me." Smith

sounded almost sincere and his lips moved in something that passed for a smile. "I feel I owe it to you because of our friendship and close working relationship in the past."

Somehow the words sounded soiled the way he used them and Max responded more fiercely than he intended. "Don't play that tune for me. That was a long time ago. I was young and not very bright and there was a war on—a lousy war, but a war all the same. It's finished. Don't bring up a comradeship that never existed. We both know where we stand. We've known for a long time—since that stinking little hut outside of Saigon."

Just the faintest twitch of the man's lips told Max his shot had found its target and he went on, less fiercely, "It doesn't surprise me that they've put you on this case. You've always had a stronger stomach than mine. But tell me, was it really strong enough to condone what they did to Leo Weber? There may have been some excuse for our little Vietnamese friend, but not Weber—not Weber."

"I'll give you this much—Weber was none of my doing."

"That's not news. You told Judith that. What you're saying then is that someone slipped under your guard. You used to be more efficient than that—or did you let them slip under? The fire, of course— the clean-up, as you told Judith—was your affair. But right from the start this whole thing must have suited your purpose. Leo Weber was halted in his search— brutally— and Judith knows now how far you're willing to go—or you hope she does."

"She's no fool. She knows what she's doing."

"My God, how can you say that! Of course she doesn't." He flung his cigarette to the ground, trying to fight off the wave of apprehension that swept over him. It was hopeless to try to appeal to this man who was motivated by old hatred and the cold pleasures of his profession. "I loved Leo Weber. I love his daughter. . . ."

Smith's face was stony, not a muscle moved.

"It's too late for the father," Max went on, his voice hardening, "but I'm warning you, Smith, don't let your guard slip where she's concerned, or I'll tear you apart limb from limb."

"Dramatic—very dramatic. With all you have to lose?"

There was the faintest shadow of doubt in the gray eyes that peered out at Max from under the hat brim. Perhaps he had shaken him a little bit. "I'm putting it to you straight. Don't count on my ambition too much. See that she doesn't get hurt."

Smith shifted his position, shoving his hands deeper into his pockets and hunching his shoulders. "I didn't know," he drawled, "that our suave, elegant darling of the State Department could be capable of such passionate, self-sacrificing, pulp-fiction love. I thought—"

"Now who's doing the baiting? And isn't *love* a strange word on your lips, Smith?"

A small and worthless triumph, Max thought wearily, as he watched the brief flash of emotion darken the cold eyes as the two men stared at each other across a span of ten years. In the heavy silence in the cold courtyard, their thoughts met in a hut, oppressive with heat and the stench of urine, and focused on the ghost of a tiny Vietnamese woman, her small oval face made ugly with pain, the skin broken and bruised with the beating she was taking. By the time Max had reached the hut, she was barely conscious except for the large eyes fixed in mute and terrible appeal on the broad-shouldered man as he turned his back on her and walked out of the hut.

He turned his back on Max now and pulled the flask from his pocket, treating himself to a long drink. He didn't offer any to Max this time. The drinking had begun in earnest, Max remembered, the flask always full and ready at hand, after that scene in the hut.

"You can't tell me, Smith, that this doctor is all that important to you." Max spoke softly through the shadows to the broad back. "It's hard for me to believe that so much effort—dangerous effort—would go into protecting one ex-Nazi medical scientist, so-called, unless someone important is involved. As you're on this case, I'd say it's someone—"

"It may be hard for you to believe, but that's your problem," Smith said, turning toward Max, his face cold and impassive again. "And jumping to conclusions can be dangerous."

Max grinned at him suddenly. "Well, I'm living dangerously at the moment. But never mind about that. Whoever this *someone* is, his name must be important enough to make good headlines, this someone who helped an ex-Nazi sadist, gave him the necessary papers to turn him into something acceptable to the human race, gave him another name—Klausing. He helped him come here—when? Forty-seven? Forty-eight? He was declared officially dead by the German courts in nineteen forty-eight. That could make a difference. It could give the man who helped him the benefit of a few doubts. If it was forty-eight, he could have been deluded into thinking that he was helping a war refugee, some poor, persecuted guy caught in the middle. There were a lot of fraudulent innocents in the refugee camps after the war and many of them found their way to places all over the world—safe from prosecution, from justice."

Smith had been standing motionless, his head bent forward, listening impassively, and when Max finished he made a sudden, restless movement with his shoulders and said harshly, "You should know without my telling you that there are people involved in this who can't be bought off with anything—fanatics

—willing to protect Wallner at any cost. That's why your Judith—"

Max cut in sharply, "And they're the ones who slipped under your guard."

"Let's strike a bargain," Smith said, his mouth twisting in a thin smile as he added, "for old times' sake. We both want the same thing, don't we? If you see that the letter and photograph, when they're found— and if they're found—are given to me personally— along with those damned books—then I'll see that Judith Weber doesn't get hurt."

"We've reached the heart of the matter, haven't we?"

"That's right."

"And, of course, I can trust you."

"Do you have any choice?" Smith reached into his pocket and brought out a small notebook. He wrote a number in it, tore off the sheet and handed it to Max. "You can reach me at this number. If I'm not there, leave a message. Quite like old times, isn't it?"

"There's a difference, though perhaps you can't see it. Anyone is fair game to you in this racket, and that puts the odds all on your side."

Max looked steadily into the man's cold eyes and again their thoughts met in the barren land of Southeast Asia. Max had never been convinced that the Vietnamese woman had betrayed Smith to the Vietcong, to the knife that took a finger and almost an eye. Max felt sure she had really loved the man and he knew that Smith had certainly loved her. It had been a passionate love, perhaps the only one Smith had ever known, and when betrayal came, how he had hated her with equal passion. The visible wounds from that time were long healed, but the real one still festered deep inside. Perhaps the woman *had* gone over to the Vietcong after Max had secretly ordered her release, but he didn't think so. A few weeks later he had heard via the rumor market that she had killed herself and that seemed somehow more characteristic of her than betrayal.

Smith was lighting a cigarette and the flare of the match lit up the hard, somber lines of his face, the thin, compressed lips. Not knowing why, Max found himself remembering the few times he had seen the man smile and how startling the transformation had been—from dark to light, from cold to warmth. How long, Max wondered, has it been since the man smiled like that? Almost unaware that he was saying it, Max murmured, "She's dead, Smith. What's the point of hating anymore?"

Like an animal preparing to charge, the man's big head came up and jutted forward. His eyes glittered, his face flushed. He started to speak, changed his mind, started to speak again and then abruptly swung away from Max and walked toward the street with the precise, measured steps of a man who has had a great deal to drink and tries not to show it.

Max called after his departing back, his voice loud and desperate in the quiet courtyard. "If I can't find her and persuade her to drop this, you'll turn your back on her, too, and walk away, shrugging off the consequences? A job is a job? Never mind how ugly it is or who's involved?"

The broad-shouldered man neither answered nor turned around. He maintained his exaggeratedly steady pace to the sidewalk where he hailed a cab.

Smith gave the cabbie an address on Houston Street and then slumped back into the seat, reaching for the flask. He shook it. His experienced ear told him it was about a quarter full. His hands weren't quite steady and he stared at them for a moment as though they were guilty of betraying him in some subtle way, then he drained the flask and slipped it back into his pocket, muttering under his breath.

"How's that?" the driver wanted to know.

Smith's voice rose, suddenly, loud and slurred. "And Weber's spirit, 'ranging for revenge . . . ,'" he declaimed, "'Cry havoc!' man, 'and let slip the dogs of war . . .'" His voice sank to a whisper. "That's what it's all about, anyway, isn't it?" The sound he made could hardly be called a laugh and it frightened the driver, who twisted his head around to look at his passenger. The man's eyes were closed, the face was blank.

I got a loony back there, the driver thought, and maintained a vigilant silence for the rest of the trip.

Sixteen

During the long and gloomy wait for her plane's departure, Judith had sat in her own private island of silence, surrounded by the sea of noise in the dining room, drinking coffee that was as black and bitter as her thoughts. At the table next to hers a little girl with golden hair and a sulky face was having a passionate affair with a new music box. "Jingle bells . . . Jingle bells . . . " Around and around the tinkling tune went.

She looked at her watch. At last it was time to go. She rose, picked up her suitcase, and paid her check. As she turned from the cashier to the door, a man appeared in the doorway, suddenly, out of nowhere. She was unable to check her stride in time and they collided. She stepped back with a startled "Excuse me," and stared at him. Why did she think the collision had been deliberately planned? He was a thin, ferret-faced man with a sallow, dirty complexion and he was bowing and excusing himself with exaggerated politeness, a sly, mocking performance. By the time he stood aside to let Judith pass, her heart was pounding with fear. She clutched the suitcase, holding it close to her. One of *them*? While he was play-acting the courtesy, his sharp, little eyes had darted from her face to the suitcase. Was it only her imagination, working overtime? She pushed past him and hurried away.

The squat little man with the musical voice had watched the pantomime in the doorway from his secluded corner, peering through his dark glasses over the inevitable newspaper. When Judith was safely out of sight, he rose and paid his check, and, while waiting for his change, he glanced casually around the room. He saw the ferret-faced man join someone, a great hulk of a man with the bulging muscles of a wrestler. They were approaching the cashier and he heard the ferret-faced man say, "We've met now, though not formally, but it'll do until the real thing comes along," and he giggled. It was a high, foolish sound, a nasty sound, and the little man hurried away as fast as his short, thick legs would carry him.

Her footsteps seemed much too loud on the ramp, threatening to expose her alien presence among the holiday-bound. Soft footsteps in a secret place . . . Is that what had informed against Leah? False words whispered in the dark? A shadow falling where it shouldn't?

Her mind was a restless jumble of thoughts, her body numb with fatigue. She had read somewhere that a person could go without sleep for two days, was it?—three?—before he began to hallucinate. She shook the thought away with a surge of unaccountable anger. She would be able to sleep on the plane and forget for a while.

But once settled and having gone through the seat belt ritual and put out the cigarette she hadn't wanted in the first place, sleep wouldn't come. Behind her closed eyes her thoughts darted like will-o'-the-wisps, settling on images briefly, then flying to another. Max's relationship with Smith must go back to his service in Vietnam, about which he had never talked to her, might never talk about, and what difference did it make? There was an ocean between them—or soon would be!

She had reached the conclusion that the "Ted" Max had talked to on the phone at the hotel must be the reporter, Ted Rosen, who had written the story about the doctor six months ago, the story which had started the whole nightmare—had made a recluse of her father, shut him up in the confines of his apartment, set him writing, writing, feverish with an infection that fed on itself and grew.

But why should Max think that Rosen could persuade her to give up her father's search? Didn't she already know everything he knew? Hadn't he been the first person her father had talked to? "He's convinced," her father had told her, "that this man Klausing is really Wallner, and he spoke with a fine passion about the magnitude of the man's crimes and how he shouldn't be allowed to remain free, but he had nothing much else to offer. He's a humane man, Rosen, and an intelligent one. He went after the facts with great thoroughness. He tried to pick up Wallner's trail—and he did, for a while. He met people who knew him, had known him in the early thirties, forties. He met people who knew he had served as a doctor for the SS during the war. He even saw a picture of him as a young man. He said there was a resemblance, but it would be hard to pin it down. The photo was forty years old. It showed Wallner with a dueling scar. Klausing has no such scar. In any event, Wallner's trail stopped, a dead-end, in nineteen forty-eight in Germany. He had seen the records showing death from natural causes, heart attack, and that was that as far as official interest was concerned." "But," Rosen had finished grimly, "as far as *un*official interest is concerned, if you can bring me proof, maybe together we can nail this bastard!"

Her father had left the apartment only when he had to—to go to the university the few necessary days a week and for three or four trips to Washington. He had seen Max and Babcock there. That she knew. He may have seen others whom she didn't know about.

Babcock . . . A man in a very sensitive position. As director of the State Department's Bureau of Intelligence and Research, he might have had information, or known where to find it, that would lead her father to those who had helped Klausing-Wallner, but Babcock was adamantly opposed to her father's mission.

"Forget it, Leo," he had said. "It's thirty years ago, it's history. Let nature take its course. Don't make yourself ill over something you can't do anything about."

Feeling that way, Babcock wouldn't have been very cooperative. "He's a weak man anyway," her father had said sadly after he had seen him for the first time. "He needs to work within that kind of power structure. It gives him the support he needs. He's not about to do anything that might rock his boat."

Judith found herself wondering suddenly with cold hatred what the doctor was doing now. Preparing for a jolly Christmas, no doubt, decking the halls. . . . Was he married? Did he have family? How strange that it had never occurred to her to wonder about these things before! She had never thought of him as having the ordinary relationships and pleasures that other people had.

She twisted restlessly, opened her eyes, and unbuckled the seat belt. Sleep was hopelessly beyond her reach. She leaned down and opened the suitcase where it stood touching her left leg. "I have work to do," she had told the steward grimly, when she had insisted on keeping it with her. She pulled out the Dinesen book, *Seven Gothic Tales*, thinking it a grievous irony that it should hold a part of her father's own gothic tale.

Penciled in the margin of the first page was a scribbled note: *Ask Max if he can find transcripts of the Doctors' Trial, '47.*

Max ... Why did it always come back to Max? *No loose ends of love dangling* ... The intensity of pain she felt when she thought of him made a lie of the words. As though he were beside her, she could feel his presence—his sensuous grace, his charm and humor—his duplicity. Hopelessly she told herself that love stories didn't always have happy endings.

Seventeen

It was late afternoon and almost dark when Max pulled up in front of the house. The heavy gray sky seemed to have lowered itself closer to the earth in order to tighten its cold grip on it. The wind was rising and snowflakes were mixed with the sleet.

The moment of confrontation. He had done many difficult things in his life, but none quite like this. He drew in a deep, steadying breath, switched off the ignition of the rented Thunderbird, and climbed out.

The country stillness was complete except for the soft crunching sounds his feet made on the white-graveled driveway. It enveloped the house as well—a very modern house in its isolated rural setting, all jutting planes and angles, softened a little by the small forest of trees that surrounded it. The great square picture window facing the front was covered with heavy draperies. No glimmer of light showed through. Max noted with a kind of dull horror the elegant Christmas wreath hanging on the door. He pushed the bell, heard its muffled reverberation inside the house. Silence. No sound of footsteps.

Of course he's here. He must be here. Max jabbed the bell again impatiently, unable to bear the thought of the wasted time if he had traveled here for nothing. Hadn't Rosen told him that the doctor, a man of precise and rigid habits, always spent Christmastime at home? When he had called Rosen again to tell him Judith had disappeared, he had said, "I'm sure he'll be

118

there, but I don't know what good it will do you, Max. You'll see what I mean when you talk to him. I'll want to know about Judith, so keep in touch. Anything I can do, anything at all ..."

Max frowned and moved around to the side of the house. From there he could see light from some window in the back gleaming palely on a small pond that was covered with a thin coating of ice. A tree beside it held a bird feeder and a chickadee perched there, cocking his head at Max.

It was all too perfect, unreal, like a stale scene etched on a Christmas card. This rich, antiseptic Connecticut community was a thousand years distant from the doctor's youth, from the mud and filth and cold of the Nazi death camp, from the screaming agony of innocent people. Here, not even an echoing memory of a scream. Perhaps that whole time had been a nightmare the world dreamed long ago.

Max roused himself, clapping his arms around his body to drive away the chill and the memories, and strode back to the door where he raised his fist, ignoring the bell, and beat a sharp tattoo on it. A second later the door swung silently open.

At the sight of the man standing in the doorway, Max took a startled step back. He had seen only the old, faded newspaper photo and he thought he was prepared for this meeting, yet suddenly he felt that it was going to be more than he had bargained for. If it weren't for Judith . . . But that's what it was all about, wasn't it? And anyway, how could he have hoped to see a different face? That would have been against all reason.

The man in the doorway nodded at him and said, "Yes, yes," as though he were reading Max's mind. He smiled briefly, a quick revealing flash of secret malice, like a curtain parting and closing.

"I'm Max Halman, Doctor Klausing."

"I know. You've been a long time coming. I've

been expecting you." His voice was hollow, without resonance or inflection. If dead men could speak, Max thought, this is what they must sound like. "Perfect, perfect," he went on, gazing into Max's face and nodding again. Then he opened the door wide and said, "Come in out of the cold." With a slight, formal kind of a bow, he ushered Max into the hallway. His English was almost perfect, a little too precise, perhaps, with only the faintest trace of an accent to reveal his country of origin.

"Who is it, Karl?"

It was a woman's voice, quietly fretful, and over the doctor's shoulder Max could see her standing on a landing halfway up the stairs that faced him, framed in the gray light from the window behind her.

The man didn't bother to turn around as he answered her. "No need to concern yourself, Nina. Mr. Halman is a business acquaintance, that's all. Go back to bed."

"You're sure there's nothing you want me to do?" the voice asked quietly.

"Nothing. If there is, I'll ask Ernst for it."

"But Ernst had to go away. You told me."

"Yes, of course, I'd forgotten. But never mind, I won't be needing anything. Go to bed."

He waved a dismissing hand at her and the woman obediently turned and walked up the stairs. Max was relieved to see her go.

The man locked the door and said in his precise English, "My wife will not be able to join us, which is just as well. She has the flu."

"The contagion is all around us, isn't it, Doctor?"

"Always." Again the swift, malicious smile flashed and was gone. "We'll go to my study," he said, and turned to lead the way down the hall. It ran the full length of the house, front to back, and was lit only by the dim light that came through the long, narrow window in the rear. The window steamed with moisture and a few drops of snow clung to it.

There were no signs or sounds of life anywhere in the house that Max could distinguish as he followed the doctor down the hall. The two people seemed to be alone. Ernst, whoever he was—a manservant?—had gone on his errand.

When they reached the study, the doctor opened the door and stood aside for Max to enter. Soft strains of music drifted through the room. Oh, yes, the doctor was a great music lover, he remembered. It was a Bach flute sonata, probably Elaine Shaffer playing. Judith would have identified it specifically if she had been standing beside him. He noted the expensive stereo equipment built into the wall on the far side of the room, surrounded by bookshelves which rose from floor to ceiling. A man's retreat, a masculine room without frills, simply and comfortably furnished. Max wondered, without really caring, if the wife Nina was ever allowed in here. There was a desk of teakwood in modern design at one end of the room, at the other end, a large fireplace where a fire leaped and crackled. In front of it were two deep upholstered chairs and a low table. On it was a squat bottle of brandy and a glass. Two windows on either side of the fireplace looked out on the Christmas-card landscape Max had seen earlier. Snow was falling gently now on the pond and the trees.

There was nothing here from that other world of horror—not an echo—except for the man himself. He was leaning down, placing a fresh log on the fire. The fire hissed under the burden while the doctor remained bent over close to the flame, holding his hands to it, beautifully shaped hands, slender and strong with long fingers.

"I like a fire," he murmured in that flat, hollow

voice. "It's strange. Sometimes I get cold and despite all the central heating, only a real fire will warm me."

Was the cold an old infection, Max wondered bitterly, caught in the death camp during that bitter winter of 1944? While their victims froze in the dirty snow, fires and woolen clothes and thick, polished boots kept the supermen warm. Even their dogs, Max remembered with a shudder, wore their own special blankets, trimly decorated—black SS on a white circle. Perhaps the cold had crept from the bodies of his victims through his clothing to settle forever in his bones.

Max studied the man by the fire. A casual observer would see a tall, strong man, still attractive, carrying his sixty-odd years lightly. The close-cropped hair was iron-gray, but otherwise there were few signs of age. The skin was smooth over the broad planes of the face, the body lean and hard. But with his senses acutely aware, Max noted the gray, bloodless quality of the skin, the lifelessness of the deep-set eyes, and felt something unhealthy like a sickness in the air around him.

As Max watched him, a sudden and astonishing change took place. The revealing curtain parted fully. The man rose to his full height and turned to face Max. The gray cheeks were flushed with color, the mouth curved in its malicious smile, the dark eyes flashed with excitement. His whole body seemed to be seized by the force of some powerful emotion that was almost uncontrollable. He clenched his hands into fists.

"It will be interesting after so long," he said, the hollow voice loud in the quiet room.

"You know why I'm here?"

"Of course, of course. The hunt is on, isn't it? The hunt is on."

Stiffly, Max answered, "In full cry, Doctor Wallner."

"Wallner . . ." He seemed to roll the name around

on his tongue, tasting it with pleasure like his fine brandy.

"Yes," he said, his wild eyes intent on Max's face. "In full cry, as you say, but the hounds are after more than one quarry, aren't they?"

All Max could say was, "Yes," as he stared into the wild eyes.

"Like old times," Doctor Wallner replied.

Eighteen

The steward had brought her coffee and Judith sipped it slowly and smoked a cigarette while she read what her father had written in the Dinesen book.

I must leave out of this account some of the horrors Franz told me as he lay in the hospital—horrors he spoke of with a kind of compulsion to purge himself of guilt—false guilt, certainly, that he felt for having survived while most of his friends were already dead. The last one died the night before he made his escape from the camp of the damned.

It began after the long roll call in the icy dawn of a morning in early January 1945. Franz carried his dead friend out of the barracks and put him in his place in the snow. Even the dead had to answer the roll call.

Then came the shouted announcement over the loudspeaker: "All prisoners under orders to the gatehouse!" And Franz's name was on the list. Panic seized him. He could scarcely force his numb legs to move. What were they going to do to him?

He broke off in his story and smiled at me, a sad, apologetic smile (My dear Franz—apologetic!) "You must understand," he explained. "We weren't human beings anymore, only a series of responses, of conditioned reflexes. At the sight of a dog, we ran, at a shout, we cowered, at the lash of a whip, we whimpered. Years of conditioning, Leo. We used to speak of such things, you remember?"

I remembered, but then it had been a calm, academic discussion. This was real—my friend's wasted body, his fevered eyes, the fact that he couldn't really believe that he might have water whenever he was thirsty and food when he was hungry.

An SS guard met him at the gatehouse, Franz continued, and told him he was wanted by the camp medical officer. Terror drained him of the little strength he had. No one ever went to the hospital to get well. It was a place to go to die, more often in agony before death brought release. He tried to steel himself against the lethal injection, the bullet, or worse, and he wasn't aware that they had moved out through the gate, across the neutral zone and away from the electrified barbed wire, heading in a direction new to him.

He didn't have to run. He was allowed to walk at a leisurely pace while the guard accompanied him quietly without shouts or blows. This unusual treatment struck more terror into his heart. What new form of sadism were they planning?

It was a long walk. The day was bitter cold but Franz, dressed only in the thin, zebra-striped prison garb with wooden clogs on his bare feet, was nevertheless drenched in perspiration by the time they reached their destination. They turned up a well-paved road, lined on each side with luxurious villas, or so they seemed to Franz at the time. These were the homes of the supermen, built with the blood of slave labor, far removed from the wasteland Franz inhabited. They were tasteful, commodious buildings surrounded by large plots of ground with tall trees, and in the summertime there would be grass and the sweet smell of flowers. He told me how the sound of his wooden clogs on the clean pavement astonished and frightened him. For four years his feet had known only the mud and snow and ice of the dead ground of the prison compound.

At the door of one of these houses the guard knocked softly. The door was opened immediately. The man who faced him was close to Franz in age, somewhere in his thirties, a tall, strongly built man, dressed in an elegantly tailored uniform with captain's insignia. The lightning strokes of the SS were embroidered in gold. In silence he motioned for them to come in. In silence he directed the guard to the kitchen. Then with a quick imperious gesture he beckoned Franz to follow him and strode on ahead to the living room, walking with long, strong steps.

Franz followed slowly, pausing midway to catch his breath. At the entrance to the room he stopped, dazed. It was like coming from dark into full sunlight. The room was beautiful and full of light. There was a grand piano, fine, soft chairs, gleaming tables, a flowering plant by the window. The floor was thickly carpeted and a log fire burned in the fireplace. The man was offering Franz a chair beside the fire. The long walk in the cold had depleted his strength; added to that was the numbing fear brought on by this unusual treatment, and Franz was near to fainting. But he refused the chair and stood swaying slightly, thinking with his last bit of courage that whatever this man planned to do to him, he would take standing up.

The man's smile was cruel, he understood what Franz was thinking. "Sit down, Halman. I'm Wallner, an assistant to *the* camp doctor. I know you're not disappointed at not seeing him. Sit down, you fool! I'm not going to eat you."

And Franz sank weakly into the chair, thinking that the man almost could eat him if he wanted to. He seemed charged with a ferocious kind of vitality. He stood beside the fireplace, one black-booted leg crossed over the other, drumming with the long, strong fingers of one hand on the mantel.

"No, on the contrary," he went on in his strange, hollow-sounding voice, "I'm going to offer you your freedom. You will travel with me to Hamburg in one of the camp's supply trucks. We will leave today. The guard who brought you here is trustworthy. He will drive us. Hamburg will be in British hands soon. Your safety and freedom carries only one condition—your signature on a paper I've drawn up which states that I was kind to you and the other prisoners, that I tried to help whenever possible, that I saved your life." His tone was arrogant. He wasn't asking a favor. He was demanding compliance.

Franz only dimly understood what the man was saying. He asked hoarsely, "Why me?"

"Because you have a foot in both camps—" He paused and smiled thinly at his own macabre joke. "You have an American wife and American friends. You have German friends who are of the right persuasion—the right persuasion, that is, for the immediate future—and, furthermore, because I consider you worth saving. You'll understand that later on. You have a good Nordic background despite the Jewish grandfather mistake in the past. And coming right down to it, I have no other choice. I would prefer to surrender to the Americans but they are farther away and I can't afford to take any chances. And never mind," he finished with arrogant impatience, "my reasons are no concern of yours. You only have to sign the paper." He left the room.

Hamburg . . . Franz had friends in Hamburg. Freedom . . . He sat in the soft chair by the warm fire and for the first time in four years he allowed himself to think of life outside the camp—of Mary, his wife, of the son he had never seen. He stroked the arm of the chair and closed his eyes and thought of them with a gnawing kind of hunger.

He was aware that the doctor had returned and was thrusting an official-looking sheet of paper at him. In a kind of daze, Franz had taken the paper and read its glowing description of the doctor's kindness to the inmates, the lives he had saved by special medical treatment and special food, how he had performed only a few operations, and those under strict orders and supervision. It went on and on and Franz felt his stomach twist with nausea as he remembered some of the patients Wallner had "helped"—of the men castrated by X-ray and moving in an agony of burns and abscesses; of the women, their wombs injected with irritant chemicals, screaming . . . Leah . . . Dead now, her letter buried in a secret place in the ground. Scarcely aware of it, he spoke her name aloud.

"Your cousin is dead, you fool. There's nothing you can do for her. Sign the paper."

Franz looked up at the doctor and shook his head. He was a dead man anyway, today, tomorrow . . . What difference did it make? He had pushed himself up out of the chair and had stood there—this dear, dear friend of mine—barely human, barely able to stand, with his knife-sharp face and shaven skull. "No," he said. "No," and let the paper fall to the floor.

Wallner had stared at him for a moment and then, suddenly, using no effort at all, he had reached out and poked Franz in the chest with one long finger and Franz had collapsed like a rag doll into the chair.

The doctor leaned over him and asked in a soft, savage voice, "How long have you been here?"

"Three years," Franz gasped.

"Before then?"

"Treblinka."

"How much did you weigh before the camps?"

"One hundred and—and seventy, I think."

Still in the soft voice, the doctor asked, "And now?"

In a flash of bravado, Franz grinned up at him out of his death's head and said, "Weighing scales are one of the few luxuries we're not permitted, Herr Doktor."

The doctor slapped him savagely across the face, his eyes wild. He picked up the paper. "Sign it!" he screamed and pushed it into Franz's hand.

Franz was on home ground. This was the kind of treatment he was used to. He simply turned his head away and waited for the next blow. It didn't come. Wallner had swung away abruptly and left the room.

Franz put his hand out toward the fire as though in farewell to this brief taste of what life used to be. Back soon to the mud and the cold, the shouts and the dogs, the icy sky—until the bitter, lonely end.

When the doctor returned, he carried a bowl of thick, hot soup. Its fragrance filled the room and turned Franz's knees to water. He tried not to look at it as Wallner placed it on a table in front of him.

"Eat it, you fool," the doctor told him harshly,

and Franz ate, slowly and carefully, so he wouldn't get sick.

"You know, of course, that the Russians are close."

Franz nodded and swallowed a spoonful of soup.

"And you know what will happen in the camp as they get closer?"

Franz nodded again. It was already happening. Daily the transports were leaving the camp, some on foot, some in trucks or boxcars. No one knew where they were going, no one dared ask. For those who remained it was no longer fear of the crematoria. They had been blown up in November by order of Himmler, but death still came daily to hundreds and the gentlest was in the form of sickness or starvation or the casual bullet. Fear of the approaching Russian army was a disease that drove the SS and the Kapos to sudden, barbarous acts of violence as though only the blood of their victims could cure the disease.

"Then you know that we won't be leaving any live witnesses, don't you?"

Franz put the spoon down. The food was choking him.

"Finish it! You'll go with me anyway." He folded the paper and put it into his pocket. "And I don't want a corpse on my hands. I'll work it out by some other means."

In a sudden rush of insight, Franz whispered, "You *need* me—you're afraid!" He was astonished not only by his boldness in saying it but by the fact that it was true. Time had run out for the superman. He needed a victim to protect him.

"Of course, you idiot," the doctor said, his eyes bright and wild looking. "But that adds to the excitement, sharpens the senses. I rather enjoy my fear. I make it work for me."

Though Franz wasn't at all sure he would survive the trip, he finally agreed to go for reasons of his own, not the least of which was to smuggle Leah's letter out. How glad he was that he had done so!

The guard accompanied him back to the barracks where he was allowed to pick up his few pitiful belongings. He concealed Leah's letter under his shirt and later stole the picture of the doctor from Wallner's own house.

Shortly before he died, Franz said to me, "There's no need to tell you why I accepted Wallner's offer, but I made no commitment— none. *You* are not committed." Then he murmured his son's name, "Max," and tried to smile. He couldn't. There was only the faintest glimmer of life in the hollow eyes.

I told him, "Don't worry. I'll take care of him, Franz, as though he were my own son."

His life passed out of him with a sigh. His body was so wasted it made almost no impression on the narrow, white hospital bed, but he had been warm and fed and lovingly cared for. He had that, at least, at the end. But Leah . . . for her . . .

Her father had found no words to finish the last thought.

Judith folded the book in her lap and looked out of the window. The plane seemed to float in the dark sky above the clouds. Looking down she caught a fleeting glimpse of cold water.

What was the use, she thought, in trying to understand what happened to Franz and Leah? It was beyond understanding, beyond imagining. She could only finish what her father had started. If only . . .

She felt a sudden surge of anger at the thought of her father's secretiveness. How simple it would have been if he had merely told her where the letter was. Her anger evaporated as quickly as it had come because she knew what agonies of conflict he had suffered—his guilt over Leah's fate, his fierce, vengeful feelings toward Wallner, his desire to protect her. How could she judge his behavior by any normal standards after having watched that slow process of deterioration?

Her thoughts went questioningly to the books. Why these six? A random selection? They were all small, easy to pick up and carry. All right, but why six? So far, those parts of the story that she had read hadn't been all that long. They might easily have been condensed to fit into three or four of the books. Was it for purposes of concealment? Perhaps. Easier for someone to overlook two or three pages when they were riffling through a book.

Memorize them, her father's voice whispered in her ear, *Memorize them.*

Judith's head was pounding, her cheeks were flushed. She returned the book to the suitcase and went to the rest room where she took two aspirin and drank several glasses of water. On the way back to her seat, the plane suddenly dipped sideways and threw her against a passenger. She swayed back with the roll of the plane and said, "Excuse me," and was about to start away when the man rose quickly and taking her wrist in a surprisingly strong grip, asked, "Can I help you?"

She backed off, startled by the eagerness in the high-pitched nasal voice. She had seen him before— the man in the restaurant doorway with his elaborate pantomime of courtesy. She shook the hand off her arm frantically—its nails, she noticed, were chewed to the quick and were black around the edges—and hurried, stumbling, back to her seat. Everyone seemed to be staring at her. She huddled down, trying hopelessly to make herself small. In her exhausted, feverish state she imagined every passenger on the plane to be the enemy, all with cold blank eyes in strange, hostile faces. She twisted around toward the window and closed her eyes, shutting them out.

Nineteen

Max left the house in Connecticut and drove with reckless speed through the dark and the driving snow back to New York, cursing himself for having gone in the first place, for having been naive enough to expect to find a spark of humanity in a man whose past had been dedicated to inhumanity and who, during the brief interview, had come to life only when some memory of that murderous past had stirred him. At those times excitement flashed in the burned-out eyes and the mouth curved in malicious enjoyment. The transformation would come and go so fast, like a match flaring in the dark, that Max was left wondering if he had really seen it.

For Judith's sake he had had to try it. And yet . . . His thoughts stumbled over the fear that perhaps he had opened another area of danger for her. No, he rejected the thought immediately. The danger was already there. He believed Smith—that those around the doctor had been responsible for Leo Weber's death.

He left the car with the rental people and taxied to the hotel where he picked up his key and hurried toward the elevator. His next move . . . ? On the remote chance that Judith might have been in touch with her, he would phone Sheila. After that, Smith . . . ? Strange to have even the most tenuous working connection with him.

Halfway to the elevator Max became aware that someone was following him, so close, in fact, that when Max swung around he trod on the man's toes.

The man grimaced with pain and stepped back, ducking his head into his collar, his dark glasses glittering vacantly at Max.

With a faint threat in his voice, Max asked, "Are you following me?"

"Yes." The musical voice was furtively low. "I wonder if I could speak to you for a moment, Mr. Halman?"

"How do you know who I am?"

"That's not important."

"What is it, then?"

"It's about a mutual acquaintance."

"I'm listening."

"Not here. Could we just . . . ?" A gloved hand plucked nervously at Max's sleeve as the man gestured with his head toward a dim corner. "It's quieter over there."

"Darker, you mean."

In the shadows the man removed his sunglasses and peered up at Max with small, rather sly, eyes and whispered, "I know you're looking for her and—"

"For her?"

"Oh . . ." He made a small, impatient movement with his gloved hand. "Do you think you have time to play games, Mr. Halman? You haven't, I assure you. I'm talking about Miss Weber, as you well know. I've been following her—"

"Following her?" The frustration and fear he had felt in Wallner's study turned to rage against this man and he leaned forward and seized his coat lapels roughly in both hands, jerking him upward so only his toes touched the floor. "Say what you have to say," Max said, his voice low and savage. "Then you can crawl back under your stone."

"I'm trying to," the little man gasped. "If you'd just . . ."

Immediately ashamed of his loss of control, Max released him and said stiffly, "Go ahead."

"I'm only trying to be friendly," the man said in an aggrieved tone.

"All right. Be friendly. Did Smith send you?"

"No, no." The man's face paled and the tongue licked out around the lips. "I was following her, you see. And I lost her at the department store—"

"You're the one . . . ?"

"Only I didn't really, of course. It was kind of an arrangement and afterward she took a taxi to the airport and I followed her there—"

"An arrangement? She gave you money, you mean, not to follow her, so you followed her?"

"Oh, I'm sticking to the agreement, Mr. Halman," the little man said with a semblance of dignity.

"Get on with it."

The man hesitated, took off his hat, and smoothed his hair, put the hat back on, all the while probing Max's face with sly eyes. Finally he said, "I spent a lot of money. It was expensive—taxis and things. And I had to sit in the restaurant a long time—food, drinks, tips . . ."

Max looked down at the man in disgust as he reached for his wallet. "I'll pay for your expenses, nothing more." He counted out two twenties and a ten and handed them to the man. "That should cover them."

The man spread the bills out fanwise, studying them doubtfully, debating, perhaps, as to whether he might get more. It had been easy with Miss Weber. She had handed the money over without question. He wished he had asked her for more. But not this man, no, so he gave the bills a last regretful look and tucked them into his pocket.

"She went to the airport," Max said sharply. "She took a plane. Where?"

"It was Lufthansa—to Bonn."

"That confirms my suspicion, so I guess it's worth the fifty. Thanks." Max started to turn away toward the elevator when the soft, musical voice stopped him.

"There's just one more thing. Two men—no one I know—were following her too. A small, thin man and a big burly guy. I heard the small one call the big guy 'Ernst.' I think—I'm quite sure—they went on the same plane as Miss Weber. They didn't look like very nice types. That's why—you understand . . . Well, the truth is, I don't like to see a woman like that—she's very beautiful. I felt I owed it to her . . ." The little man seemed to have trouble finishing his thought and the soft voice trailed off into the air.

Max didn't speak, just stood there staring at the man as though he were a million miles away.

"Well, that's all." The man smiled sadly and shrugged. Then he turned and waddled off through the lobby and out of the door, pulling his coat collar up against the snow.

Max roused himself, shaking his head slightly as though to clear it. He saw the back of the man disappearing down the steps and he experienced a fleeting moment of warmth for him. After all, he thought, he needn't have come to me at all. He could just as easily have walked away and forgotten the whole business. Was it sympathy for Judith that motivated him? The money? Both, probably. Judith must have given him a good bit of cash if he was content with only fifty from Max. Unhappily, he thought of some of the unsavory rules she must be learning in a hurry for this game, that she would have to learn if she were going to reach her objective.

He went on with his brooding thoughts as he headed for the elevator. That last bit of information had been worth the money. Two rough types—a big, burly man named Ernst—on the plane with Judith. Wallner's manservant was named Ernst and he had gone away on an errand. Wallner had lied to him, but why should that surprise him?

The elevator lifted him up to the fifth floor but it was the surge and lift of a plane he felt. Judith was off and away now, flying into the heart of the danger. She would land at the Bonn-Cologne airport early tomorrow morning, probably rent a car there and drive the short distance to Aachen and the border of Holland.

Head bent, absorbed in thought, Max hurried down the corridor to his room. Once in Holland, he was thinking, she would have to do some searching around. She didn't know exactly where the letter was. Or had she discovered its secret in the books somewhere?

I have a chance to catch her if I hurry, he thought, as he fitted the key into the lock. Hurry . . . ? An ocean between, holiday traffic and lousy weather! Pass a miracle, Halman, old man, pass a miracle.

It was then he smelled the cigarette smoke and saw a small cloud of it rise over the top of a chair—one of those stiff, forbidding chairs even the best hotels place in corridors. A figure rose from the chair and moved toward him.

"I've been waiting for you. I want to talk to you. I called Washington and Sara told me you were in New York. It came as a surprise to me."

Damn! Damn! Max cursed silently as he stepped aside to let Babcock walk past him into the sitting room. He was his usual neat, precise self, smelling subtly of expensive cologne, and the bland voice held only a faint accusing tone as he said, "I've been sitting there for quite a while."

Not all that long, Max thought as he flicked the light switch and noticed the melting snow still glistening on the man's hat and coat. "Sorry," he said curtly.

"Let's make it brief, shall we? I have only a few minutes."

"Good of you to give me that much."

Max ignored the sarcasm. "I spoke to Sara this morning. There was only routine stuff that she was handling with her usual efficiency. What's up?"

"Strictly speaking, this isn't office business."

"Ah . . ." Max said softly. "I didn't think so."

He dropped his own coat on the chair beside the door and watched Babcock go through the ritual of removing his outer garments. He peeled off his gray suede gloves slowly and placed them on the sofa. Beside them, tucked into the corner, lay Judith's forgotten rain hat, looking crumpled and pathetic. Max's glance strayed automatically to the window. The wet snow was coming down heavily now and he thought of her as an anxious parent would think of a child: she was catching cold, she should have a hat on. What if she got ill, alone, wherever she was, with no one to look after her?

Babcock paid no attention to the hat, though he must have seen it. He removed his own hat and placed it on top of the gloves, then took off the dark blue overcoat, which he shook twice to get the water out before he draped it carefully over the back of the sofa. Every movement was slow and deliberate as though he had all the time in the world. Max held back his anger. That would be utterly useless. Babcock himself was in a rage though his face didn't show it. His face rarely showed any feeling. Only the vein in his temple gave him away. Babcock's barometer, the people in his department called it. It was swollen and throbbing now as he sat down, stretched out his legs, and pulled up the trousers so they wouldn't crease—as though he had come for a quiet cup of tea . . . !

"You know about Leo Weber?" Max asked, knowing he must know but wanting to get on with it.

Babcock turned his smooth, tanned face to Max.

"Yes, I know about Leo Weber and I'm—sorry." He seemed to choose the meaningless word with delicate precision. "And that's why I'm here. To come straight to the point, I think it's time this fruitless, silly quest is finished. I would like you to convince Miss Weber to give it up." Babcock held up a small, well-manicured hand as Max started to speak. "Let me finish. Toward the end, as everyone knows, Leo Weber was quite— distraught." Again the delicate choice of word. "Despite that, however, he was able, it seems, to convince his daughter of the justice of his cause, though it was based on the slimmest evidence—" He shrugged. "—if one can call it evidence at all—that this man *might* be a former SS doctor who *might* have committed some kind of crime. The man we're talking about is an American citizen now. He has his rights under the law. His name is Klausing and there is no real evidence to connect him to Wallner, who, so the records state, has been dead since nineteen forty-eight. One can't prosecute a dead man. Only further unpleasantness can result if she pursues this. She would be wise to drop it."

"She won't drop it, I'm afraid, and if Leo Weber lost touch somewhat with reality, Judith hasn't, and certainly Ted Rosen, the reporter who wrote the story, hasn't. He's a practical, intelligent man who made a careful investigation. You know that. He came to see you shortly before the story was published."

"But he was not able to say for certain that Klausing was Wallner." The voice was smoothly skeptical and Max realized with something of a shock how much he really disliked this man. How long had he felt that way and not known?

"No," Max admitted, "he couldn't do that. Someone had prepared a very careful background for Klausing. But Rosen was personally convinced that the two men were the same and went to great lengths to build his case. He spoke to the man himself, spoke to people in

Germany who knew Wallner in the thirties and forties. He got hold of a picture of him as a young man taken sometime in the thirties. There was a strong resemblance, though the young Wallner had a dueling scar—"

"Which this man does not have, I understand."

"Nothing that shows. There's always plastic surgery."

With amused contempt, Babcock said, "Really now, Max, if I didn't know you so well, I'd say you were deluding yourself. Plastic surgery, a photo taken over forty years ago . . ."

Max felt his face go hot with anger at the man's tone and he turned away, fighting for control. He felt he had been on a kind of emotional seesaw for two days and he wanted to get off—find Judith and get off. He managed to speak calmly. "I haven't mentioned the most important connection. You must know it. A friend of Rosen's, himself a doctor, identified Klausing as Wallner. Saw him at some medical 'do' here in New York. He was terribly excited and upset. He'd been an inmate at Auschwitz for three years, had been on the receiving end of certain 'medical' treatments himself. He told Rosen that even though the man's face had changed with age, he could never have mistaken the voice—a strange, flat, hollow kind of voice—"

"Then why hasn't he come forward?"

"Unfortunately he was an old man. He died of a heart attack shortly after—but—" Max broke off, shocked by the thought that in light of what happened to Leo Weber, it suddenly made sense that the old man might not have died of natural causes at all, but of very unnatural ones. Go easy, he cautioned himself, go easy, you'll be seeing torturing brutes and assassins around every corner. Still, he'd mention it to Rosen.

"An old man, probably sick when he made the statement, now dead . . . ? Really, Max, I'm surprised. A man of your training, your ability . . ."

The silk-smooth voice, the cool, calculated reprimand

—goddamn him! Max said stiffly, "I had hoped we would find ourselves on the same side in this." It would serve no useful purpose to tell Babcock of his visit to Wallner, of the fact that Wallner had admitted his identity with pleasure. There had been no witnesses. Wallner could simply deny everything. Besides he wanted to terminate this interview as soon as possible. There was so little time.

"I'm not on any side, Max. Objectivity is the key word here and you're too emotionally involved with Miss Weber to be objective."

"I love her, if that's what you mean."

"Of course." Babcock paused to remove a cigarette from a case of beaten gold. Inserting it carefully into a holder, he lit it with a gold lighter, then he leaned back, inhaling deeply, and gazed at Max through bland, shuttered eyes. Max could only guess at the thoughts behind them. Of course Babcock sensed his impatience and was being deliberately provocative.

"Of course," Babcock repeated. "What do you intend to do now?"

"Find Miss Weber, if I can."

"If . . . ? You must find her."

"Must?" Max raised an eyebrow.

"That's the whole point of my visit, my dear Max. You must find her and put an end to this. I remind you of your obligation to the Department. I don't want it involved in this. It would be better for everyone, including herself, if she were simply to forget about it—"

"Better for everyone? By which you mean for those who were responsible for bringing the doctor—and how many others—into this country—who are afraid their guilt in the matter will be revealed?"

"Guilt . . ." Babcock waved the word away with the elegant cigarette holder as though the matter were unworthy of discussion. "My dear Max, at the end of the war everyone scrambled around for the German scientists. Russia 'recruited' her share, we took ours, Egypt, South America—"

"Which makes it just dandy. But we're not discussing legitimate scientists here, Babcock—you know damned well we're not—nor the moral and ethical justification for giving that kind of sanction to the enemy. We're discussing one man, a sadist-butcher. . . ." Like a heavy, dark cloud it swept over Max—that lingering smell of evil haunting the firelit, book-lined study, its occupant gazing at him with dead eyes.

Babcock leaned forward to tip the ash of his cigarette into the ashtray, saying gently, "It's such an old matter."

It's such a long time ago. It's of no importance now. . . . Wallner's soft, hollow voice as he leaned forward to refill his brandy glass, the firelight flickering on the gray skin while the clean snow tracked its way down the windows.

"And all the files are buried under dust, and let's not disturb the dust. No," Max murmured. He walked away from Babcock to the window. "It can't end like this, not now, not after Leo Weber . . . We have a responsibility."

"I'm asking you not to pursue this," Babcock's suave voice broke in.

Someone in an apartment in the building opposite the hotel switched on the lights suddenly and the pretty glow of a Christmas tree was outlined in the window. Max thought with a kind of angry sorrow of the holiday plans he had made for Judith and Tommy and himself—ice-skating in Rockefeller Center under the big Christmas tree, hot chocolate afterwards, walking down Fifth Avenue, the three of them together . . . He was going to have to tell Tommy something, make it up to him. Perhaps he might get Judith back in time. With his eyes still on the Christmas tree, he asked almost absently, "And if I pursue it all the same?"

"If . . . ? But of course you won't do that. We don't want this connected with the Department in any way. That would be a very foolish thing for you to do."

Quietly he persisted, "But if I do?"

Babcock remained silent for a long time and Max almost forgot about him and the drift of the conversation while he checked off in his mind the things he must do within the next hour. When Babcock spoke finally in a voice that had a slight breathy quality, the words registered slowly.

"If you do, I might be forced to ask for your resignation."

Shaking off the lassitude that had held him, Max turned to face Babcock and said, "Ask and you shall receive. Then the Department won't be inpolved in any way."

The two men stared at each other, both astonished at how easily the words had been spoken.

Unbelievingly, Babcock said, "You're bluffing."

"Am I?" Max watched the heavy blue vein in the man's temple swell and pulse with his anger while he himself made a grim assessment of the statement. Was it fatigue or was he just desperately sick of the business that had seen his friend, Leo, die in agony and his beloved Judith off on her mission, vulnerable and unprotected? He only knew he had to do something about it no matter what Babcock's reaction was. He had told Smith "I'll tear you limb from limb"—angry, unreasoning words, but true all the same. "Try me," he said bluntly.

"You're a fool," Babcock said, sitting ramrod-stiff on the sofa, holding himself rigid against the rage that wanted to break out. "You mentioned responsibility. What about the Department? You can't possibly be so irresponsible." His cigarette had gone out in the holder but he didn't notice it. His eyes were cold on Max's face. "You're slated for my spot when I leave. There's no one better qualified. You'd throw over everything you've worked for to tilt at a windmill . . . !"

"I want the job—that and more—but not enough to cover up and condone murder. I have to live with myself for a long time." And with Judith, he thought.

"Leo Weber died in a fire."

"Smith's story. Smith's doing. You accept it?"

"I have no choice." He rose stiffly and dropped the cigarette into the ashtray and pocketed the holder. Then he pulled on his coat and buttoned it. He picked up his hat and gloves, making a gesture as he did so toward the crumpled rain hat. "Find her," he said, "and bring her back and let's forget what we said here."

"I'll have to resolve this my way, Babcock. I don't want Judith Weber to find that letter any more than you do—for my own reasons."

"You know where it is?"

Max remained angrily silent.

"Because if you do," Babcock said, pulling on the gray suede gloves and smoothing the fingers carefully, "that makes you vulnerable."

"Vulnerable . . ." Max shrugged. "Smith? Whose watchdog is he?"

Max hadn't expected an answer and there was none. The two men faced each other at the door. The battle lines were drawn. Max would do what he had to do and Babcock would do what he could to stop him. Max had always been vaguely aware that this man was jealous of him. He had ignored it, thinking it pointless to delve for reasons, and except for the recent weeks when tension grew between them because of Leo Weber, they had worked well together, keeping an impersonal kind of relationship. One thing Max knew and had grown used to was that Babcock was never quite comfortable with him. No matter how hard Babcock tried, no matter how carefully he dressed, he always felt gauche in Max's presence. That casual elegance that was second nature to Max, Babcock could never achieve. It was the same in his relations with people. He was not at ease with them and just once, in a singular moment of confidence, Babcock had admitted as much to Max. At the same time he gave the subtle impression that his association with Max pleased him, that he enjoyed being Max's superior. A feeling of power ... And something else which Max had studiously avoided thinking about. There had been the one whisper of scandal some years ago. It had faded quickly and wasn't heard again. Since then Max suspected Babcock led a completely celibate life. He was drawn pretty fine on the wire sometimes, it was obvious, but his work came first. Nothing would interfere with that. Babcock had climbed to his position in the State Department the hard way. There had been no wealth to rely on, no proper schools, nor the right contacts that went with them. To succeed, he had learned to fight, not always by the rules.

A light touch on his arm interrupted Max's thoughts. He roused himself and became aware of a sudden, subtle change in the room's atmosphere as Babcock said in a soft voice, "Forget it, Max, please. Come back to Washington where you belong."

Briefly the man's guard had dropped, the veil lifted from the bland eyes and allowed Max to look into them, through them, and catch a momentary glimpse of the naked, tormented soul that lay beneath the careful veneer of polish and sophistication, a victim of its own stark, almost primitive emotions. Something was there, too, of the same driven, haunted quality he had seen on Judith's face when she had stood here earlier.

It was over in a second. The guard went up again as Max swung away, rejecting the revelation, angry at the pity he suddenly felt for the man, unwilling to accept it or cope with it. He busied himself lighting a cigarette, keeping his back to Babcock, who had stepped away, putting distance between them. Max heard him breathing deeply as though steadying himself after running.

The break was mended, the atmosphere re-charged itself with the men's hostility.

With studied calm, Max said, "I won't deceive you, Babcock. It's impossible for me to forget it. I've told you what I have to do and I'll do it."

Babcock's voice, detached, silk-smooth again: "Then I won't deceive you, Max. If you persist in this, I shall take steps to have the letter, if there is one, declared a sensational trick of forgery. I'll have you proved a person of, shall we say, unstable personality who had sympathetic connections with the Vietcong when you were in Vietnam—a Vietcong sweetheart with whom you committed certain indiscretions, and while you were not exactly disloyal, who knows what you would have done had I not brought you back in time. That shouldn't be hard to prove. There are witnesses who will state how you managed to get her released against the better judgment of others."

"Smith."

"Yes, and others."

Max tried to remember the names of the other men in that hut but they had receded beyond recalling. He had no doubt that Babcock knew them, had them filed tidily away in a draw of his neat desk.

Babcock went on. "In addition, it shouldn't be hard to have Miss Weber proved of unsound mind considering the evidence of her father's paranoia these last six months—"

"A very contagious disease indeed. You're over-reaching yourself, Babcock. Why not have us thrown into mental hospitals like they do in the Soviet Union? We disagree with you, therefore we are insane. As for *my* Vietcong sweetheart, you know damned well she was Smith's woman and that it was Smith—"

"Who made a mistake and had to rectify it?"

"He thought he had."

"Yes, you know that and I know that and Smith knows. The Vietcong woman is dead, of course, but then her word wouldn't have counted in any event. If I were a gambler, Halman, I wouldn't bet on your chances."

"And if you expose my instability, as you call it, won't you find it hard to explain why I'm still in this sensitive spot, slated to step into *your* shoes at *your* recommendation?"

Babcock's dark eyes gleamed and the thick, soft lips smiled with a kind of triumph. "How deceived I was in my protégé. What clever deceit Max Halman practiced on his friends and superiors . . . !" He spread out his gloved hands in a fraudulent gesture of helplessness, stared at them for a moment and flicked an imaginary speck of dust from one. "You understand, Max," he said softly, "I don't want to go this far, but you know what pride I take in the Department's integrity. I won't have it involved in some dirty scandal, so don't force my hand." He opened the door and stepped out into the hall. "I trust I'll see you in Washington soon." He walked off down the corridor without saying good-bye.

Twenty

I'll see you in hell first, Max thought as he shut the door on Babcock's neat, navy blue back. He had never felt such anger. His body was hot and trembling with it. He knew well what damage Babcock could create with just a few nasty whispers in the right places. *No fury like* . . . He reached for the bottle of cognac that stood invitingly on the coffee table where he had placed it this morning for Judith, uncapped it, and tilted it to his lips for a long drink. "Shades of Smith," he murmured as he recapped it. But it had the calming effect he had hoped for. He was even able to tell himself jokingly that there was a strong smell of burning bridges in the room.

Tomorrow, he thought, I'll worry about Babcock. He picked up Judith's hat and headed for the bedroom remembering how, earlier in the evening, he had left Wallner as abruptly as Babcock had left him. Murmuring a scarcely audible "Good-bye," he had hurried away from that lonely house and the sickness that contaminated it, leaving the doctor standing at his window gazing out at the poetic winter scene. As he stood there with the glass of fine brandy in his hand, did he see a double image? Hollow-eyed women standing in the dirty snow, the pale lavender of death painted on their gaunt faces, shaven heads etched in sharp distortion against the raw Polish sky. Leah one of them. When he listened to a piano concerto, didn't he see Leah's small figure bent over the keyboard, working her magic with music? Or was he never troubled with the nightmares that had haunted Leo Weber?

Max picked up his suitcase from the floor and put it on the bed. He had to pack and get to the airport, though luckily there was little packing to do because he hadn't really unpacked. He flipped the lid open and saw the maps. He had forgotten they were there. While Judith stood talking to her brother with the suitcase at her feet, had she noticed them? She must have, else why had she agreed so readily to take a nap and slipped away at the first opportunity? He had bought them after Sheila had called him and told him about Leo. He could scarcely remember what he had in mind then. Had he hoped to be on his way to finding the letter, destroying it, and never let the contents be known? Sheila had urged him in that thin, hysterical voice to do that. There's still a chance, he thought grimly.

He rummaged through the suitcase, checking its contents: change of underclothing, clean shirt, tie, socks. He arranged them carelessly, without his usual fastidiousness, and on top he placed Judith's hat. Then he headed for the bathroom. A quick shave and he would be on his way. He could eat at the airport if he had to wait, otherwise, on the plane.

He stared at his reflection in the mirror before he applied the lather, hearing Wallner's flat voice saying, "Remarkable. You're the image of your father. The blond hair, that fine, long bone structure of the head, tall, slim . . . The elegant, aristocratic bearing—the perfect Nordic specimen. Only the best of breeding—"

"Nordic!" The man's words had made him feel soiled. "My father was a Jew." Max glared down at the old man in the soft armchair.

"Not altogether. A taint only. I forgave him for that. One must make certain compromises sometimes for the right ends. Your father resembled his mother, who came from an old and noble German family. The fact that your grandmother chose to marry a Jew—stupid. But the taint can be bred away . . ."

Max went on shaving mechanically remembering that strange, terrible interview, the sense of dislocation, of walking between two worlds. He hadn't taken off his coat, he hadn't sat down. He paced the room except when disbelief shocked him to stillness.

Instead of the positive hatred he had thought he would feel for the man, there had been only a negative kind of revulsion. Wallner had sat for the most part in the armchair in front of the fire, broad shoulders slumped forward, his feet in soft slippers propped on a footstool, sipping his brandy. Max's pointed refusal of a drink hadn't disturbed him, if, in fact, he had noticed it at all. He seemed a dead man, a shadow, except for the few times when some memory of the past had brought about that sudden, startling transformation. Then the wild excitement flashed in his eyes and the smile of malice curved the lips. At those moments he straightened in the chair and seemed to grow bigger, broader, younger, the superman his father had known; but the malevolent flame of life would die as quickly as it had come, leaving him empty and exhausted, a shell of a man waiting to be filled again by his memories. Most of their discussion seemed simply to have bored him.

"That is why," he had continued, "out of all the rabble, I considered your father worth saving. It would be necessary, I knew, to rebuild the master race, necessary to prepare a broad base of healthy Nordic blood from which the Heroes would arise again . . ." The hollow voice rumbled forth its rotten mixture of Hegel and Nietzsche out of Rosenberg and Goebbels. "The leaders—lords of the earth—above and beyond the legal and moral laws of ordinary men, who will rebuild from the ashes . . ."

Perhaps he believed it, perhaps it was just a kind of mental reflex, for when Max interrupted to ask harshly, "Surely it was simply a matter of insurance? My father might have saved your neck, if it came to that," the man had peered up at him, his eyes sharp for a moment and said, "Of course, why not? *All good things approach their goal crookedly*. Nietzsche? Yes, it must be Nietzsche—poor, demented man—but useful."

"Unfortunately, my father didn't live long enough to do you or himself much good."

"I couldn't foresee that, of course." He smiled slyly at the fire, then he shrugged and whispered, "It all happened so long ago," and lapsed into weary indifference.

For the burning questions Max had brought with him, the man had shown little interest.

"What of Leo Weber's death?"

"That's what brought you to see me finally? You have no real sense of destiny, Max Halman. I understand he died by accident in a fire."

"How did you know?"

"My man, Ernst, brings me the papers." With one long arm he reached for a newspaper that lay on the floor beside the chair and handed it to Max. It was an afternoon edition, open to the page which held a brief story of Weber's death, obviously put in just before the paper went to press.

Max tossed it on the table and said bluntly, "He didn't die in the fire. He was tortured."

"Your imagination is too vivid." He said it calmly enough but the eyes he turned to Max gleamed for a second with a kind of hunger.

"His daughter, Judith Weber, found the body before it was burned."

"Did she? Then she must go to the police."

"It was done to protect you. Leo Weber knew of a letter that could have exposed you."

"A letter . . ." In the brief silence the fire hissed and crackled and Max saw the transformation begin as though some of the fire's flame leaped into Wallner's body. The dark eyes blazed at him, the gray skin flushed with color. "The letter—I've been told of the possible existence of so-called evidence." The traces of accent were stronger in his speech, so was the arrogance. "Evidence manufactured by sick, crazed minds—"

"Made crazed by your ministrations—"

"And this manuscript put together by Weber, grown paranoid in his old age—"

"No, only tormented by the memory of how his wife died and the knowledge that her murderer still lives—and how did you know about that?"

One strong, white hand waved in the air. "That's not important, but you're deceiving yourself, Max Halman, if you think these stupid documents, if they exist, will make any difference. They have nothing to do with me. Kurt Wallner is dead. You know that."

"If the letter is found, there's a photograph with it that can bring Kurt Wallner back to life."

The man might not have heard. The fire in him had gone out. He slumped back in the chair, one hand dangling loosely over the arm and the other toying with the brandy glass, his listless eyes on the flames leaping in the fireplace.

Max persisted, though he felt he was swimming against a strong current. "Your wife? Your family? Publishing the letter will hurt them."

"I'll explain something to you, Max Halman, though I don't know why I'm doing it." The hollow voice spoke from a great distance. "It doesn't matter. Noth-

153

ing really matters. It's been a long time since anything has. Family? A few people in Germany. As far as they're concerned, I'm dead. My wife is not important. You've seen her. She's useful to me, she cooks, she keeps house. I take care of her in return for services rendered."

One of Bach's flute sonatas was spinning its notes in the air. "Judith Weber . . ." Max offered the last feeble hope of reaching him. "She's a talented pianist. She's worth saving."

"Yes." He nodded broodingly at the fire. "I heard her play once. It was—it was an exciting experience. She should stick to her music and let vengeance alone."

"Call off your dogs if it doesn't matter to you. Tell them to leave Judith Weber alone."

"I have none to call off." A weary hand was raised in a weary gesture. The voice was plaintive. "And if I had, why should I? Life has grown very dull. This little hunt might provide some excitement for me. And if it doesn't, why should I deprive others of their fun?"

"If you're caught in the hunt, what of the people who helped you?"

"You're being subtle, Max Halman. It's your State Department training. You mean, would I reveal their names? Why not? What are they to me? I'm more important than they are and I paid a very handsome fee for my safety. I wasn't the only one. A small fortune was made . . ." The voice trailed off indifferently as he leaned forward to pour a little brandy into his glass and then rose from his chair and walked to the window. The silence in the dim, twilit room lengthened while Bach played softly in the background.

The man was motionless for so long, staring out of the window, that Max thought he had forgotten him. Then he heard him whisper, "History . . . You and Weber's kind pay minor tribute from time to time to thirty-year-old history to relieve thirty-year-old guilt. To what purpose? Does it ease the nightmares of the survivors? Will it prevent *our* coming again? History is tricky, Max Halman. Millions and millions of words have been written about—our solution. The world must know that it happened—" He turned to face Max, the burned-out eyes staring from the dead face. "—but do you think that they really believe it's true?"

The words echoed in Max's ears as he strode from the room and the house without looking back, the weight of his anger and hopelessness heavy inside him.

Some of that had dissipated. At least he was doing something. He wiped his shaving things and put them in the case. He splashed water on his face and wiped it with a towel, thinking of Judith and the dangers surrounding her about which she probably knew little and against which she had no defense. The doctor's man, Ernst, "away on an errand," Babcock, with that hidden rage of his, Smith in his cold mechanical pursuit.

The phone rang. He dropped the towel over the rack, picked up his shaving kit, and went to the bedroom.

Sheila's voice, thin and strained, said without preamble, "Max, have you heard anything from Judith?"

"Nothing. I was about to call you to find out if you had."

"She won't call me, I'm sure. Haven't you any idea where she went?"

"Yes, and I'm going there now."

"Where? Where are you going, Max?"

"To Bonn first, Sheila. From there I'll just have to feel my way. But remember what I asked you. Don't discuss this with anyone, please."

A second's hesitation, then, her voice sharp with

anxiety, she asked, "Bonn? Do you think that's where the letter is? Do you think that's where she is? Do you, Max?"

"That's what I'm going to try to find out."

"Because she won't stop, you know, Max. Judith will just go on until something terrible happens. You have to find her!"

"Yes. I'm leaving now, Sheila. I'll talk to you as soon as I can." He hung up.

"He didn't say much—poor Max. He sounded so distracted."

"But he is going to Bonn?"

"Right now. He said he'd have to feel his way from there so I suppose that means he's not staying there. . . . Oh, Mr. Babcock—" Twisting hands, wide blue eyes, thin, plaintive voice. "If you could find her, if we could put an end to this. My poor Leo—he went a little mad, you know, when he saw that picture in the paper."

Babcock stood, neat and precise, in front of the partially decorated Christmas tree. Beside him on the couch lay the pretty disorder of tree decorations. "A little mad, yes," he said as he picked up one of the ornaments and turned the glittering, delicate ball in his hand, staring at it with cold eyes. "Perhaps we're all a little mad, Mrs. Weber, each with our own obsessions. But—" He laid the ornament carefully back on the couch and began to button his blue overcoat which he hadn't removed. "I'll do what I can."

"It's so good of you to concern yourself with this. I know how much you must have on your mind." She ran a thin, nervous hand through her hair and smiled defensively. "The past has to be relegated to the past sometime, finished and done with. After all, there isn't anything we can do about it, is there?"

Babcock looked at her for a long moment, thinking

with contempt, *She's a rich, selfish, stupid woman;* but aloud he said courteously, "We all want the past to remain in the past, Mrs. Weber."

She opened the door for him, tears gleaming in the china-blue eyes. "I'm so glad you understand that. It's what I tried to explain to Judith, but she's so stubborn, like Leo. I hope when you find her you'll tell her that."

"I'll be glad to."

Sheila sat silent and sad on the couch after he left. Babcock had arrived so suddenly, had asked questions so rapidly, it had confused her. She had called Max at his insistence. Now that he was gone, she felt a vague uneasiness. She wished she hadn't suggested that Betty and Andrew go to a movie. She didn't like being alone.

Surely she had done the right thing. Max had said not to discuss it with anyone, but Babcock wasn't just anyone. Robert Babcock was not only Max's superior but he was an old friend of Leo's, had worked with him during the war. This problem, as he had explained in his gentle, courteous way, was his problem too, and they must work together to solve it. Yes, of course she had done the right thing.

For a moment before Max closed the suitcase, his eye rested on Judith's hat and he remembered with a tightening in his throat how she had looked here in this room a few hours ago—the white, translucent skin stretched so taut over the bones of her face, the dark eyes somber and haunted and at the end so hostile. Where, he asked silently, could I have found the words to explain? He lifted the suitcase off the bed, facing unwillingly the cheerless prospect that he might never find the words.

He was stepping out into the corridor when the solution came to him. How is it he hadn't thought of it before? Charlie—Charlie Forrester. Pass a miracle ... ? Charlie was his miracle. If anyone could help him, Charlie could. He dropped the suitcase and hurried back to the phone. He glanced at his watch. Midnight in Bonn. Well, if Charlie wasn't awake, he soon would be!

Twenty-one

"Is this all?"

The customs man was surprised and a little suspicious at the limited amount of luggage Judith was carrying. With sidelong glances he looked her up and down while his nimble fingers poked and pinched through the few articles. How could a woman who looked like she did be content with one small suitcase? the eyes seemed to ask.

She was alone in Leah's country now with no sense of safety at all and she found herself explaining too rapidly and with too many words, "I never travel with much luggage. Easier to travel light, don't you think? I'm not staying very long. Just a change of clothing, a few books to read . . ." How stupid the eager explanations must sound! How strange it must seem—six books and one change of clothing.

She kept her dark eyes possessively on the books as he examined them, riffling through the pages, pressing the covers, searching for contraband, humming softly under his breath. As he finished, he stacked them on the counter beside the suitcase.

"Good story." He smiled over the Hammett book. The last one, Camus, brought a frown to his face and he muttered something about never having been able to understand what that Frenchman was getting at.

Judith stared at the pile of books as the customs man turned his attention to the suitcase itself, probing with inquiring fingers into the corners and along the quilted lining. She would find a quiet place to stay, she decided, where she could rest and finish reading her father's manuscript and find the directions to the letter's hiding place.

"Miss Weber?" The voice was very close and it startled her. She turned to see a colorless-looking man wearing a uniform, motioning toward a door on the other side of the customs counter. "Would you step this way for a moment?"

"But why ... ?"

"A formality only."

"I don't understand. Is there anything wrong?"

He repeated in a loud voice, "A formality only," as though she were deaf or had difficulty understanding the language though he was speaking in English.

He took her by the elbow and started ushering her toward the gate while the other passengers in the room fell silent and stared at her, their eyes blank and uninvolved.

"My suitcase." Judith pulled back.

"It will be all right." The petty official had his orders and the urgent hand on her elbow became more urgent. There was nothing to be done. Judith went with him helplessly through the gate toward the office door. Looking back over her shoulder she saw the customs official carefully replacing the books in the suitcase and setting the case on the floor at his feet. She felt a little reassured at that.

Her escort knocked once on the door, waited for the shouted, "*Herein!*" from within and then swung the door open.

"Miss Weber is here, Herr Baum!" He clipped out the words as Judith walked past him into the office and the door closed behind her.

She found herself facing a fat man sitting behind a desk. He didn't look up, only waved a hand and said, "One moment, Fräulein," while he continued to study a file folder open on the desk in front of him. There were several filing cabinets placed along the wall behind the desk, a table under the window held a carafe of water and a glass upside down. On the desk she noticed a brown paper sack torn open and revealing the remains of a doughnut. Beside it stood a plastic cup of coffee. On the desk, also set at an angle so she could just make it out, was an enlarged photograph in a leather frame of a group of young soldiers in stiff poses, wearing the World War II uniform of the Wehrmacht. It looked dusty.

Judith noticed these things only peripherally. None of them really concerned her. She stood rigid, waiting, while the silence stretched on interminably. He hadn't asked her to sit down. What part of the game was this? Was he one of them?

Finally, with a huge sigh that shook his jowls, the man closed the file folder and placed it on top of a pile of them at the side of his desk, aligning it neatly. He looked up at her then and pointed to a chair opposite him. "Do sit down, Fräulein."

Judith shook her head. "I prefer to stand, thank you. What is this all about?"

"A formality only, I trust. May I see your passport?"

"That's already been checked," she said, her hands tightening on her handbag. "It's in order, or else they would have said something at immigration. . . ."

"It will only take a moment." He held out a fat, imperious hand and waited.

Fighting a growing sense of panic, Judith reached into her purse and brought it out. She felt lost as his fingers closed around it. He waved again at the chair but Judith felt it would be impossible for her to move to it. Her legs felt so weak she knew she wouldn't be able to take a step without betraying their weakness. The air in the room seemed stifling. She pressed her handkerchief to her lips and watched the man page through the passport with agonizing slowness, studying each page intently. What on earth could he be looking for? At her photograph he paused the longest, looking from her to it and back again, an official kind of frown creasing his forehead.

This is ridiculous, Judith thought, the passport is in order, the picture is a perfect likeness.

"Well, Fräulein," the man said finally, "you have come here to spend the Christmas holidays, no doubt, with friends?"

"No doubt," Judith said a little hoarsely. "My name is Miss Weber. I prefer to be addressed that way."

"Yesss." He hissed it out. "Weber . . . A good German name."

"I'm an American. My passport is in order and I'm asking you why you are detaining me here." She seemed to have lost control of her voice. It rose until she was half-shouting.

"Detaining?" His smile was puzzled as though he was having trouble understanding the word.

"Yes, detaining—holding me here. I would like to contact my embassy—"

"No need for that. Do not distress yourself. How long do you intend to be here, Miss Weber?"

"Does that matter? A week, perhaps. I'm visiting some friends." She added with a boldness she didn't feel at all, "At the American Embassy."

He nodded. "At the Embassy." He looked down at her picture in the passport again but not before Judith caught the look of fear that the words "American Embassy" seemed to have put there. He pulled a pad toward him and busily scribbled some notes on it while Judith took out a cigarette and lit it, glad to see that her hand wasn't too unsteady. The fear in his eyes had dissipated some of hers and she felt the stirrings of a helpless kind of anger.

"Am I free to go, Herr Baum?" She had regained control of her voice and she laid particular stress on his name, telling him she knew it and would remember it.

Before he could answer, there were scuffling sounds outside the door and raised voices. Baum's head came up with a jerk as the door swung open and two men stumbled in. The one was the official who had brought Judith to the office. His face was flushed and he was breathing very hard. The other was a stranger and though his brown eyes were sparkling with anger, he was otherwise quite unruffled. His round, boyish face was pale, if anything.

"Charles Forrester," he said in blunt introduction, looking from Baum to Judith. "Press officer for the American Embassy." He smiled briefly at Judith and then turned a severe gaze on Baum. "I understand you are detaining Miss Weber and I would like to know why."

"Detaining? Detaining?" Baum blustered, having trouble with that word again. Judith saw real fear in his eyes this time. His upper lip was very damp as he pushed his clumsy bulk out of the chair to face Forrester. "Not at all—not at all, Mr. Forrester. Simply a matter of mistaken identity. We mistook Miss Weber for someone else." He spread out his hands in a gesture that was part helplessness and part apology. The heavy jowls trembled with sincerity. "It happens, you know. We do have to check these things. My apologies to Miss Weber. I hope she will forgive any inconvenience we may have caused her—"

"If you're finished, then," Forrester said curtly and held out his hand. Baum grabbed the passport from his desk and slapped it smartly into Forrester's hand. He started to bend his gross body in what he hoped was a bow, but Forrester simply nodded, took Judith's arm, and they left the office. Behind her Judith could hear harsh, guttural German—Baum cursing the lowly, erring official.

Forrester retrieved Judith's suitcase from the floor at the feet of the customs official, who gave them a wary smile and moved away quickly as though afraid of some contagion.

Still holding Judith lightly by the arm, Forrester guided her out of the building, chattering in her ear in an easy, pleasant voice.

"Stupid, petty officials. God save us from them. Particularly if they make a mistake. They can't afford to admit it gracefully. They have to compound it with all kinds of foolishness. I'm certainly glad I happened to be here to help you. I just saw my wife off to New York. Lucky chance." Only a small lie, Forrester thought. He had brought Ellen to the airport yesterday. And don't overdo the light chatter bit, he reprimanded himself. "Of course, I'm not at all sure that I had the right to barge in like that—legally, that is—in case you had just poisoned the pilot or something." He smiled down at her. Like Max he was slender and several inches taller than she was and for a foolish moment she found herself liking him just for that. She smiled back at him.

He stopped beside a battered Opel and opened the passenger door. "I'll be glad to take you to wherever you're going."

Judith hesitated. A cold rain was falling. Snow in New York. Rain in Bonn. Didn't the sun ever shine on this godforsaken world? She was shaking with cold and the aftermath of the incident with Baum. She flung her cigarette away and looked at Charles Forrester. He was smiling at her, an innocent smile that made the boyish face even more so. Press officer for the American Embassy . . . Is that what he really was? How could a face that open and honest hide a malicious secret? He was forty, perhaps, though it was hard to tell. Faces like that never really showed age. He had a head of thick brown hair with a stubborn cowlick. He was running his hand over it now and saying, "I'm going to Bad Godesberg—the Embassy.

I won't let you take a cab. My good deed isn't complete until you let me deposit you on a doorstep—any doorstep."

Judith was suddenly too tired to distrust anymore and she smiled into the warm brown eyes and said, "That's very kind of you. There's an inn—a hotel—on the river. Somewhere near here . . . ?" Was it Max who had told her?

"There are several. One rather pleasant one—in Bad Godesberg actually. Old, but charming and nicely run. I can recommend it. Queen Victoria slept there when she was in the neighborhood, as well as some of her countless relatives."

Judith let him put the suitcase on the back seat of the car and help her into the front seat. As Forrester climbed in behind the wheel, he jerked a thumb toward the case and said, "You really do believe in traveling light."

"Yes, I do," she said, and then, "Light . . . ? Just a moment."

She twisted around and unsnapped the lid. There lay her few articles of clothing, a cosmetic bag, a small container for her toothbrush and toothpaste, and that was all.

A manufactured case of mistaken identity to get her out of the way while someone removed the books. No wonder Baum had been afraid. She had no doubt that he had been bribed to hold her there while the books were stolen. The customs official, too, must have been paid off—or was he one of them? Good God, how efficient they were—how terrifyingly efficient! Smith had warned her that they could take the suitcase any time they wanted to, but he had also said that they would do it the easy way and let her lead them to the letter and the photograph. Why, then, if that was so . . . ? Should she go back and accuse the customs official? What was the point, she had no proof. And whoever took them was well on his way. She was afraid and angry at the same time. *They won't stop me. I've come this far. I'll find a way.*

"Is there anything wrong?" Forrester's voice seemed to come from a great distance.

"Wrong? No, nothing's wrong," she said wildly. She snapped the suitcase shut and swung around. "How far is the hotel, Mr. Forrester?"

"About ten minutes, and my friends call me Charlie," he said lightly, smiling.

"I would like to go there quickly." The face she turned to him was haggard, the eyes feverish.

"Are you all right?"

"I have a cold. I'm tired, I need to rest."

"I'll get you there fast, don't worry—as fast, that is, as this old heap will take us."

Charles Forrester, press officer, so he said, yet even if he were, didn't *they* come in all shapes and sizes? But he had no luggage, no briefcase, there were no bulges in his pockets. If he had taken the books, where would he have put them? How fortuitous for her that he had been at the airport. Was it too fortuitous?

Around and around in a giddy circle her thoughts went while she listened vaguely to Forrester's pleasant voice ramble on about airports.

"They're the same all over the world. A diabolical plot. Once they've got you in, they're not going to let you out—not unless you can come up with the right combination of letters and numbers."

A dim, shapeless thought stirred in the back of Judith's mind, but Forrester went rattling on and drove it away.

"Driving in Europe is always two-thirds luck and one-third skill—though I may be overrating the skill." He pushed on his left indicator, stuck his head out of the window, followed it with an arm which he waved wildly, and then saying, "Oh, what the hell!" he swung recklessly into the left lane while Judith waited for the crunch of fenders. None came.

"Luck, you see? What's so irritating is that everyone else always seems to know where they're going. It's very hard on my ego." He chuckled and glanced sideways at Judith, who sat silently staring straight ahead through the windshield. Her head was bent forward slightly and the heavy black hair fell around the white face, partially screening it. She seemed absorbed in watching the rain beat down on the pavement. Her arms were folded tightly across her chest.

"I wouldn't let it worry you." His voice was gentle.

"I beg your pardon?" She turned a kind of sleep-walker's face to him.

"What happened back at the airport."

"A case of mistaken identity, they said."

"It happens. Forget it. It's finished."

She stared at him for a moment as though she were trying to make up her mind about something. Then she said, "Look at me."

"With pleasure!" He grinned at her.

"I don't mean that. It's my size. I'm not a made-to-order size. Do you think they really mistook me for someone else? You can change the appearance of your face more easily than you can alter the shape of your body."

"I hope you weren't thinking of doing either of those things."

"Please."

"Sorry. Just trying to bring a smile to that sad face. Still, what else could it have been? If you want to lodge a complaint, you're free to do so, though I don't know what good it would do. I'd just forget it if I were you." He fell silent for a moment as they swung onto the main street and stopped to let a streetcar clang past. Then he eased the car slowly through the rainy morning traffic. "We'll be there in a few minutes now."

"How long have you been at the Embassy, Mr. Forrester?"

"Just under two years," he said promptly. "Before that it was Egypt. God, that was a hot one!"

"What does it involve—being press officer?"

"Oh, good Lord, everything! I'm more of an errand boy than anything else—for the ambassador on the one hand and the press corps on the other. But it's not a bad job—keeps me on my toes. I like it."

After a few moments of silence they entered Bad Godesberg, the foreign embassy center of West Germany, spread out along the same main road leading from Bonn. Forrester turned down a narrow, sloping street that ended abruptly at the river's edge. A few yards short of it, he brought the car to a halt.

"There you have it." He waved at the river. "The fabled Rhine of the fabled castles and Rhine maidens all lying at your feet. Have you ever been in Germany before?"

"No," Judith said. No, only in the nightmare memories of my father, she thought, as she gazed out at the broad, fast-flowing river. The rain splashed down on it and answering wisps of mist curled up from it. Sturdy tugs and large barges and heavy freighters moved up and down, conversing with each other in the noisy river language of horns and whistles.

"A pity," Forrester murmured.

"Why do you say that?"

"Polluted. Absolutely filthy. Periodically thousands of fish float to the surface, dead—oh, I may be exaggerating a bit—but they just can't cope, poor things. The government's been trying to clean it up, not making much headway, and now they're running out of money—like everybody else, I might add."

Forrester turned right off the road and entered a broad courtyard, enclosed, except for the driveway, by a low stone wall. He pulled to a halt at the entrance to the old hotel, a sprawling L-shaped building that had been added on to at one time, the newer addition not quite matching the old. That part of the courtyard facing the river was obviously a patio for summer dining, though now there were only a few stone benches set along the wall. Over it the lonely, winter-dead trees drooped their leafless branches. Steps led down from the patio to a broad public walkway along the river.

Judith climbed out of the car slowly as Forrester held the door open. She hadn't been aware until now just how exhausted she was. She swayed a bit and the man took her arm and looked anxiously into her face.

"Are you all right?"

"I will be—after a rest."

"All right. You'll be in a comfortable bed in a couple of minutes."

He took her suitcase from the car—that useless suitcase—and holding her arm firmly, helped her up the steps.

"The plane trip isn't long but it seems that way, doesn't it?—with the time change. Takes a couple of days to adjust."

He led her into the lobby and Judith received a quick impression of a large room with elderly-looking sofas and chairs placed haphazardly around, of doors leading off into smaller lounges and an old-fashioned writing-room, of an overall shabby gentility and a relaxed, unhurried atmosphere.

Set into an enclosed nook beside the stairway was the reception desk where a slender young man assured her there was a room with a bath for Fräulein Weber. "In the old building, but," he added hurriedly, "I'm sure you will be comfortable." He explained to her unnecessarily that it was Christmas and they were very busy.

Yes, Judith nodded as she signed the register, she was sure she would be comfortable. Her fatigue was so complete now that she felt nauseous and was forced to lean against the counter while the clerk called a porter and gave him the key to her room and her suitcase. She handed the clerk her passport reluctantly, remembering Baum.

It didn't really matter about the room, though she couldn't tell this polite young clerk. All she wanted was a bed to lie down on for a while, to rest and plan the next stage of her trip. In her mind she had already said good-bye to Charlie Forrester and the hotel. She was transient here. This afternoon she would rent a car and be on her way to the border.

The porter started toward the stairway and Judith turned to Forrester, holding out her hand. "You've been so kind—rescuing me. I don't know how to thank you."

"I should thank you. Coming to the aid of a beautiful lady made me feel very noble." He held her hand in a firm clasp and wouldn't let her turn away. The brown eyes were grave as he added, "But if you want to—to show your gratitude—I wonder if you would let me take you to the Embassy Christmas party tonight."

"Tonight?"

"You'd really be doing me a big favor. My wife, Ellen—well, she's on her way home to get a divorce—"

"I'm sorry." Judith made a mechanical sound of condolence.

"No sympathy called for. It was mutual and amicable. We just agreed to go our separate ways, but it will be a little strange rattling around on my own for a while. Think about it. I'll call you this afternoon. It will be just the usual embassy 'do'—I'm sure you know what I mean. You look like you could stand a little fun, if you don't mind my saying so. There'll be some nice people there and plenty of ham and turkey and booze."

"I'm really too tired to think now." If she agreed, he would let her go and that's all she wanted at the moment. "Yes, call me," she said and smiled at him.

The smile had a strange effect on Charlie Forrester. He blushed, then frowned, then stammered. "When— shall I call?—two—three—you name it."

"Three will be fine."

"Good, good!" He pumped her hand enthusiastically, beaming at her. "I'll see you later then. Rest well." And he hurried out of the hotel.

Judith started to climb the steps to the second floor slowly. There seemed to be only three floors in the big, sprawling building. Surprisingly, she found herself counting the steps as she used to do when she was a child. Eight, nine, ten . . .

She was trying to remember something—something Forrester had said that disturbed her—but her mind was dull with fatigue. "The usual embassy 'do.' I'm sure you know what I mean." That was it.

Why should he be sure she would know what he meant? Why should he think that a strange American woman he had met by accident at the airport would know what embassy parties were like? She had been to countless of these "do's" with Max or her father but how could Charlie Forrester know that?

She was breathing hard and her heart was pounding fearfully when she reached the second-floor landing. To her left at the end of the corridor she saw the porter waiting for her in front of an open door. He ushered her into the room and made a great ceremony of showing her the bathroom, all gleaming chrome and tile and snow-white towels. Then he opened the big, old-fashioned wardrobe in the bedroom for her inspection. From there to the bureau . . . Would he never finish with this stupid show, Judith wondered? He was like a tour guide pointing with pride to the great historical sights of his country. Hampered by her lack of language, exhausted almost to the fainting point, she kept nodding and saying, "Yes, yes," and, "Never mind."

She looked around for her suitcase and saw that the

porter had placed it on a luggage rack at the foot of the bed and—it was open. Since when did porters open guests' luggage? He seemed so innocuous, this little man, but when she looked at him now she saw that his eyes were on the suitcase, too. My God, how many of them were there! She remembered her father's dark-shadowed eyes after a sleepless night and his telling her with a terrible kind of sadness, "I don't know how many are concerned in this—and I'm not yet sure why—but it's best just not to trust anyone."

"*Frühstuck?*" the porter asked and added loudly, "*Essen?*" as he made a dumb show of eating.

"No, just go." She walked to the door and held it open. He understood that. Certainly he understood the expression on her white, frozen face. She handed him a coin and he scuttled off down the corridor trailing "*Bitte's*" behind him.

She was wet and cold. She dropped her shoes beside the bed and her coat and jacket on a chair as she looked around the room. The furnishings were old but everything was clean and attractive. The wide floorboards slanted a bit like a ship's deck at sea. It was a corner room. One of the windows looked out over the Rhine, its water cold and swift under the mist. Directly below it was the patio, which was filled with small muddy puddles. The other window, facing out on the rear of the building, had a narrow balcony running alongside it. A tree's branches, heavy and black with rain, trailed over the balcony's railing.

Judith turned away from the window and padded on silent, stockinged feet to the door and turned the old-fashioned key in the old-fashioned lock. No bolts or chains to keep out intruders.

Shivering, she removed the rest of her clothes and climbed into bed, drawing the blankets well up to her chin. Gradually she grew warm but sleep was elusive, her mind questioning with feverish urgency: Charlie Forrester, friend or foe? The thought struck her suddenly that it was curious he had not asked her what she was doing in Germany. Wouldn't it have been a natural thing to do? Perhaps he was too courteous, would have waited for her to offer the information. She wanted to trust him. She needed an ally. She was adrift in a never-never land. Losing the books had severed her from the only solid link with her father, and whatever messages they had for her were gone.

Words stirred in the back of her mind as sleep began to fog her brain. Charlie Forrester's voice: *... the right combination of letters and numbers ...*

Twenty-two

If he could have, Charlie Forrester would have kicked his own behind, but as he was sitting behind the wheel of his car, that was physically impossible so he slapped the wheel instead with a sharp, stinging blow.

"Stupid!" he muttered. "What a stupid slip. Where are your brains, Forrester?"

... the usual embassy "do." I'm sure you know what I mean.

Had she caught it? If she had, it would send her running like a hare. Max had warned him. Remembering how downright ill with exhaustion she had looked, he consoled himself with the hope that the words might have slipped by her. Maybe he should call her now to make sure. No, that would look suspicious. This was supposed to have been an accidental meeting.

He turned into the Embassy compound and the old car rattled into its parking place almost without guidance, like an old horse into its stall. He switched off the engine but didn't move to get out for a moment, thinking that if she had not been frightened off by his slip, and if she agreed to the party tonight, that would take care of today. But what about later tonight? She could slip away easily in the dark. And tomorrow . . . ? If Max didn't get here by then? And why in hell couldn't Max have given him more details?

If you find her, keep her there by fair means or foul, as long as you can. I don't care how you do it. If she

*seems disturbed, ignore it. Her father just died under
—unhappy circumstances. This is important, Charlie.
I'll tell you more when I get there. But this is
important.*

"You can count on me, old man," Charlie had said.
Yes, you can count on me to put my foot in it, he
thought bitterly. All right, so if she's here tomorrow,
if I haven't scared her off . . . ? Sightseeing?
Beethoven's birthplace? She played Beethoven like an
angel, he understood, and looked like an angel, too, or
would if she weren't so tired. A woman too beautiful,
Charlie thought, to be so troubled. And that smile—
my God, what a smile! It had turned his knees to water.

A trip down the river? No, he didn't think that
would do it. She was being driven, hell-bent, to
something he couldn't see. There wasn't anything
frivolous about her, and castles on the Rhine, he was
sure, would hold no interest for her at all.

"Charlie, old chump!"

A shrill, nasal voice broke into his thoughts.

"Here you sit like the proverbial bump on the
proverbial log, and lucky for me."

The door on the passenger side opened and a man
climbed in, a thin man with a narrow, pointed face
and sallow, acne-scarred skin. He had always reminded
Charlie Forrester of a weasel with his sharp little eyes.
Right now Charlie would have preferred the company
of a weasel.

"I've got a favor to ask of you, Charlie old chump."

The "Charlie old chump" grated on Forrester's
nerves as much as the high, nasal voice did.

"Glad to see your old rattletrap is still running.
Mine's in the garage. Give us a lift there, hmm? It'll
only take a few minutes."

"Us?"

"My friend, Ernst there, from the garage."

Someone else whom Forrester hadn't noticed until

now was climbing into the back seat without waiting to be asked and Forrester caught a glimpse of a big, burly man, all heavy shoulders and creased bull neck. In the rearview mirror, as the man settled himself into the seat, his flat, black eyes met Charlie's. Their expression gave him a very unpleasant sensation down his spine. He looked away from him to the man sitting beside him.

"If your friend, Ernst, is from the garage," Charlie said slowly, "why doesn't he have his own transportation?"

"You're quick, Charlie old chump. No doubt about it, you're quick." The man's voice hardened and one hand went into his pocket and came out holding a revolver, the business end pointing at Charlie's stomach.

A fleeting memory came to Forrester of something he had read—that a gunshot wound in the stomach was horribly painful. He didn't dwell on it.

"Just drive," the nasal voice said. "I'll ask the questions."

This is ridiculous, Charlie Forrester thought; something out of an old movie. Here he sat in the familiar compound, his office only a few yards away. . . . He looked from the gun to the man's face. He had never liked this man, a sort of hanger-on in the newspaper world, a stringer correspondent for small papers and magazines that couldn't afford a fulltime correspondent. It had occurred to him more than once that the man's credentials might not be bona fide but he had never taken the time to check. He was sorry now that he hadn't.

"If this is some kind of a joke . . ."

"No joke, Charlie. Serious, Charlie—d-e-a-dly serious." He jabbed the gun painfully into Forrester's ribs. "Now just drive, and while you do, tell me about the books."

"The books?" Charlie backed the car out reluctantly and swung it in the direction of the road.

"That's what I said—the books. Turn right here as you leave. The—a—garage is in the country, where it's quiet and we can talk and won't be disturbed. Just keep strictly to the speed limit or a little under and don't try any fancy driving. And as there isn't a lot of time, it'll work out better if you don't stall or tell any lies."

"I don't know what the hell you're talking about! Books . . . What books?"

"Where are they?"

"There are a lot of books in the library—"

Forrester let out a cry of pain as the gun smashed into his ribs and the car swerved.

"Knock it off, Charlie, and watch your driving," the nasal voice snarled and the big man in the back seat stirred restlessly and licked his lips. "This isn't a joke, I told you that. You met her at the airport. She doesn't have them anymore. A friend of mine at the hotel checked. You've stashed them somewhere. A matter of simple deduction, see, Charlie? Where did you stash them?"

The garage, when they reached it, was a garage, but not for servicing cars. It was attached to a small house that was set well back from the road and isolated from its neighbors by a fence and a thick hedge.

With the doors closed and a portable radio playing at full volume, no one could hear Charlie when the big man took over the questioning. While he could talk, Charlie insisted he didn't know anything about the books. He was telling the truth, of course, but they didn't believe him. If he had known, Charlie would probably have given them the information they demanded. He wanted to go on living and he didn't have Leo Weber's reasons for silence.

177

In the end, the nasal-voiced man put a bullet in his head. They left the body in the garage until it was dark and then they took it and dumped it in a spot where Judith Weber was sure to know about it.

Twenty-three

The dark came early on that December afternoon. Judith watched it enclose the small piece of world she could see through the window of the hotel dining room. The gray mist hung heavy on the river and the foghorns from the black barges and freighters sounded their lonely warnings.

In front of her on the table were two open-faced ham sandwiches and a pot of coffee. The coffee was welcome but she ate the food without enthusiasm, only because she had to.

It was almost four o'clock, later than she wanted it to be. She had finally slept, only to dream at first—a long, fragmented dream in which she was running in that terrible slow motion of dreams from hard-faced men, from menacing figures lurking in shadows. Max had appeared from time to time, standing on the sidelines, elegant and casual, looking on with aloof interest as though he were watching strangers in whose lives he was not involved. She had jerked half-awake from the dream, moaning, and then immediately had sunk into a deep, drugged-like sleep.

She had awakened the second time totally disoriented, had spent moments of heart-pounding terror before she located herself in time and place. A hot shower had eased some of the tension. She had put on the few clean clothes she had brought, exchanging the soiled turtleneck sweater for a white cardigan and wrapping a silk paisley scarf around her neck. The black slack suit went on without concern for its crumpled state.

All the while she had been listening for the tap on the door that would tell her there was a phone call. There was no phone in her room. He would have to call the desk. She found herself wanting very much to see Forrester—the round, open face, the smile, the warm, friendly eyes. She couldn't say that she trusted him. She could only say that she wanted to trust him which was as close as she could get right now to the real thing.

Downstairs at the desk she had picked up her passport and then had called Forrester's office, partly to find out if he was what he said he was. She had been put through immediately to his secretary, who told her that Mr. Forrester had not been in all day and that, except for a phone call in the morning, she hadn't heard from him. Her voice sounded puzzled as though this were unusual behavior for Charlie Forrester. Was there any message she could give him when he came in? No, Judith, told her, she would call back.

She sipped her coffee, thinking that the phone call had confirmed the fact that a Charles Forrester was press officer at the Embassy, but she couldn't know if that was the same man who had rescued her at the airport. And why hadn't he called? He had seemed so eager. . . . She shrugged, thinking it was academic whether he called now or not. She would soon be on her way.

A sudden clamor of voices, loud and argumentative, broke into her thoughts. Four young men seated at a table across the room—the only occupants of the dining room besides herself—were carrying on a noisy discussion, heated but without animosity. The one who seemed to be the oldest held up his hand in an arrogant gesture to silence his friends and rose from his chair. He took a stance, setting his feet slightly apart and firmly planted on the floor. Then he brought his hands together as though holding a heavy object. Saying something to the others, he raised the imaginary thing up to a level with his head and with a fast, swiping motion, he swung it diagonally down through the air. Judith could almost hear it whistle, so graphic had the demonstration been. She shuddered. It had been ugly and clumsy and frightening. The young man spread out his hands in a gesture that said, There, you see, that's how it's done, and then he sat down smiling broadly while the other young men broke into applause, looking at him with envious admiration.

A platter of sandwiches sat in the center of the table and each had a stein of beer at his elbow. They toasted the superior young man with a clash of steins and then resumed their argument as noisily as before.

They could have been brothers, so alike they looked. All tall, gracefully slim, their very blond hair clipped short, and despite the heat of their discussion, they sat very erect in their chairs in military perfection.

The one who had given the demonstration seemed to lead the discussion while the others deferred to him. On his cheek he had a long scar and from its red, angry look, Judith concluded that the wound must be of recent origin.

From time to time the quietest of them, and perhaps the youngest, glanced covertly in Judith's direction. Once he caught her eye and smiled shyly. Judith gave him a vague smile in return and then looked away.

She was finishing her coffee when they rose and left the room. The youngest one held back, looking from Judith to the door and back to Judith. He stood there for several moments and then suddenly he squared his slim shoulders and walked to Judith's table. He stood beside it ramrod stiff and silent until Judith looked up at him. Then, as though someone had pressed a button, he clicked his heels sharply together and bowed from the waist. He held a funny-looking little peaked cap in his hands, twisting it with thin, nervous fingers.

"Dieter von Traban, at your service," he said in clipped precise English. "Please forgive me. I only want to say that I hope myself and my friends have not disturbed you. We were too loud, is it not so?" He ended the brief speech, breathless with his boldness, fair brows frowning anxiously over deep blue eyes.

"You didn't disturb me, but it's kind of you to be concerned."

"I only want you to understand," he pressed on eagerly, "that we are not lacking in manners. We were excited."

"I could see that."

"Yes, you see, Gottfried has just—how can I explain —has just fought his *Mensur*—his duel. He has the *Schmisse*—"

"*Schmisse?*"

At her look of bewilderment the young man ran his finger down his cheek. "*Schmisse*—a scar from dueling. It is a great thing. He is a *Bursche* now—a man— with honor." He smiled down at her with youthful arrogance.

Judith remembered then with revulsion her father's description of these bloodletting rituals he had seen as a student at Heidelberg, so-called duels between students where the purpose was simply mutilation, having nothing in common with the grace and skill of fencing. It was only fought for the scar, the badge of manhood. She thought they had been banned. She looked up at the young man's handsome face, the blue eyes wide with his excitement as he described the duel and how someday he would fight his *Mensur*, and she tried to visualize the smooth cheek broken open with the ugly, gaping wound. She heard herself half-whisper, "But why?"

Like a schoolboy reciting a lesson, he told her,

"Tradition. It is good to keep some of the old traditions."

Like Max, she thought with a stab of pain. She stifled a sudden urge to reach out and touch the boy's slender wrist with its protruding wristbone. It could be Max standing beside her, fifteen years younger. He wouldn't be talking of duels, no, but of something else, with that same youthful eagerness. They were cut from the same mold—that elegant grace, the bright blond head, the deep blue eyes.

Some of the pain she was feeling must have shown in her face for he relaxed suddenly and leaned down, asking like a troubled child, "Have I upset you, Fräulein? I did not mean—"

"No, no," she assured him. "You remind me of someone. . . ." She wanted him to go and not go at the same time. She couldn't afford the luxury of sitting here any longer, but if he went, she would be alone again, and her eyes clung to his face as her lonely thoughts clung to Max. She put out her hand finally and said, "I'm Judith Weber and I'm glad you came to talk to me. May I call you Dieter?"

"Please. I should like that." He took her hand, shook it once shyly and then released it, accepting the handshake as his dismissal. Once more he resumed the military bearing, clicked his heels, bowed rigidly from the waist, and left the room. Judith watched the slim back, very stiff and very young, disappear through the door and she felt a sense of loss as though Max had gone from her twice. Judith shivered. The dining room was suddenly dark and cold.

She dropped a tip on the table and rose, firmly turning her thoughts to the next stage of her journey. Charlie Forrester would have called by now if he had been going to. She wanted to be in Maastricht by tonight.

From the river a foghorn sounded in the distance and from somewhere inside the hotel, as she ap-

proached the desk, came the sound of a piano—
stumbling fingers picking out a Chopin étude.

She asked the clerk about renting a car and he told
her there was a large car rental service in Bonn and
he would be glad to call and have them send one. It
could probably be here within the hour. Would that
suit her? Yes, that would be fine. And what kind of
a car would she like to rent? Most Americans enjoyed
driving a Mercedes. His spectacles gleamed earnestly
at her. Perhaps Judith disappointed him by saying
that it didn't really matter just as long as the car was
in good running order.

"Have there been any phone calls for me?" she
asked.

"If there had been, I would have brought you the
message immediately, Miss Weber," he said primly.

She had offended him. "Of course," she apologized.
"I'll be in my room until the car comes."

But the sound of the piano, close by, in some room
at the rear of the hotel, drew her like a magnet, and
she found herself walking automatically toward it.
The car wouldn't be here for an hour and she certainly had no packing to do.

It was a big, high-ceilinged room and, like the rest
of the building, furnished haphazardly and with
shabby gentility. Reading lamps leaned over comfortable armchairs with worn chintz covers, magazines were
scattered around on small tables. A bookcase stood
against one wall, its books worn and with cracked
bindings. Two card tables in a corner were fully
occupied, the card players gravely concerned with
their game, the inevitable beer steins at their elbows.

This was the heart of the hotel. A Christmas tree,
softly gleaming, stood on the far side of the room.
From the ceiling dangled the traditional Advent
wreath, three of its four candles burning. The last
candle would be lit tomorrow.

Judith stared around at the festive room, feeling

lost, as though she had wandered into the living quarters of a large and rather untidy family. It all had an air of unreality. The only real thing for her was the grand piano, a Steinway of ancient vintage and shabby like the rest of the room, but she could hear its full, rich tone as the young pianist, a girl of fourteen, perhaps, picked her way slowly over the keyboard. Hardly aware of what she was doing, Judith moved to it and stood close, her hungry eyes on the clumsy fingers.

A woman, one of the card players, said something to the girl in German and the girl turned, saw Judith, and rose immediately. With a gesture toward the piano, she asked in schoolgirl English, "Did you wish to play, Miss?"

Judith started to say, "No, thank you," but the words didn't come out as she had planned. Instead she heard herself saying, "May I? For a moment only?"

In answer the girl pulled the stool back, smiling and motioning to it, and Judith sat down, feeling her hands begin to tremble. She clasped them together tightly, the white skin straining across the knuckles, then she let them rest on the mellowed ivory keys. She played some soft chords and immediately, as the sound flowed from the piano, the room and its occupants vanished for her and, as always happened, she was alone. With a faint, dreaming smile on her lips, she bent over the keyboard and began to play the Chopin Ballade in G-Minor. This was like growing well after a debilitating sickness, like finding home after being lost for a long time. Perhaps her father was there, and Leah, dim shadows, sitting beside her, but she felt lightheaded, giddy with joy at the reunion. The opening, then the gentle, melancholy notes filled the room, halting the card game, hushing the children, until the last dramatic, reckless rush of sound, and then silence. Judith dropped her hands into her lap and bowed her head; her face was flushed, her eyes shining.

From what seemed a long way off she heard a burst of applause and she turned to see an audience she hadn't been aware of—not only the people in the room, but other guests and some employees had gathered in and around the doorway. She recognized the desk clerk and Dieter, smiling. And then behind them, suddenly framed in the doorway, appeared a big, broad-shouldered policeman. He must have just come in. His uniform was very wet. He was tapping the clerk on the shoulder, bending over to speak in his ear, and the clerk in turn nodded and looked puzzled and pointed to Judith. The policeman moved through the crowd in the doorway while the people fell silent, making way for him.

"Miss Weber?"

She nodded.

"Miss Judith Weber?"

She nodded again, unable to speak. She had risen, tall and pale, one hand clutching the piano for support. The policeman, who was young and serious, was distressed by her white, strained face but he couldn't allow himself to show it.

"It is—some questions, Fräulein—my superior— could you come with me, please?"

They walked from the quiet room. The people who had just applauded enthusiastically for Judith watched her now with hard, suspicious eyes. Only Dieter made a move to go to her, but the policeman shouldered him rudely aside. Judith tried unsuccessfully to smile at him.

They went through the lobby and out of the door. The chill wet night struck an answering chill in Judith's heart. She stumbled on the steps. The policeman took her elbow and guided her across the patio, down the stone steps toward the mist-clouded river.

She could see several people grouped around a figure lying on the broad cement walk. As she approached, a short, heavyset man separated himself from them, saying something in a low rather mournful voice. Some of the people moved away. The more stubborn ones remained.

Like a bright dream the interlude of the piano had come and gone. Judith moved alone in the dark. The voices of the people, the sounds of the boats on the river, even her own footsteps were muffled and distant in the fog.

The policeman's hand on her elbow urged her forward to the huddled figure. The onlookers stepped back, their curious, unfriendly eyes on the tall woman.

The body lay in a twisted position, the face turned up to the sky. Rain sparkled on the eyelashes and glistened on the dead face like tears. The once warm, brown eyes stared glassily up at her. She wanted to lean down and close them. She wanted to lean down and touch his cheek and tell him she was sorry. She saw his hands were broken and swollen like her father's had been. There was no need to ask if he had been her friend but it was too late to give her trust. A moan came from deep in her throat; she flung out an arm to push the sight away, to find support, while waves of nausea swept over her, beading her face with perspiration. She would have fallen if the young policeman hadn't held her arm in a firm grip.

She heard a murmur of voices around her, one of them saying, "She's big enough to have done it," and a nervous, answering reply. Then the heavyset man stepped forward and said something with quiet authority, and with a few mutters from the bolder ones, the spectators reluctantly turned and left. When they were far enough away to satisfy him, he walked up to Judith and said gently, "I'm Inspector Kemmler, Miss Weber. I would like to ask you a few questions, if you don't mind."

But I do mind, Judith thought. What can be said about Charlie Forrester that his poor body doesn't already say? Aloud, she said simply, "All right."

The young policeman left her side to take a blanket from a hurrying porter. He covered the body with it as carefully as she had covered her father's. He looked at Kemmler who nodded and as Kemmler took Judith's arm and guided her back up the steps to the patio, the young policeman remained standing stiff and silent beside the body.

Kemmler said a few words to the clerk who was standing in the doorway, staring out at the river with a frightened look on his face. The clerk said, *"Bitte, bitte,"* and ran to open the door of a small office behind the reception desk. Kemmler ushered Judith in and helped her to a chair. She was cold and wet and had begun to shake uncontrollably. Again a few sharp words from Kemmler sent the clerk running with his urgent *"Bitte, bitte."*

Judith felt the shaking would tear her apart and she clasped her arms around herself, holding tightly. When the clerk reappeared, he carried a tray with a bottle of cognac and two glasses. Kemmler took it from him in silence and closed the door in his face.

He filled the glasses and handed one to Judith and watched her drink it. Then he refilled it, motioning for her to drink that as well. She did. He nodded in approval and took a slow sip of his own, watching her with large, sad, dark eyes. He had a long woolen muffler wrapped several times around his throat. His nose was red and he blew it frequently and mournfully into a large handkerchief.

"Can you talk now?"

Judith nodded.

"I'm sorry I had to subject you to that. I thought—perhaps . . ." He shrugged. "I know who the man is, of course, not only from his identification but we've had occasion to meet in the past—on friendly, social terms, of course. He was a—good man. Unusually so. And I don't like his being killed like that. I don't like it at all." His large eyes were angry as he swallowed his brandy and refilled both glasses. "I would appreciate your telling me all you know—anything at all that will help me find out who killed him." His English, American English, was spoken with fluency. "You knew Mr. Forrester?"

Judith nodded, then shook her head.

"You knew him or you did not know him?"

Why did he think she knew Charlie Forrester at all? Just because they were both Americans? No, the clerk, of course, must have told him that Forrester had brought her to the hotel this morning. "I met him for the first time this morning," Judith said.

"Where did you meet him?"

"At the airport."

"You arrived here this morning from New York?"

Judith nodded.

"I have good memories of New York," he told her. "I spent a year there with your police force. It was very instructive." He sneezed into his handkerchief and wiped his red nose while his sad eyes watched her. He asked, "Did Mr. Forrester go to the airport to meet you, Miss Weber?"

"No, it was a chance meeting. He had just seen his wife off for New York. He offered me a ride—"

"He had just seen his wife off for New York?"

"Yes."

Frowning, Kemmler reached into his pocket and brought out a crumpled pack of cigarettes. He put one in his mouth, then remembered his manners and offered Judith one. She took it and he leaned forward to light it for her. He lit his own, blew out the smoke and asked mournfully, "Is there any reason you can think of why Mr. Forrester should have lied to you?"

The smoke caught in Judith's throat. She choked and coughed and finally gasped, "Lied?" The small, stuffy room seemed to whirl around her. There was nothing she could hold on to, nothing.

"I happen to know that he took his wife to the

airport yesterday. They were getting a divorce, if my information is correct. I wonder then what reason he could have had for going to the airport today, if it wasn't to meet you?"

He waited for her to speak, perched on the edge of the desk, swinging one short, thick leg and letting it bang from time to time against the desk.

Judith fought against the whirling room and the giddiness of her fear, trying to put her thoughts in order. She had convinced herself that Forrester had been her friend, now she found he had lied to her in that light, pleasant voice. Yet if he had been her enemy, why was he sprawled beside the river in the rain, his body as bruised and battered as her father's had been?

The bones of her face were sharp under the taut skin, the eyes haggard as she looked up at Kemmler and said, "I know nothing about him except what he told me—that he had come to the airport to see his wife off, that he was press officer here at the Embassy." But he *had* come to the airport to meet her, of that she was certain now—smiling and open-faced—and lying.

A knock on the door interrupted them and the clerk poked his head in and after excusing himself several times to Kemmler, he told Judith that her rental car had arrived and what did she want to do about it?

"We'll take care of it in a few minutes," Kemmler told him and waited for the clerk to close the door. "You were going somewhere, Miss Weber?"

"I was going—to visit some friends—in Holland."

"In Holland?"

She waited fearfully for him to ask, what friends, where in Holland? and wondered what she would answer. I'll be visiting ghosts, looking for a letter written by a ghost. What would he say if she told him that?

"—talk about?"

"I beg your pardon?"

"I said, what did you and Mr. Forrester talk about?"

"Talk about? Nothing, nothing important. I had been detained and he had helped—"

"Detained?"

What had made her say that? She wasn't thinking clearly—how *could* she think clearly? "It was a mistake—mistaken identity—nothing. Then he drove me here to the hotel." She broke off, coughing. Her head was aching. She was shivering again. From the rear of the hotel came the sound of the piano.

With a sad smile Kemmler said, "I see that you are suffering from a cold, too. I won't keep you much longer. Perhaps Mr. Forrester told you something about himself—something that might be important to me."

"Only what I've told you—and he invited me to the Christmas party at the Embassy tonight."

"And did you accept?"

Judith stared at him. "What difference can it possibly make? I said I might. He was going to call this afternoon, but . . ." She spread her hands open in her lap and looked down at them, listening to the piano. "He couldn't, of course," she said softly. She put her hands into the pockets of her jacket, carefully, as though they hurt her.

Kemmler reached into his pocket and brought out a slip of paper and held it out for Judith to see. "Is there any reason why Mr. Forrester should have written your name and hotel on this paper? We found it in his pocket. It's unlikely that he would forget you and where you were staying, isn't it?"

Judith glanced at the paper with its scrawl of writing and said hoarsely, "There's no reason I can think of," while panic shook her. That's what had led Kemmler to her so fast. *They* had put it there. They wanted to be sure that she would know about

Forrester. They must have killed him somewhere else and then brought his body here in the dark and left it by the river.

The room seemed very still. She looked up to find Kemmler's mournful dark eyes intent on her face. She looked down again quickly so he wouldn't read the fearful knowledge in her eyes.

Kemmler asked, "There is nothing more then?"

Judith didn't speak and he leaned toward her and said earnestly, "I intend to find out how and why Mr. Forrester died the way he did, and who was responsible. Naturally—that is my job. So if there is anything—anything at all—that you can tell me . . ."

She shook her head and said through bloodless lips, "Nothing."

"Perhaps later you may think of something." He sighed, blew his nose and rose from his perch on the desk.

The interview was coming to an end. Judith drained the rest of the cognac in her glass as though it were water and put out her cigarette in the crystal ashtray on the manager's desk that advertised the name of the hotel. She rose, too, very pale, and walked to the door. Kemmler held it open for her.

"I would appreciate it if you wouldn't leave the hotel for a while. You weren't planning on going to Holland tonight, surely. There may be more questions I'll have to ask." He smiled at her gravely. "You are free, of course, to call anyone at your embassy if you want to."

"Yes, thank you. I'm sure that won't be necessary."

He watched her walk slowly up the stairs and then Kemmler left the office and went out to where his duty lay. The young policeman had been joined by other officials. The cameraman was photographing the body; others had set up lights and a search of the area was being made. Kemmler felt sure nothing would be found. His friend, Charlie Forrester, hadn't been killed here.

The police surgeon saw him approach and got up off his knees, saying, "Nasty, very nasty."

"Yes, nasty," Kemmler agreed. He wound the wool scarf another time around his throat, thinking with restless dissatisfaction that there was much more Judith Weber could have told him. Something was hiding behind those haunted eyes. Detained at the airport . . . ? Mistaken identity? How could *she* be mistaken for someone else? About that he could find out easily enough.

Kemmler sent the young policeman back to the hotel, outlined certain phone calls for him to make and told him to see that Miss Weber didn't leave the hotel. He would want to talk to her later.

Twenty-four

The silence was broken only by the rain hissing against the window and the creaking of the old, slanting boards under her feet as Judith paced the room, back and forth, back and forth, measuring the area with hard, angry steps.

By now her fear had given way to something close to rage, rage against the heartless brutality that had killed Charlie Forrester and left him in the cold rain beside the river, the round, boyish face that would never have looked old, swollen and blood-encrusted with the small, neat hole in the forehead. Her father's death had been almost impossible to accept but there had been some preparation for that, if such a thing could be. But Charlie Forrester had been innocently caught in the middle, or so it seemed, and that was a brutality not to be borne. Now more than ever the letter must be found. They must not be allowed to win this game. If Kemmler held her here until tomorrow, she could be too late. Whoever had stolen the books might find the letter's hiding place before her.

Her rental car stood in the courtyard but it might as well have been a hundred miles away. Perhaps Kemmler had already sent it back to the garage, telling the clerk in his mournful voice that she wouldn't be needing it. She put her cold hands to her hot cheeks

and paused at the window looking out to the river.
There must be a way! They had taken Charlie Forrester's body away, she noticed. The rain had formed
a deep puddle on the spot where it had lain. They
would be notifying his next of kin . . . And then it
came to her suddenly why Charlie Forrester had met
her at the airport. Max had sent him—Max. It was
stupid of her not to have thought of it before. Easy
to understand that they could be friends. Everyone
knew everyone else in diplomatic circles if they were
around long enough. Forrester was to kidnap her, in
a friendly way, of course, and hold her here until Max
could come, keep her occupied somehow . . .

Again the floorboards creaked under her feet. Max
was probably on his way here already. How long ago
it seemed since she had seen him standing there in
the hotel corridor, tall and slim with the light shining
on the bright, blond head, highlighting the cheekbones. . . . Suddenly, against all reason she wanted
him with such physical desire that her body trembled
with it. She leaned against a chair, forcing herself to
think coolly of why she was here—of Charlie Forrester, her father, Leah. . . .

There was a soft knock on the door. Judith pushed
away from the chair and swung around, looking for
escape. There wasn't any, of course. Two windows
and a door and someone was at the door—Kemmler
or his policeman. Hopelessly, she opened it.

Tall and slim and blond, he stood there and for a
moment she allowed the shadowed hallway and her
mind to trick her. Max . . .

Dieter von Traban stepped across the threshold
into the light, smiling shyly and twisting the funny
peaked cap.

"You're in trouble, Miss Weber? Can I help?"

Her knight in shining armor. Without thinking, she
put her hand on his arm and drew him away from the

door, closing it. "Yes," she said and then hesitated for a brief moment, knowing she had no right to involve this boy. But the choice was not hers. She was moved by a stronger claim from the dead.

"You can help me," she said.

He stiffened, clicked his heels and bowed. "Please," he said.

She felt that if he had been fully accoutred, he would have drawn his sword and rushed heedlessly into battle against whatever enemy she named.

"I have to get away from here."

"Yes."

The bright blue eyes were eager and unquestioning. Command me, they said. Was he just a young man, smitten for the moment with romantic ideas or was he someone else . . . ? The wind blew with a sudden, quick gust, driving the rain against the windows, scraping the branches of the tree against the balcony railing. Judith shivered. It seemed very dark all at once.

She whispered, "Do you have a car?"

"Yes, a small one." Dieter whispered in his turn.

"That doesn't matter."

"It runs. It's in good condition."

"Can you take me to the next town—or to Aachen, perhaps? If that's too far, then to Cologne."

He said simply, "If you want to go to Aachen, then I shall take you there."

His tone implied that if she wanted to travel to the moon, he would do his best to get her there, no questions asked. She knew nothing about him, this eager young knight. She hesitated, agonizing over the decision she knew she would make anyway. She had to take the help he offered.

"Your parents . . . ? Are you expected home? Will they miss you?"

"My parents are dead. I live with my aunt."

"I'm sorry."

"It has been so for a long time." He put it away quite easily. Finished. A thing of the past. Everyone died at one time or another.

"All right." She smiled at him sadly. "You understand, Dieter, that I haven't done anything wrong. I haven't broken the law. I wouldn't involve you in anything like that."

"Of course not." It wouldn't make any difference to him if she had broken every law in the land, his eyes told her. "Anyone," he added with his shy, schoolboy smile, "who plays the piano as you do couldn't do anything wrong."

"If it were that simple . . . I must go without anyone seeing me. Where is your car?"

"In the courtyard."

"It would be better if I didn't come there. Can you drive up the road to the corner and wait for me there?"

"Yes, but will you be all right?"

Judith nodded and asked, "In case I'm delayed, you'll wait?"

"Of course," he said. Forever, his eyes said.

Again doubts nagged her. What right had she to involve this fair-haired romantic, this schoolboy in uniform? His uniform conjured the images of other uniforms, of black-booted legs and swinging truncheons. Which side would you have chosen, Dieter, forty years ago?

"Is something wrong?" he whispered.

"No, no," she said. How sensitive he was to her every mood! "No," she said gently. "I'll see you in a few minutes." She put her hand on his arm as she opened the door for him, wanting to say something loving, trusting, but she couldn't find the words. All she could say was, "Thank you, Dieter."

She watched the slim back move off down the corridor. At the stairs he turned and waved his cap at her and then, like a boy heading for great adventures, he leaped down the stairs two at a time and disappeared from view.

She closed the door quickly on the sounds that drifted up from the floor below—voices singing and laughing and talking—meaningless sounds. She locked it and left the key in the lock. Pulling on her coat, she buttoned it as she contemplated the view of the window overlooking the river. If she left through the lobby, Kemmler and his young policeman would see her. Perhaps the clerk had received instructions, too, to watch out for her.

The fog had thickened and that was good for her purposes. A ghost ship moved stealthily on the water, its ghost horn muffled by the fog. Lights coming from the ground floor cast a dim reflection on the wet surfaces of the patio below. No exit there.

The other window would have to be her escape hatch. There, one of the old tree's branches extended over the balcony railing. Well, all right, she thought grimly, how long has it been since I've climbed a tree?

She rolled her slacks up to her knees, pulled on her gloves, tucked her purse under her arm, and then looked questioningly around the room. She had the sense of something forgotten. Her eyes fell on the almost empty suitcase and she realized that was it. For almost two days it had been a part of her, an unnatural kind of appendage, but it was useless now. She turned her back on it and slid the window up softly, climbed out on the balcony, and slid the window down just as softly. Leaning over the railing she dropped her purse and heard it land with a soft thud. She reached out and grasped the branch firmly in both hands and stepped up onto the railing. It was

198

old, she felt it move a little under her feet. Her breath caught in her throat. She teetered on the railing, unable to go forward, unwilling to go back. She felt giddiness overtaking her. She could be killed if she fell. *The prisoner, attempting to escape, slipped and fell to her death.*

Don't look down and move, she cautioned herself.

She swung a leg out slowly into space. She knew there was a branch somewhere beneath her but for a while all she felt was emptiness. Her searching toe touched it finally and before she could let herself think, she stepped down firmly on it. For a frightening moment she straddled air until she forced herself to pull the other foot from the railing to the branch. She heard no cracking sound as the branch sagged under her weight so she took a deep breath and with agonizing slowness, like a tightrope walker, she crept along, inch by inch, her arms encircling the branch above, until she reached the juncture of branch and trunk. She released first one arm and then the other until she was clinging to the trunk in a tight embrace, her cheek against its wet, reassuringly rough surface. She closed her eyes and rested for a moment. So far, so good. She slid her arms down the trunk and lowered herself to a sitting position on the branch, still encircling the trunk with one arm.

She had to look down to assess the drop, estimating that it would be about ten feet if she swung from the branch she was sitting on. The earth beneath looked soft and muddy from the rain. It would cushion her fall.

She let her legs swing in the air for a moment while she gathered courage and looked around. There was a big house neighboring the hotel, separated from it by a stone wall. It was a small island of blazing light in the mist. Voices and music came through the closed windows. A broad veranda fronted the house facing the river and as she looked, a man stepped out. He held a glass in his hand and his walk was unsteady. He looked down toward the river and she saw him shake his head and then look up at the sky. His eyes described an arc across the sky to the hotel and, in passing, to the tree. Had he seen her? He stood only a few yards away. He moved uncertainly in her direction and squinted up. Every muscle in Judith's body froze. If he makes a scene, calls out to her . . . ? She waited, saying silent prayers. Suddenly he waved his glass in her direction, shouted something, drank, and then, laughing and weaving, he went back into the house. He's drunk, Judith thought, and probably thinks I am. The good old Christmas spirit. But he's drunk enough so if he describes this strange bird in the tree, his friends might not believe him. Without humor, she laughed softly, her throat filled with the cold fog.

And then, giving no further thought to anything, she twisted sideways on the branch, placed both hands on it, and with sudden, reckless courage, shoved herself off. She dangled helplessly for a moment in mid-air, then, taking a deep breath, she let go and dropped. She landed in a crouching position, hands, feet, and knees hitting the ground so hard the impact jarred every bone in her body and forced a cry of pain from her. The fall had been longer, the ground harder than she had anticipated. The dark had deceived her.

She rose and limped around cautiously for a moment. Nothing seemed to be broken though her right ankle gave her some pain. It would probably be all right after a rest. It would have to be.

She retrieved her purse and rolled down her slacks, brushing off some of the mud as she limped clumsily toward the far wall of the hotel, away from the river. There she turned and moved slowly, keeping against the wall and listening for sounds. As she neared the courtyard, she heard voices, young men's voices, loud and teasing. She peered around the corner of the building. Dieter's three companions had him backed against the Volkswagen and from their attitudes and the expressions on their faces, they were enjoying themselves at Dieter's expense. The tallest one, the oldest with the scar on his face, had his hand on Dieter's shoulder and was saying something. Whatever it was, it annoyed Dieter, who pushed the hand away angrily and tried to get into the car. But they hadn't finished their teasing. One of them held the door closed, laughing and saying something about *"Tante"* in a sarcastic tone.

They're teasing him about me, she thought, and there's nothing I can do until they've played out their silly game. She leaned against the wall in the shadows, putting her head up, receiving the cold rain on her face. Concentrate on taking one step at a time, she told herself—to Dieter's car, to Aachen, a rental car, to Holland. . . . They seemed very long steps and she had no way of knowing where they would lead her.

She heard other voices, not the boys', but muffled and quite close. She shrank deeper into the shadows and looked around for the speakers. She was standing beside the window of the room that led off from the lobby, a small room set aside for guests who wanted to read or write letters or enjoy a quiet cup of coffee. She edged up to the window and looked in. Kemmler was there, talking and pacing with slow, deliberate steps, back and forth in front of the window. His thick brows were pulled down in a heavy frown over his sad eyes and at first Judith thought he was talking to himself, until she moved closer. Then she could see the tall, young policeman standing in front of the door. As she watched, Kemmler stopped his restless pacing and planted himself squarely in front of the window and began to fire rapid questions at his subordinate which were answered just as rapidly. At one point she made out Forrester's name and the word *"Zimmer"* and the policeman made sweeping, violent gestures with his arms indicating tearing and breaking and she heard him half-shout, *"Kaput, alles kaput!"*

It wasn't hard for Judith to understand that the same vicious search that had destroyed her father's apartment had taken place in Forrester's and that the people who had killed him did not have the books and that, therefore, Smith had them.

The familiar waves of fear swept over her and she turned away from the window and leaned against the wall, overwhelmed by the hopelessness of her task. In the dark the harsh, whispering voice of her father came to her: *How could I live with myself for the rest of my life if I didn't do everything I could to bring this man to justice? It would be a betrayal. I would be turning my back on Leah.*

And she couldn't turn her back on either of them, no matter how lost she felt in this barbaric land without maps to guide her out. She closed her eyes, smiling faintly to appease the ghosts.

"Fräulein Weber . . ."

Kemmler's voice dispersed the ghosts and alerted her to present danger. She peered through the window in time to see the young policeman nod and leave the room while the sad-eyed detective resumed his slow pacing.

He's sending for me. I must get away from here with or without Dieter. Then she was aware that the courtyard was silent, had been so for some minutes. As she listened, the silence was broken by the grinding of the VW engine. Her young knight had managed to break away from his friends.

She waited until the car had swung out of the gate and then, putting as little weight as possible on her ankle, which had stiffened painfully, she hurried across the courtyard and up the narrow road. With a sigh of relief she saw the taillights of the little car ahead of her, glowing warm and friendly through the mist.

From the shadowed doorway of a small tobacco shop across the street, cold, gray eyes watched the tall blond young man leap eagerly out of the driver's seat of the VW and hurry around to the sidewalk to open the door for the woman, making a stiff little bow as he did so. They watched the tall woman climb into the car with that awkward grace he had been so aware of in the coffee shop in Penn Station. He noticed she had been limping, favoring the right leg. He shook his head as he wrote something in a small notebook. It wasn't really necessary. He already knew the young man's name, the car license number, and its destination. The notemaking was habit more than anything else—years of little notebooks filled with little notes. He put it into his pocket and pulled out his flask. As he drank, he watched the taillights of the car fade away in the night. Then he moved to the dark blue BMW parked by the curb and climbed in behind the wheel. In doing so he disturbed the small pile of books on the seat. Two of them fell to the floor. He cursed softly as he reached down to pick them up. Why couldn't the foolish old man have said outright where the letter and photograph were instead of making sly references to small towns in Holland and marvelous organs? One thing the old man hadn't been vague about—names. One in particular. And in naming that one some of his rage seemed to have burned itself into the page. Reading it, Smith felt the heat of it.

He had another drink from his flask and then lit a

cigarette, opening the car window to let some of the smoke out, some of the cloudy, cold air in.

He hadn't needed the old man's frankness about names. What he had needed was information about the letter. Watching Judith Weber move along so surely from New York to Bonn and now to Holland, he had felt sure the books had told her the secret of the letter's hiding place. He hadn't even tried to find her in New York. He had simply come here, certain of picking up her trail.

She had told him in the coffee shop, her face pale and stiff, that she didn't know where the letter was and he had been fool enough to believe her. He hadn't thought she would lie. He hadn't thought the other woman would lie either. . . .

How long had it been since he had allowed himself to think of her? And why now? Why should her face come back to him now—that small, oval face with the gentle eyes. Such a tiny creature, weighing nothing when he picked her up in his arms. *Love is a strange word on your lips.* . . . Halman's words had torn open the wound that had never really healed in the first place and now it festered inside him.

He drank from the flask again, hating the way his thoughts were running but unable to stop them.

Why should he think of her at all in connection with Judith Weber, that tall, black-haired woman with those haunted eyes, blundering toward a brutal confrontation? What had they in common? Devotion . . . ? Devotion to something above and beyond the call of ordinary duty or love? He drank again, a long drink this time, to deaden the stirrings he felt, the hot, gnawing hunger in his loins. Who was the hunger for? The dead one? This one?

The footsteps of a pedestrian fell softly on the wet sidewalk beside the car. Smith shook his head sharply, sat up, and roared the engine into life with a savage twist of the wrist. Sentiment had withered and died in the hut in Vietnam. Let it stay buried there. He had a job to finish and he had to finish it before they finished it for him. Clumsy, brutal fools! First Weber, now Forrester . . .

The tires shrieked in protest as he swung the car in a U-turn and set off in the direction the VW had taken.

Twenty-five

"All the same," said Dieter, resuming an old argument, "I shall find a pharmacy in Aachen and get something to bind your ankle with."

"I don't want to take the time. It will have to get better by itself."

With sudden and surprising firmness, Dieter said, "All the same, I shall."

Judith was too tired and there was time enough for arguing about that, so she let it go and they drove along the wet autobahn in silence. Judith's thoughts were vague and jumbled in her head until out of all of them one grew sharp and clear and all of a sudden she burst out laughing, a shattering, joyless sound verging on the hysterical, rising and swelling like a tide. It frightened Dieter, so the car swerved and he slowed quickly, pulled over to the side of the road, and stopped, staring at her in helpless confusion. The laughter died finally in a fit of coughing and through it Judith gasped an apology.

"It's all right. I'm sorry. Drive on, young knight, drive on!" Her voice was reckless with the remains of the wild laughter. She pulled a tissue from her purse and wiped her face which was wet with perspiration and tears. "Forgive me for startling you. I was laughing because—because I climbed down that damned tree! That's as good a reason as any, isn't it?"

Dieter drove back into the traffic again, thinking how strange she was, and how very sad, with that

206

white face and those dark, feverish eyes. She was shivering, he could see, and he pushed the heater up to its maximum. He would have taken off his coat and given it to her but he knew she would refuse. "You are sure you are all right, Miss Weber?" he asked in his precise English.

"Yes, I am, I am." Another fit of coughing seized her and she took out another tissue. "There isn't anything the matter with me that tomorrow or the next day might not cure. Can you imagine me climbing down a tree—a great, hulking woman?" The wildness was gone from her voice; it was thin and tired.

Dieter smiled shyly, keeping his eyes on the fogged road, and said, "Forgive me for disagreeing with you. You're not a great, hulking woman. You're a—a goddess." He brought the word out fast and breathlessly and then added quickly, as though apologizing for his boldness. "It's true. I thought so when I first saw you."

She touched his arm lightly and smiled in the dark at the earnest young profile. "If anything, you're my knight in shining armor. I needed someone and there you were. I'm grateful for that, more than I can say."

"Like a Valkyrie," he said, his boldness for the moment knowing no limits.

"Ah . . . Dieter—"

"It's true."

"My hair is black," Judith teased him.

He forgave her with a quick, sidelong glance.

"And I certainly wouldn't allow you to be slain in battle if I could help it."

"It is not the worst thing in the world," he said stiffly, his back straightening into the ramrod position.

"Perhaps not," Judith said gently, "but isn't it better to live usefully—"

"My father was too young to serve in the last war but my two uncles did," he said with pride. "One died gloriously on the Russian front and the other, a doctor, served long and honorably for the Fatherland."

He made it sound as though he were reading from a book. From what Judith knew, no one had died gloriously on the Russian front.

"Horace said," Dieter quoted with youthful pomposity, " ' 'tis sweet and seemly to die for one's country.' "

"In Horace's time, perhaps, though I doubt it. Isn't it more seemly to live and try to make the world a sweeter place? Your uncle, the doctor, saved life, while the other took it. Isn't that strange?"

"Both sides of my family, the Wallners and the von Trabans, have never held back when Germany needed them."

"The . . . ? The name caught in her throat as the blood rushed to her head and then receded as quickly, leaving a weakness in her body and a pounding in her ears. Through the shock her inner voice cautioned her, *Wait, wait. It may be a common name in Germany.* With forced calm, she asked, "Wallner . . . ? Your uncle's name was Wallner?"

"He was my mother's brother—Kurt Wallner."

She turned her head away, staring out of the window, seeing nothing, trying to convince herself that it made no difference. The boy was not his uncle, had probably never met him. It was only witch doctors and Nazi supermen who talked of tainted blood. But what strange and terrible irony had led Dieter to her table? Out of all the young men in the country, out of the thousands in Bonn University alone . . . ? Why this boy? Why was she sitting beside him now, cold and shivering again? It had vanished—that brief illusion of cheer and warmth generated by their light talk of goddesses and knights and Valkyries. Just speaking that name seemed to have poisoned the air in the car.

"I know our countries were enemies then," he was

saying softly, "but that was a long time ago. It's all over."

She whispered, "Yes, it's all over."

The lights of Cologne gleamed at them for a moment, washing away some of the fog, and then the autobahn carried them away from the city, westward to Aachen.

"I never met Uncle Kurt," Dieter went on. "He died before I was born, in nineteen forty-eight, probably as a result of the strain of his work during the war, my mother and aunt told me. He was a fine man, they said, dedicated to medical science. When he was my age, he had already fought his duel, earned his *Schmisse*."

That's what the two women had told him, this slim, handsome boy whose blue eyes had shone so fanatically when he talked of dueling. Were they lies the women themselves had believed when they had Kurt Wallner declared legally dead, or had they known the truth? *He* should know, he should be told the truth, Judith thought. How could he grow up believing in fairy tales of Valkyries and butcher-doctors in concentration camps? *I* could tell him! Yes, I could tell him. Judith was shocked by the sudden savagery of her thoughts. Some of the youthful glow would leave those blue eyes. I *should* tell him. . . .

She rested her hot forehead against the cool window, knowing very well that she couldn't possibly do it. Vengeance on a boy for his uncle's crimes? The boy's only crime, perhaps, was his over-willing acceptance of what he was told.

"Have I offended you somehow?" Dieter asked.

That incredible sensitivity to her mood. Even Max wasn't as quick. But the question had caught her before the heat of her angry thoughts had cooled and she said roughly, "No, of course not. Why should you think so?"

Turning to face him she saw the spasm of pain cross his face and hating herself for hurting him so unjustly, she leaned toward him, touched his hand, and spoke quick, gentle words of apology. "Forgive me, Dieter. That was cruel of me. I'm tired, you understand, and you mustn't take too much notice of what I say. You didn't offend me. I'm tired, that's all." And then she had to turn her face away again because all of a sudden she was crying. Silently the tears rolled down her cheeks, unchecked.

"You must have some food," he said. "I'll get you some in Aachen."

She managed to say no, that she wouldn't have time.

"Let me come with you. Let me take you where you want to go."

"No," she said softly to the window, fighting the seduction of his words. "I can't let you do that—and I can't explain."

Judith put her head back and shut her eyes against the dark road and her dark thoughts. She must have dozed a bit, for when she opened them, her head rested on Dieter's shoulder and the car was swerving onto the exit. The gleaming lights of a town swam up out of the mist to meet them.

"That's Aachen," Dieter said as she raised her head.

He drove first to a pharmacy, ignoring Judith's protests, saying simply, "I will do it. If you get angry, very well, then, you must get angry."

He left her waiting in the car and when he returned shortly, he carried not only a large roll of gauze but coffee and a bun he had picked up for her somewhere along the way. From romantic schoolboy to competent young man, Judith thought, as she watched him bandage the sore, swollen ankle with hands that were quick, skillful, and gentle. He explained as he did so that the pharmacist had had no elastic bandage but that the stretch gauze was really better in a way.

"There," he said, rising and brushing off his trousers, "it should be easier for you now."

"Yes." She smiled at him over the rim of the plastic cup. "It is already."

It took some looking, but they finally found a car to rent in a small shop under the long shadow of the cathedral, owned by a fussy, irritable man who lived in an apartment behind the garage. He was closed, he complained bitterly, in answer to their loud knocking on the door, and why did these Americans think they could get something after hours that he wouldn't give to his own countrymen?

All of which Dieter translated, taking some of the sting out, as he explained the man's rudeness in light of the fact that there had just been two other Americans there for a rental and that the man was hungry and tired and wanted to get back to his wife and his dinner.

"Please tell him that I'm sorry to put him to so much trouble."

Dieter explained with great tact and courtesy and the man lost some of his irritability and even smiled briefly as Judith brought out her passport, signed papers, and paid him money, adding something extra to compensate for the lateness of the hour.

The car was a Saab, of all things. It was all he had. There had been a Mercedes, but the other Americans had taken it. "This is clean and it runs well," he said, and he backed it out to the curb and then promptly disappeared into the garage, closing the doors with a loud, firm bang.

Judith turned to Dieter. This was the difficult part and she didn't want to prolong it, for both their sakes. He no longer looked like the responsible young man who had handled the car rental with such tact and efficiency and had been so firm about her ankle. He was just a boy now as he stood beside the VW waiting, hesitant and forlorn in the rain.

Too young, she thought, too young to carry an old and hateful burden. Let her father's generation carry it and his uncle's. And wouldn't her father be the first to agree? No doubt, yet . . . Leah at twenty was older than this boy would ever be and she was already marked for death.

She went up to him and took his face between her hands and kissed him gently on the smooth cheek.

"Thank you, Dieter, for everything you've done for me—everything. Now I want you to promise me something."

"Yes, anything," he said hoarsely. His face flushed and grew warm under her hands and she felt him stiffen as she released him.

"No, don't go all stiff and start to bow. You're too charming the other way. I want you to promise me you'll go straight back to your aunt's, as quickly as possible—"

"I'm quite capable," he said formally, "of taking care of myself."

"Certainly. I didn't mean that. I want you to promise that you won't discuss this trip, where you left me, with anyone. It will be better—safer—if you don't."

"Safer?"

She hadn't meant to say that. She was tired and the fear was coming back now that she would be alone again. "I only meant that I don't want to involve you in my troubles. For the time being anyway, forget we came to Aachen, forget you know me at all. Do you promise?"

He nodded unwillingly because he had no choice. Her dark eyes were staring fixedly into his, drawing the answer from him. He didn't want to leave her. He wanted to put his hands on her shoulders and hold her there, not let her go away from him. He didn't know what was in her heart or mind or what trouble brought the haunted, driven look to her eyes, but they were demanding that he accede to her request. He nodded dumbly and took her hand in his and bowed over it, clicking his heels.

Then she was gone. He watched her climb into the little Saab and drive away through the rain. Her hand appeared in a brief wave through the window as she turned the corner and disappeared from view.

Twenty-six

Judith brushed a strand of damp hair out of her eyes and looked again into the rearview mirror. Yes, it was following her and had been for some time. She was sure of it. The car was close enough behind her so she could make out the familiar grill and emblem of the Mercedes. Other cars on the highway had sped up and passed her or dropped behind and turned off. This one had maintained a steady pace behind her, slowing when she slowed, speeding up when she did. She realized this had been so since she left Aachen.

She was sure of something else, too, though she didn't know why—that the car's occupants were the Americans who had rented the fussy man's Mercedes. They weren't making any effort to conceal themselves from her.

She would have to think of something. The border was just ahead. She could see the checkpoints, dimly lit in the mist. There was no hope at all that the Saab could outspeed a Mercedes. She would simply have to think of something to slow them down, to give her a few minutes of extra time. What?

She slowed the car and pulled off the road for a moment and pretended to be consulting a map, one of several that the last renter had left in the glove compartment. She thanked him silently, whoever he was, as she lifted it high over the steering wheel, unfolding it with large movements while she glanced

214

again into the rearview mirror. The Mercedes had pulled off the road too, about fifty yards behind her. No doubts now.

By the time she had folded the map up again and returned it to its compartment, an idea was forming in her mind. She concentrated on it as she drove slowly back onto the highway. The Mercedes hadn't started up yet. They were thinking, of course, that they had plenty of time. She would be held a few minutes at both checkpoints.

Approaching the gate, another thought occurred to her—that Kemmler, having missed her at the hotel, might have her stopped at the border. It shook her. Why had she told him she was going to Holland to visit friends? Or would he think that because she had told him where she was going, she wouldn't be stupid enough to go there? Yes, he might think like that. How important was she to his murder investigation? I'll soon know, she thought grimly.

To her relief, it was all amazingly simple. The German official was sleepy and casual. Anything to declare? Nothing, she was only going over to visit friends for a few days in Heerlen. She saw the map in her mind's eye and the name of the town, close to the border, came to her without hesitancy. He looked quickly at her passport, the car's papers, and her international driver's license, kept up-to-date at her father's insistence, yawned, wished her a Merry Christmas, and waved her on with a smile.

The Dutch official, slower, a little ponderous, but very courteous, went through the same routine, asking in addition how long she would be staying in Holland. She answered truthfully, "A few days only," and untruthfully, that she was visiting a friend who lived near Maastricht named Cornelius Steen. She watched his face carefully as she spoke the name but he simply nodded and smiled and said he hoped she would enjoy her visit. A shot in the dark. Too much to hope for that a border guard would know a Cornelius Steen who might live near Maastricht.

It's now or never, she thought, as he handed back her passport and papers and she said slowly, looking doubtful, but very earnest, "The car behind me . . ."

"Yes," the official said helpfully.

He spoke English well. She hoped he understood it equally well.

"I don't know what it means—only that it looked suspicious—and I know how much drug smuggling there is. . . ." She had the official's close attention at the word "drugs."

He glanced behind her and then leaned against the window, nodding and waiting for her to go on.

"In Aachen at a gas station, that car was there too, the Mercedes behind me. The driver pulled off into the shadows, I noticed, and took some packages out of the trunk of his car. It looked suspicious—I'm not sure why. He put these packets—they weren't very large but there were quite a few of them—" The story came out of her complete and of its own accord, almost. She was astonished. "He put them inside the hubcaps of the wheels and secured them with tape."

She had hit a snag, she could see that. He didn't understand the word "hubcap." She excused herself and she opened the door as he stepped back. Out of the corner of her eye she saw the Mercedes pull up to the German checkpoint. She had to make him understand—*now*. She leaned down and took the hubcap in her hands and pretended to pull it off, motioning underneath it. "In there," she said. He was nodding rapidly up and down with a gleam in his eye. It was all right. He understood. She rose, dusted off her hands, and climbed back into the car.

"I did think you should know." She spread her hands helplessly and smiled at him. "I wasn't sure. . . . I hope I've done the right thing."

"You have, you have." He nodded some more and

smiled and then looked over his shoulder at the black Mercedes and stopped smiling. The look on the good man's face told Judith that he was prepared to go over the car bolt by bolt. He thanked her and wished her a good journey.

She sped away, watching in the rearview mirror as the Mercedes was stopped and directed off the road by a firm official. She saw the driver climb out, obviously arguing, making angry gestures with his hands. She couldn't make him out very clearly through the mist but he seemed to be a small, rather thin man. He was joined by his companion, a bigger man, and the last she saw was the two of them walking slowly up the steps of the customs shed.

She felt sure she knew them. Twice she had had contact with the small one—at Kennedy Airport and on the plane—and though she had lost sight of them at Bonn, they had not lost sight of her. The locked doors of the car, the warmth from the heater, and the good sound of the engine gave her a sense of security, if only temporary. She had borrowed a little time, not much. They had a powerful car and once the customs search was over, they would be after her again. Abruptly she swung off an exit into a secondary road. There must be many little roads that would eventually take her to Maastricht and this way it would be hard for them to find her.

She rounded a curve and began to climb a long, slow-rising hill. The mist was clearing. A cold wind was rising, sending the clouds racing across the sky and the last drops of rain spattering against the windshield.

Twenty-seven

The weather had changed abruptly in the night and it had started to snow. Large white flakes drifted down, covering the ground. Only a few bare patches still showed, emphasizing the purity of the snow cover.

Lost in the night on small back roads that led past quiet farmhouses and sleeping villages, Judith had been afraid to stop in any lighted area for fear of seeing the black Mercedes loom up out of the dark like some huge monster. For the same reason she had avoided inns and hotels.

Finally, half asleep at the wheel, she had looked for some kind of protection, some hiding place, and had found it in a small clump of trees. She pulled the car off the road and parked in the center of it.

The night had passed slowly, in twisting and turning to find comfort in the cramped space of the car, in fitful stages of waking and dozing, in snatches of dreams that were no more than images of dead faces, hers among them. She shivered, waking, and realized she must have slept for a couple of hours, for she had been unaware of the snow until now.

She groaned as she moved to get out of the car. Every joint was stiff, every muscle ached. Her ankle had stiffened so it was almost useless. Her numb fingers switched on the engine and fumbled for the heater. A blast of cold air struck her and she pushed it off. Leaving the engine running to warm up, she began to walk, slowly at first, limping unsteadily up and down the country road—it was no more than a lane, really—until some circulation began to return, stinging, to her limbs. Then she forced herself into a kind of half-hop, half-jog, gritting her teeth against the pain in her ankle. She paused now and then to clap her arms around her body and stamp her feet, sending up small clouds of fine snow.

She was on a hill. Pleasant, prosperous-looking farms were spread out around her and in the distance was a village. Softly through the gently falling snow she heard church bells toll the hour—seven o'clock.

She left the lane and walked out into an open meadow and found herself looking down into a valley where a city sprawled in all directions and a domed cathedral sent its tall spire exploring upward into the gray sky. *I could see its spire reaching for the bare sky.* She stared at it for a moment, then her eyes went beyond it. Were they the lanes of the autobahn? And closer, were those the border checkpoints?

Was this some kind of hallucination—or hand of fate? She felt stupid with cold and hunger and fatigue as she looked around her, trying to make sense out of what she was seeing. The signs at a small crossroads on her left pointed to vaguely familiar towns: Vaals, Kerkraade, Heerlen—Heerlen! She had gone in a large and tortuous circle and was back where she had started last night—on a hill looking down at Aachen.

My walks led me out of the town into the country. On a hill overlooking the German border, I could see Aachen lying below in its pleasant valley.

Excitement quickened her breathing. She was no longer aware of the cold. She felt the ghost-hand of her father on her shoulder, she heard his ghost-whisper in her ear: *You're almost there. The answer is close at hand.*

Here somewhere in this small corner of Holland it had all come together for her father. The roads she had traveled last night had been rutted and laid waste by war when her father, torn between hope and despair, had walked over them in 1945. Over one of them, Franz Halman, near death, had come to the final and tragic meeting with his friend.

Without conscious effort, thoughts and images began to race through her mind. The books. *Memorize them.* Charlie Forrester's light voice joking about airports: . . . *the right combination of letters* . . . A specific number of books memorized in specific order. Was that right? Was she remembering correctly? Had he always said them in a certain order? She closed her eyes to concentrate and saw the books as they had been stacked on the customs counter at the airport: Hammett, O'Connor, Lawrence, Dinesen, Updike, Camus. Forget the titles for the moment. Her father's attention had always seemed to be on the authors' names. The simplest code would be the first letter of each name. H-O-L-D-U-C. She opened her eyes and looked at the road signs. She knew there wasn't a Holduc there but that didn't really mean anything. The name certainly sounded Dutch. It must be. It had to be.

She ran back to the car and took the map from the glove compartment. Dusting the snow off the car's hood, she spread it out. Her trembling finger described a circle east of Maastricht and she spoke the strange names aloud: "Vaals, Valkenburg, Hoensbroek, Beek, Margraten, Heer, Wittem, Mheer, Meerssen . . ." And over again . . . And again . . . When she found her finger straying too far north or south, she brought it back to the proper area.

It was a detailed map but her searching finger found no Holduc. She had been wrong—wrong! The heat of her excitement drained away, leaving her colder than before. She stared at the map in angry disbelief for a moment and then, suddenly, with a violent sweep of her arm, she sent it flying from the hood to the ground as she swung around and walked with hard, heavy strides to the meadow. Gazing down at Aachen, her eyes black with despair, she whispered aloud with savage disappointment into the stillness, "I tried, I tried."

I tried, she went on silently, but it's all been madness, a nightmare. There *is* no letter. There *is* no photograph. Mother was right. So was Max. It's finished, Father, done. Your death, Charlie Forrester's . . . For nothing.

She flung her head back and looked up at the gray sky, her face white with bitterness. The record is closed, she thought. For Leah, for the others—no justice. For Klausing-Wallner—no retribution. He will die comfortably in his bed and that will be that for the victims of sterilization, of bone-breakings, of the mad-scientist operations without anesthesia. This is the final defeat, the book is finished, Father. *They've* won.

Judith didn't know how long she stood there with the snow falling damply on her face, a tall, silent figure in a creased raincoat. Time might have stood still, raced ahead, or fallen back. It was all the same. It was only when she heard the church bells toll again that she turned finally and limped on cold feet back to the car, brushing vaguely, like a sleepwalker, at the hood of snow on her head and shoulders.

She retrieved the map from the ground, folded it with care, climbed into the car, and restored it to the glove compartment.

With one hand on the steering wheel, the other on the stick shift, she was ready to go. Where? The question roused her from the dreamlike state she had fallen into. Where was she to go? Without the compass her father had marked for her with his goal of vengeance, she was lost, adrift, with no course to follow. She gazed uncertainly around at the hills and valleys surrounding her, the white ground dotted here and there with the dark shapes of houses. Her eye was caught by thin ribbons of smoke curling out of one of the chimneys of a farmhouse several hundred yards down the hill. It was a solid, prosperous-looking place with several sturdy outbuildings behind it and sprawling fields surrounding it. It looked secure, safe, somehow. She would go there and ask directions to Bonn—or Maastricht. To take the map out again and study it was an effort she was too tired to make.

The truth, if Judith had been conscious of it, was simply that she had a sudden, overwhelming urge to *see* someone, anyone, to make small talk, trustingly, with a friendly stranger, to escape from this state of terrible aloneness.

She glanced back at the meadow to say good-bye to her ghosts, wavering shadows in the pale morning light, waiting with patient faces. With aching despair she put the car into gear and drove quickly away, leaving them there with their empty, scarred hands. She had nothing to give them.

The beckoning fingers of smoke guided Judith down the bumpy road, along level ground for a few yards and then into a lane that led her up to the door of the farmhouse. A little girl knelt by the stoop, playing in the snow, a dog beside her. They looked up as Judith climbed out of the car and studied her silently with innocent eyes.

Judith smiled and said, "Good morning."

The child smiled back and the dog rose, stretched, licked the child's face, and walked unhurriedly over to Judith. He sniffed her feet with great thoroughness, then her ankles; reached a decision, sat down, and looked up into her face, sweeping the snow with his tail. He was a strong, stocky animal who looked like the result of breeding husky with a wolf, but he was smaller and had a gentle, intelligent face.

"Do you speak English?" Judith asked the child. She nodded and repeated, "English." She was no more than six, with large blue eyes, a pert nose, and a wide, smiling mouth. One long strand of blond hair had escaped from beneath her cap and straggled down along her cheek.

"I'm an American. I'm lost, you see. I want to go to Maastricht," Judith said.

"Maastricht." The child nodded solemnly.

"Can you tell me what road I take?"

"Yes," the child said and fell silent.

"Which road is it?" Judith pointed first in one direction and then another and shrugged her shoulders.

The little girl laughed at the game they were playing, pointing with small mittened hands as Judith had done and shrugging her shoulders.

"You don't really understand English at all, do you?" Judith said gently. "You're just being polite, aren't you?"

The child nodded and smiled and said, "Yes."

"Is your father here?" Judith asked, gesturing at the house. "Or your mother?" The child certainly wouldn't be alone here with the dog.

"*Opa*," the girl was saying as she rose and came to Judith. "*Opa*," she repeated, taking Judith's hand and pulling her toward the door. Just then it opened.

"Mariet?"

An old man stood in the doorway. He was tall and lean with strong arms and broad shoulders and tanned, leathery skin, a man used to working long hours in the open. His eyes were pale blue, keen and intelligent, crinkled at the corners now as he smiled at the child and then looked inquiringly at Judith.

Mariet ran to him, saying, "*Opa*, American!" and launched into a noisy explanation, pointing at Judith and giggling sometimes. Throughout, the old man kept his eyes on Judith's face. Even after the child had finished, he continued to gaze at her with a curious intensity.

Judith realized how dirty and unkempt she must look and launched into her own explanation—of losing her way in the night, of sleeping in the car. "I came here hoping—hoping you could help a lost stranger find her way." She gave him a feeble smile. It was all she could manage.

To the farmer she looked like a lost soul without hope of any kind wandering in some kind of purgatory. The broad-boned face was haggard, the black-shadowed, deepset eyes were too bright, too full of pain. Once many years ago he had seen a face like this on someone who stood where she was standing, looking up at him, trying to smile in that same forced way.

He opened the door for her and stepped aside. "You must come in out of the cold," he said, then spoke a few words to the child, and dog and child, leaping through the snow, disappeared around the back of the house.

In the hall the old man insisted she remove her coat and gloves, saying, "We will be having breakfast soon. You will join us." Judith protested weakly, but the old man simply shook his head.

"Have you traveled far?" he asked.

"Only from Bonn. Before that, of course, from New York."

"New York . . . You are visiting friends here for the holidays?"

"In a way."

"Friends in Maastricht?"

"Yes—that is—friends of friends." Her voice was husky with fatigue. She was beginning to be sorry she had come. It had been a mistake, better to have followed the map. Certainly he had a right to ask questions of a stranger he was inviting into his home but there was more than casual, courteous interest behind the questions. The old man was in a state of agitation, his excitement barely suppressed. The pale blue eyes studied her face with a kind of wonder in them. Judith leaned back against the wall to get away from the eyes, so close to her, frightened by something she didn't understand. Clumsily, she changed the subject. "It's kind of you to take a stranger into your home and not too presentable a one at that."

There was a split second silence. Then the old man said softly, "You are not a stranger, I think, unless . . . But, no, I couldn't be mistaken. You are not a stranger."

The hall was cold, the doors leading from it were closed, probably to save heat, but that didn't account for her trembling or for the pounding of her heart as she stared at the old man and saw that he was trembling as well.

Without another word he took her by the arm and led her to a door on the right of the hall and opened it. Judith walked mechanically beside him, unwilling or unable to think at all. They entered a rather formal sitting-room that was clearly little used. It was colder than the hall and the fireplace at the end of the room was empty and black. The hand on her arm shook slightly as he urged her toward the mantel over the fireplace which was crowded with pictures of all sizes: informal snapshots, stiff portrait-photographs, some old and faded, some of recent taking.

He placed a long, brown finger on one of them, a glossy photo in a cardboard frame showing a group of young men in uniform. It was grainy from enlargement and faded with age.

"The resemblance is remarkable, except perhaps . . ." His voice was thin with excitement as his finger moved to one of the figures and Judith leaned closer and found herself looking at the youthful face of her father. "He wrote me that if he could not come, you would come. I'm his friend, Cornelius Steen. He must have spoken of me. That must be why you are here. Tell me I'm right. My eyes haven't deceived me."

Judith shook her head, dazed, and whispered, "They haven't deceived you."

The old voice went on in an excited murmur, "He wrote me—every year about this time. His last letter arrived only a few days ago—a strange letter—not like the others at all. It puzzled me. Wild, he seemed, out of control. I wondered if he was ill. Now you're here, you can tell me."

Judith turned to look into the troubled blue eyes and nodded and then looked back at the picture, her mind just beginning to cope with what had happened. Was it only fifteen minutes ago that she had told the gray skies she was giving up, conceding defeat? Was it only such a little time ago that she had turned her back on the hollow-eyed ghosts? Now she stood in Cornelius Steen's home.

"I had no idea . . ." Her voice sounded strange and distant in her ears. "Yes, I wanted to find you. That's why I came to Holland, but I didn't know where you were. I came here because—something must have guided me." Judith smiled faintly and added, "The smoke from your chimney, perhaps."

In the same thin, excited murmur, the old man went on, "Your father sat with me here in this room, Miss Weber, in front of this fireplace. Late into the night we would talk, drink gin, get a little drunk. I did, that is. He never could, though he tried so hard. I always hoped he would come back to visit, bring you with him—how much you resemble him!—but he never could bring himself to come. I understand why."

The picture had been taken out of doors. The men were standing in front of the door where she had entered. It was winter. There was snow on the ground. They all wore their army trenchcoats with the collars

226

turned up. Her father was the tallest of the group and looked painfully young except for the too-solemn eyes. She leaned closer, her eye caught by the man standing next to him, a small, dapper man wearing captain's bars on his shoulders, a familiar face. . . . She pointed to it. "This one is . . . ?"

"Bob Babcock." Steen nodded. "He was here, too, at that time. Leo didn't like it. I remember that he—"

"Was he here when Franz Halman arrived?" *Bob came back to report . . . He stayed on and on. I wanted him to go but he told me he thought I needed company. . . .*

"Yes, he left shortly after." The old man hesitated, his lined, leathery face tense with pain for the answer he already knew. He asked, "You came because your father couldn't come?"

"He's dead." Judith's whisper fell heavily into the cold room.

"How long ago?"

"Only—only—" Only when? Time had blurred and she fought to remember. "Two days ago." Was it really only that? She started to speak again but Cornelius Steen laid a hand on her arm and said gently, "Later. You can tell me later."

"Yes, later."

They stood in silence for a moment, the old man retreating to happier memories to ease the sorrow of the present, while Judith's mind raced ahead to where she had to go. Perhaps it's here, she thought, right here in this room. Perhaps this is the end of the search.

She wrapped her arms around herself and turned to face Steen. In a voice hoarse with fear of disappointment, with fear of a fate that would say, *I've let you come this far but no farther,* she said, "You know then about the letter and the photograph Franz Halman brought my father."

She watched the frown wrinkle the leathery face

and the eyes grow puzzled. She heard him say, "Halman brought . . . ?" Then he broke off and shook his head, looking away from her.

"Yes, yes! Halman brought—what?"

"A letter? A photograph?" he mumbled. "I know nothing of them." Still he didn't look at her. "We left them alone most of the time, you see, my wife and I. They wanted it that way. They had so much to say to one another and Halman . . . We all knew he had only a little time to live. The day after he arrived, I believe, your father took him to the hospital and he died not long after."

Fighting a new wave of despair, Judith broke in passionately. "You *must* know why I've come here. Surely while he was here or in his letters, my father must have told you about the evidence—" For a moment she hesitated while the wild thought ran through her mind that he was one of *them*. No, no. She felt she was losing her grip on reality altogether. This man was her father's friend. "Evidence, Mr. Steen, that Franz Halman brought with him from the camp, that my father hid somewhere in this area, evidence that will convict an SS doctor, Kurt Wallner, who lives in the United States now under the name of Karl Klausing, evidence that will force his deportation, bring him to trial in Germany. He was responsible for Leah's murder—you *must* know!"

Steen reached out and clasped Judith's hand in one of his warm ones. "The man who was responsible for his wife's death," he said. "I understand now why he was so troubled in his letter. Believe me, my dear child, I would like to help you. If I knew where this evidence was, of course I would tell you, but I don't. Leo never mentioned it—but wait . . . It occurs to me. The brother might know."

"The brothers?"

"There were other people in this house at the time. If Leo really wanted to hide something safely, he wouldn't have hidden it here. He would have found a much better hiding place somewhere in the monastery at Holduc. One of the Capuchin monks could have—"

"Holduc—a monastery!" The despair was swept away again by the pounding excitement. "Not a village? Holduc is a monastery?"

Steen nodded, bewildered by her swift changes of mood from angry despair to this almost uncontrollable excitement.

"And of course it wouldn't be on a map!"

"Your father spent a great deal of time there, playing the organ in the chapel. That's why it seems possible . . ."

What was it her father had written? . . . *my brothers, my dear, dear friends . . .*

"Brother Joseph would be the one most likely to know," Steen said.

Twenty-eight

How long had the monastery stood here on its hill, brooding over the villages and farms spread out around it? Three centuries, perhaps. It was a massive, gray stone building with a bell tower topping a central section and two wings coming out at right angles to form an open square. In the center of the square on a large concrete block stood a towering statue of Christ, arms spread wide to encompass saints and sinners alike. But despite the welcoming arms, there was something forbidding about the scene to Judith, something . . . final? Was that the word she wanted? Shivering, she hesitated at the foot of the steps leading to the massive double doors and looked around. The sky was dull and dark and heavy. Pale plumes of smoke drifted from chimneys, losing themselves in the falling snow. Something beyond the actual chill in the air touched her across the shoulders. *Déjà vu* . . . Almost as though she had been here before. Through the clean, white snow that fell, covering history, her tired, overwrought imagination heard the voice, startlingly clear and urgent, calling to her.

Leah . . . For you the snow had been ugly and cruel, spotted with blood, flecked brown with diarrhea and in the end, deadly. What died in it thirty years ago was barely human, a thing with shaven skull and transparent skin over bones. What a small area of ground those bones must have covered!

She pulled the bell and heard it reverberate hollowly inside the stone hall, and after a moment one of the doors swung open slowly, shuddering and creaking with the effort. A small, round monk with large, dreaming eyes in a smooth, round face peered up at her from under his brown cowl. He was dwarfed by the massive door.

"My name is Judith Weber. I've come to see Brother Joseph, if I may. Cornelius Steen sent me." Judith found herself whispering into a vast silence and the words came whispering back from the huge hall.

The little monk stepped back, nodding for her to come in. The door creaked shut after her.

"Might I—would it be all right if I waited for him in the chapel? You have an organ . . .?"

Tucking his hands into the drooping sleeves of his robe, the monk nodded again and as he turned away, Judith thought she detected a smile on the ageless face.

He led her away from the great-arched whispering hall down an endless corridor. Her crepe-soled shoes were soundless on the worn stone floor and the monk's sandals made soft, slapping sounds as they walked side by side through the silence of centuries.

He turned right and padded down another corridor at the end of which Judith could see ornately carved double doors. The monk pushed against one and stepped in, holding it for her to enter. The door swung closed after them with a *whoosh* and the little monk disappeared quite suddenly, leaving Judith alone. She had a sense of great size, of a high vaulted ceiling, of dim lights and deep shadows, of old stained-glass windows and new incense. Candles flickered in wall holders. On a long brass chain suspended from the ceiling the vigil light glowed through the red glass.

Large though the chapel was it was almost dwarfed by the organ which stood in all its magnificence to the left covering a third of the wall, its pipes gleaming and no doubt stretching to heaven. An awesome instrument. She walked to it and fingered one of the manuals. When she heard a sound, she jerked her hand away guiltily and looked up to see a monk appearing mysteriously from the shadows on the other side of the organ. He walked toward her slowly, limping a little, and when he was near enough for her to make out his face, she saw that he was incredibly old, the face shriveled with skin like crepe paper. But behind the steel-rimmed spectacles, keen brown eyes studied her face and his smile was gently youthful.

"Miss Weber?"

Judith nodded.

"You do not speak our language, I suppose? No, well, you needn't worry. My English was learned in your country, in Wisconsin. I spent some time there with some of my brothers before the war." He beamed at her. "And how is my friend, Cornelius Steen, and little Mariet?"

"They seem to be very well, Brother Joseph." Again that sense of *déjà vu* unsettled her. Why should she feel she had always known this man? Had her father ever spoken of him?

"I'm glad. They are learning to live with their tragedy then."

"Their tragedy?"

"Ah, you don't know. Only a year ago, the little one's parents, Cornelius's son and his son's wife, were killed in a car accident. His son had survived the war —against all odds, I might say. He was one of the leaders of the resistance, and then . . . For a while, though he is not of our faith, Cornelius came here regularly to talk to me, to try to make some sense, spiritual sense, you understand, out of what happened. Perhaps he succeeded."

"I hope so."

He had come up to her and was looking closely into

her face, eyes squinting behind the spectacles. "We've met before. Remind an old man. Where? When?"

How very old he was! How could he possibly remember?

"You knew my father, I think. I look very like him. He was here in nineteen forty-five shortly before the end of the war. He used to come to your chapel to play the organ."

"Weber." He continued to gaze into her face, frowning. Then he nodded. "Leo Weber." The youthful smile told her he was pleased with his memory. "A good man, but such a sad one. He sent you to me?"

"Yes, he sent me to you."

"He sent you to see my beauty, perhaps." He caressed the gleaming wood of the organ case with a fragile hand. "My weakness. But the good Lord knows it and forgives it, I hope." A faint twinkle in the eyes told her he was sure of forgiveness. "When I play Bach, I play it as Bach wrote it for Him. It is a Silberman, built sometime in the mid-eighteenth century. That was the golden age of organs. No one is quite sure what it is doing in the chapel of poor Capuchins. Probably a gift from some rich burgher buying his way into heaven. I've always hoped he made it, if only that I could see him there and thank him. But never mind, never mind. You shall play it yourself after the Mass."

"I should like nothing better," Judith said, "but I haven't really come about that, Brother Joseph. My father sent me for something he left here for safekeeping—at least, I feel he *must* have left it here. You're my last hope of finding it. A letter and a photograph—in an envelope about . . ." Her hands trembled a bit as she sketched a vague size in the air. "During the war, in January nineteen forty-five, it would have been." One hand remained held out to him in a gesture that pleaded: Let the letter be here.

A moment's hesitation as the keen eyes studied her

face. Perhaps something he saw in her eyes prompted the question. "He could not come himself, your father?"

Judith shook her head.

In a low voice the monk said, "He came here so often at that time, a haunted man, looking for peace here—" He touched the organ. "I wonder if he found it."

Judith whispered, "Perhaps—at the end."

"I will pray for him," the monk said simply. Then he took her hand between his own fragile ones and said, "There is no need to distress yourself. I have the envelope safely put away where it has been since your father gave it to me."

Judith stared at him, mumbling stupidly, "You have it? You have the letter?" After all the hopelessness and despair, could it be this easy in the end?

He assured her, "I have it. Your father searched for a hiding place where it would be safe. I did not know what was in the envelope—only that he was terribly concerned about it. He didn't want to involve me, he said, but I pointed out to him that he had no choice, unless he started pulling up stones from the floor. . . ." He smiled his youthful smile. "And we wouldn't have approved of that. Besides, I told him, if he secreted it so carefully and was not able to come back for it himself, how would anyone find it? It wasn't easy to persuade him. It was a long time ago but I remember well how he was. The letter seemed to have touched him with madness for a while. He gave it to me in the end and we agreed that if I died before he returned for it, I would see that another brother held it and communicated with him. But, as you can see, the good Lord has been kind to me, has kept me alive to play the organ for him—but never mind. You want the envelope. Wait here a moment. I shall bring it to you."

He limped away through the shadows toward the

234

small door on the other side of the organ which probably led to somewhere behind the altar. As he reached it, he paused and turned, looking at her doubtfully. "But, surely, there was something else?"

"Something else?"

"A child? Your father's friend, Mr. . . . Mr. . . . ?"

"Halman?"

"Halman, yes, poor man. He brought a child with him—an infant, really."

"No-no . . ." Judith shook her head, staring into the shadows at the old man. "How could that be? My father would have told me."

"I seem to remember trying desperately to find enough milk. I believe the Steens . . ." The voice trailed off and he stood nodding to himself with a doubtful expression creasing the parchment skin. "It could have been someone else," he murmured. "There were so many who came here during those terrible last months of the war, helpless, in trouble . . ." He limped through the door, pulling it shut behind him.

Her legs trembled suddenly, too weak to hold her. The twisted ankle throbbed with pain. Judith sank down onto the organ bench, closing her eyes. Brother Joseph was alert for his age, certainly, she thought, but some confusion must exist in the old mind after all these years. How many hundreds of refugees, fleeing from one side or the other, had passed through this building? Quick, frightened footsteps on the stone floors, whispers echoing in the corridors.

Her father had talked to her always and only of Leah—her death, the letter, the photograph, Wallner —of Leah, Leah, Leah.

No, time was playing tricks with the old monk's memory. The letter would soon be in her hands. The job would be finished.

But if Brother Joseph's mind played tricks with him, hers was not going to let her rest. *When Franz Hal-*

man reached me after traveling hundreds of miles—
so her father had written in the O'Connor book—
he had accomplished something that amounted to a
miracle. What he brought me gave me more pain than
I have ever known. How could it help but do so? But
that was the letter her father referred to—the letter.

Judith raised her head at the sound of the door
opening. Brother Joseph came toward her, holding
a manila envelope in his hand. She wanted to stand
up but found that she couldn't. She remained motionless, making no move to take it from him. She was
just too tired, all of a sudden, and too fearful, to make
the effort. When she had walked mechanically, a blind,
mindless creature, from her father's apartment such a
long time ago, had she really believed she would ever
find it?

Brother Joseph laid the envelope in her lap and
she saw that it was sealed as her father must have
sealed it thirty years ago. She saw the monk watching
her, smiling and nodding down at her. What am I
waiting for? she thought. I have the indictment in
my hands. A quick look and I can be on my way. I
won't read it, just check to see that the letter and
photo are inside. Her fingers were clumsy as she tore
open the envelope, felt inside the smooth surface of
the picture, pulled out some dirty, ragged sheets of
paper. Where had Leah found the paper, she wondered? The writing scrawled and slanted across the
pages like that of a careless child. Judith visualized
the wraithlike Leah in the darkest part of that last
night of her life, writing slowly and painfully, trying
to make it legible, pausing now and then to rest,
perhaps putting the pencil to her lips.

She couldn't help herself. She began to read in
the dim light.

This earth is not your earth. This sky is not your
sky. It is like nothing you have ever seen. Who

can know outside these wires of death what we have become, what sicknesses seize our minds?

Leo ... Leo ... Leo ...

Now I can say your name. Now I can think of you. I closed you out of my mind all these years. To dream of life outside is like a poison, leaving us weak and vacant, without defenses, exposed to the whips and the dogs. To survive here we must think only of how to survive.

Now I try to remember what you look like, it is too late. Your face is blurred. Only your eyes are clear as they were long ago when we first met—so blue—so serious. Was it a dream?

Are you there, Leo? Are you really out there somewhere? Did you ever really exist? I know nothing anymore—only Hell—and it makes no difference.

It is hard to keep my attention on what I write. My mind wanders. But I must. When this reaches you, I will be dead and you must know who it was and how it happened. My dear Franz will get this to you if he lives.

It isn't such a long story. They took me to Theresienstadt after they found me in Prague. How that was I don't know. Not my friends. A betrayal by a neighbor, perhaps, who heard the piano or a strange voice. I kissed my friends goodbye. No doubt they were taken, too, for helping me. No one must help anyone in this world. It is too dangerous. The Gestapo broke the piano before they took me away—smashed it. They have done the same to me. It only took a little longer.

Doctor Kurt Wallner. Remember him. He is responsible. I was his housekeeper, his mistress. I went with him willingly—yes, willingly—for when I first saw him I had hope. I wonder now how that could have been—how fate could have played such an ugly trick.

He recognized me in the selection line on the platform the day I arrived. He had heard me play in Berlin once. He loved music. No one is all bad, are they? My God, *he* loved music! It amused him to have me in his house, in his bed, at his piano.

One offers one's body to the rack, keeping the spirit inviolate!

The time spent in his house was easy. What comparisons are there? He was a sadist in bed as well as out—it didn't matter. I was willing to pay the price. I had the piano. For that—anything! I do not apologize, you see. I thought I could stay alive. Debased and in Hell, I wanted to stay alive.

God forgive me. Leo forgive me. When I've thought of you sometimes, I've hated you. Forgive me!

It was the music I wanted.

There was a child. I gave birth to it in his house—his child. I never saw it. Was it a boy or a girl? It doesn't matter. It's dead, I'm sure, and good that it is. Nothing grows here. Nothing lives. It is the land of the dead.

After that he sent me away. The months I had been his thing must be wiped out. To the clinic, a guinea pig for their sterilization experiments. I cannot describe it—the pain. Women screamed —died screaming all around me. *He* performed many operations. *He* was head of it.

Kurt Wallner—remember.

I don't know if the world will make it through the night. My mind wanders. Others will put their names down here.

I am ill. My body burns with fever. It is thirst that is the worst torment. In sleep my dreams torture me with visions of clean, cool water. I drink and drink but I wake with the same burning thirst and fight with the others for the morning "tea." We are animals here. Morning— morning starts at three. I drink the tea slowly. It's dirty and it smells but it is liquid. Afterwards the *stubhovas* wash themselves in what is left. That is all that it is good for.

Alles raus! The stinging belt on the face, the legs. We go out for roll call. How long does it take to count fifteen thousand women standing in the snow? Sometimes for punishment we stand until night time. I faint. How many times I don't know. My friends hold me up.

The wind blows and blows across the cold frozen marshes. The wind blows and blows through us, ghosts in zebra stripes and tattered jackets. We bend to the rocks with the dogs at our heels. We lift the rocks and put them in carts, the truncheons on our backs. Pain, my hands are torn and ugly. All day. Every day. *Schnell!* *Schnell!* Shouts and screams. No one speaks gently here. Nothing lives here. This is the end of the world. Death is king—and unreasoning brutality.

The writing had been growing more and more feeble, the letters shaky and ill-formed, as though the twenty-two-year-old writer had suddenly grown very old and palsied.

Tomorrow I will make friends with the snow. It is cold only when you fight it. If you don't fight it, it becomes a warm friend. I shall kneel and make a place in it and then lie down and stretch out and rest. Tomorrow, while the orchestra plays the waltzes, the girls in their pretty dresses playing *Wiener Blut*, perhaps. I only pray I am

239

dead before they see me, before the dogs reach me.

The screams and shouts will fade away into a vast silence. They will step over my body as I have stepped over others in the past. Later they will take me to block twenty-five.

It is Christmas, Leo. Pray for me. It is Hanukkah. Pray for me.

Is it possible . . . ? Oh, God, how is it possible that life can end like this!

That was all. There had been no greeting of affection at the beginning, no love expressed at the end. There was a list of a dozen names or so at the bottom, with home addresses after them—homes in France and Belgium and Holland and Greece and Czechoslovakia and Hungary and Poland and Austria. . . . Homes most of them had never seen again, no doubt.

Judith was shaking—cold and frightened and confused—and suddenly startled by a sound in the distance. She looked up, turning her head in one direction, then another, as though in a cage, seeking a way out.

"Are you all right?" Brother Joseph whispered, frightened in his turn by the dead-whiteness of her face. "Mass is about to begin. Stay, my child, do stay. We can talk again later."

The two of them stood in the shadow of the organ at the side of the chapel. The sound drew nearer, the sound of many sandal-shod feet moving slowly and rhythmically on the stone floor in the direction of the chapel. Two monks appeared from the sacristy onto the altar—silent, reverent shadows lighting candles.

Judith cast a quick glance at the photo in her hand. In the dim light she caught an impression of a face, a face like the one in the newspaper, but different, somehow, a face that mocked her. She found herself pushing the letter and photo frantically back into the envelope and thrusting it at Brother Joseph as he sat down on the bench at the organ.

"Please—keep this for me until after—please!"

He nodded and took the envelope without a word. It disappeared somewhere into the thick folds of his robe and then he turned his back on her and busied himself with the organ. For the time being she had ceased to exist for him.

What had prompted her to give it back to him? What was sinister about a swaying line of brown-cowled monks moving through the wide chapel entrance? Under the flickering candlelight they shuffled slowly down the aisle, breaking off, entering pews.

"Brother Joseph!" Her whispered cry of despair fell on deaf ears. The old monk, sitting a few feet away, might have been miles distant as he placed his hands on the keys, his face turned upward, an old man sending his musical prayers to God.

As the end of the line appeared in the doorway, the last two monks detached themselves and moved swiftly and silently up the side aisle toward the organ. Judith stepped back against the wall into the shadows as though to melt into them and disappear while panic swept through her like a storm. Sanctuary, she thought wildly. I should cry *"Sanctuary!"*

No, how stupid to be caught at the end. The little door on the other side of the organ was only a few steps away. She started toward it and they were beside her, one on each side, blocking movement. One was small. From under the cowl, his face peered out, thin and pointed like a weasel's. He was smiling. The other was big and burly, his thick shoulders straining against the material of the brown robe.

"Jesu, Joy of man's desiring . . ."

The music broke over her in brilliant waves of sound, clear and rich and full, winding around and up and up and around, filling the chapel with sound.

At least I've heard it, Judith thought with a hopeless kind of irrelevance as she felt the big man grip her arm just above the elbow. Relentless pressure of brutal fingers pressing into flesh against nerve sent pain flashing through her body. Weakness and nausea robbed her of voluntary movement.

Under cover of the music, the nasal voice spoke in her ear. "We'll just walk happily and quietly down the aisle and out of the chapel. We don't want to hurt any of the pious brothers, but on the other hand, it won't really matter to me if we have to." His hand came out of his sleeve holding a large, ugly revolver. "I'll use it. Make no mistake."

She believed him. Hadn't he used it on Charlie Forrester? He must have wanted to use it on her father. Drops of perspiration beaded her forehead as she nodded, white-lipped, at the small bright eyes that watched her. She stumbled down the aisle between them, thinking, only because she had to think of something to keep from fainting, how stupid to be caught in the end! If she had been just a few minutes sooner getting away . . . Or had they been here all the time, waiting?

No one seemed aware of them at all as they passed out through the chapel doors. The monks' absorption in God at the moment made them impervious to any awareness of evil.

Neither man looked at her, neither spoke as they walked down the long, cold stone corridor, made a turn, another long corridor, another turn. . . .

Twenty-nine

The sounds from the chapel had faded and were gone. Judith had no idea how many corridors they had traveled nor where they were in the vast building when the pressure of the brutal hand on her arm brought her to a halt. The thin man pushed open a door and went into a room, small, cell-like, sparsely furnished with a cot, a small table and two straight-backed wooden chairs, one with arms and the other without.

The rough hand on her back shoved her forward into the room. She would have fallen, but the thin man caught her arm, spun her around, and pulled off her raincoat. His fingers went through the pockets, then up under the lining, crumpling it. He flung it on the cot and jerked the jacket from Judith's unresisting arms. He searched it, beginning to curse softly and savagely under his breath. The jacket joined the coat. Her purse was next.

"Nothing," he snarled. "Where are they?"

"They?" She stared at him, dark eyes lost in despair.

"Don't pretend you don't know—the letter, the picture!"

"I haven't got them." Her voice seemed to come from a long way off. She stood tall and gaunt beside the chair, clinging to it, her face ghastly in the dim light.

"I *know* you haven't got them, but you know where

they are. All you have to do is tell me. It'll save you a lot of trouble and me a lot of time."

Judith stared at him without seeing him and didn't answer.

"A goddess," the thin, spiteful voice said. "We have a goddess to deal with, Ernst."

A fallen goddess. Where was her knight in shining armor now?

"Please sit down, goddess." He bowed to her. "Ernst, help the goddess to a chair. She must be tired after her long journey. It'll be easier for her to talk if she's comfortable." He bowed again and gestured toward the chair with the arms. It was the same parody of courtesy he had used in the airport restaurant.

The burly man stepped forward from the doorway where he had been standing silently. He closed the door carefully behind him and then moved toward Judith, a half-smile on his thick lips. Judith started backing away but his hand had seized her wrist, jerking her into the chair, before she had taken more than a step. He pulled a coil of wire from his pocket and began to unwind it while the thin man lounged back on the cot, watching and grinning.

Pushing the cowl from his head, he said, "He's an expert. Been at it for a long time. He enjoys it." His lips twitched. The small eyes gleamed. A devil, incongruous, in saint's robes.

Businesslike, the man called Ernst concentrated on the job at hand. He put the wire around her waist, then through the back slats of the chair, and twisted it. A deep breath would drive the wire into the flesh. He took her arm and put it on the arm of the chair and wrapped a smaller coil around wrist and chair. He did the same with her other arm. He was breathing heavily, noisily, but he didn't speak. The half-smile remained on his lips.

It was a dream. . . . A part of Judith seemed to be standing in a shadowed corner of the cell, a stranger, watching what was happening to the other woman, pitying her without sorrow, and when the big man stepped back to admire his handiwork, nodding in satisfaction, and the thin man said, "Just a couple, Ernst, to let her know what it feels like and maybe bring her to her senses," she watched the hand, broad and flat, raise itself in the air. Then it whipped down, striking her on the side of the head and she wasn't in the corner, she was the woman in the chair, her body arching in pain against the wire as the hand whipped through the air again, striking her on the other side of the head, snapping it back against the hard wood. White-hot pain rushed through her. Bile rose in her throat. She retched the bile; there was nothing else to come up. She closed her eyes to a swirling world of red and black.

Through it she heard the nasal voice saying, "All right, goddess, tell me where it is. Your customs trick cost me a night's sleep tracking you down and I'm always very irritable when I haven't had my eight hours beauty sleep."

Every breath a sharp knife, Judith whispered, "How can I tell you what I don't know?" She moved her head against the wood and looked at him. Excitement glittered in his eyes and burned on his cheeks.

"They're here somewhere, you know where, you tell me. I don't want to start tearing this place down brick by brick, so save yourself some agony and tell me."

"Didn't the books tell you? You stole them before I had a chance to finish them." Keep him talking, a voice in her mind urged. Something might happen. Someone might come—one of the brothers—Cornelius Steen is expecting me back for breakfast.

"We haven't got the books." The nasal voice spat the words out venomously. "A mutual friend of ours lifted them at the airport."

"A mutual friend . . ." Judith gasped. "Smith . . . !" She was shocked by the sudden surge of hope. Why should the thought of the cold-eyed man give her hope? And if he found her, would he be in time? And if he saved her, wouldn't he demand the letter and photo?

"Yes, Smith, that sneaky bastard. But we've got you. That's a hell of a lot better than the books—a hell of a lot. The personal touch, you know?" He lit a cigarette and waved a skinny hand at her. "So you just tell me and we can all walk away happy."

"Like Charlie Forrester walked away . . ."

"Stubborn—Charlie was."

"He didn't know."

The man shrugged. "Too late for that now, isn't it?"

"And—and my father?" Judith closed her eyes against the nausea, against the pounding pain in her head, against wanting to tell them and knowing she couldn't—while the big man stood patiently in front of her, waiting.

"Now, there was a man who wasn't human. I've never seen anyone take so much pain. I think he almost enjoyed it. But you'll never stand—or sit—up under it as long as he did. Like father, like daughter—only up to a point. Ernst enjoys working on women. The pleasure-pain principle—you've heard of it. Your pain gives him pleasure." Then abruptly, coldly, he said, "We're wasting time. I don't know what you want to prove, goddess, but we'll see. And it won't matter how loud you scream, there's no one to hear." He nodded at the big man.

Ernst looked at her face, then his eyes traveled to her hands.

"No—no!" The cry tore from her throat. "Not my hands—please! Anywhere—not my hands!"

She screamed as the hammer fist struck. Had her father cried out, had Leah? Her clenched teeth cut into her lip. The hammer fist on the other hand. She tasted blood. Someone was screaming. . . . Her body writhed and twisted to escape the ruthless hand, wire cutting into flesh. . . . She was swimming in a sea of pain. Drowning . . .

From far away she heard a door open. A voice: "Don't get carried away, you fools!"

Then she gave up and sank into the black sea.

"Don't get carried away, you fools!"

Smith's cold, gray eyes swept the scene in the room as he stood in the doorway, hunched into his wet coat. The scar over his left eye showed red against his pale face. Under his arm he carried the six books and he walked to the table and placed them on it.

"We were just giving her a sample." The voice had a touch of uneasiness in it as the man leaped from the cot.

The scarred eye held a murderous glint as he looked at the thin, sallow-faced man. "Too many samples and she won't be able to tell you anything, least of all where the letter is."

"She'll tell us."

"Good, that means she hasn't yet. But I think you're a little too excited to be thinking clearly," Smith said, looking dispassionately from Judith's slumped form to the big man standing over her. "It really turns you on, doesn't it, Beeder? You can't do the torture bit yourself, but you sure enjoy watching it, don't you? If I hadn't had a flat tire, I'd have been here before this foolishness started. You're lucky I got here in time."

"In time?"

Smith ignored both men as he moved to the cot, stripped the blanket off, went to Judith, and draped it carefully over her. He looked down at her for a moment through narrowed eyes, noting the face already swelling and discolored, hearing the shallow, labored breathing, seeing the dark marks on the long, white throat. Suddenly, in a low, hard voice, he said to the still figure, "Why, for God's sake, can't you tell them? What the hell difference does it make!" He swung around to face Beeder. "Klausing isn't paying you to kill her, you bloody fool! Tell bully boy here to untie her—"

"He's paying me," Beeder said. "My devotion to a cause comes high, but 'bully boy,' as you call him, does it for love."

"Untie her anyway. Your job is to find the letter and photograph and destroy them, the same as mine. We'll manage to finish it—"

"How in hell do *you* know what my job is, Smith?"

Smith saw the gun emerge from the folds of the robe pointing at him and he went very still. Only his eyes flickered with surprise. He hadn't expected trouble from this little man.

"Touching. Really touching." Beeder waved the gun at the blanket-draped form of Judith. "Your good deed for the day? Now *your* boss—"

"Just put the gun away, Beeder. There's no need for that. We're both after the same thing."

"I know one thing—your man wants that letter and picture a hell of a lot more than our nutty old doctor does. I ought to know. He was in at the kill with Weber."

"I've always found you to be a singularly crude liar, Beeder—"

"Ha! The left hand doesn't tell the right hand, is that it—nothing like that now!"

Smith's hand had gone to his coat pocket and Beeder took a step toward him, waving the gun nervously. "Hands out of pockets."

"I just wanted a drink."

"Still at it," Beeder snorted contemptuously.

"We all have our problems, Beeder."

"Help yourself then, but slowly."

Smith drew out the flask and unscrewed the cap, his eyes gazing vacantly into space. He took a long drink and then held it toward Beeder. "Can I offer you some?"

"I've never really liked the stuff."

"You get your kicks in other ways," Smith said as he turned to Ernst, thrusting the flask at him. "How about bully boy? A little schnapps before hard work begins again?"

"Ernst has a one-track mind. I wouldn't worry about him."

"I won't then. I haven't any choice anyway." As he spoke, Smith swung back toward Beeder. His arm shot through the air. The flask caught Beeder on the temple. He staggered back against the cot, flung a hand on it and steadied himself. Smith's hand was in his pocket. He had his gun out and two shots crashed, cannonlike, in the small room. One low cry. Judith stirred and moaned. Then silence.

"Well . . ." The nasal voice quavered a bit. "You're fast on the draw, but not fast enough. That's what happens, old chum, when you let emotion get in the way of business."

Beeder gazed down at Smith's still form on the floor, nudging it with his foot and looking distastefully at the small pool of blood. Then, grinning, he turned to the big man and said, "More fun and games later, Ernst, my efficient friend. *Später, später.* Let's go to our little hidey-hole and let the goddess come to. Give her time to think of the consequences of her silence. We'll take our misguided friend with us."

Ernst hoisted Smith over his shoulder as though he weighed nothing at all and they left the cell-like room, locking the door behind them.

Thirty

The stone walls themselves throbbed with her pain as Judith returned to consciousness and raised her head. The simple effort sent the pain stabbing into parts of her body she hadn't known existed. Panting, her stomach heaving with the waves of nausea that swept over her, threatening blackness again, she retched and moaned and retched again. She hadn't eaten in so long there was nothing to come up except her own bitter, rancid bile.

They had gone and left her alone but they would be back. She let her head rest against the chair and closed her eyes for a moment and when she opened them again she felt a little steadier. Through the narrow, slitlike window above her she could see a patch of bright sunlight in an icy blue sky. It had been snowing when she arrived. When had it stopped? How much snow had fallen? With irrelevant urgency she wanted to know, but the window was too high for her to see. She was cut off from the world around her. They will come back, she thought again in dull despair. She was lost.

Her eyes moved slowly around the room and stopped at the table, arrested by the sight of the books neatly stacked there. They hadn't been there before, had they? She tried to remember but her mind, fogged with pain, found conscious thought almost too great an effort. Things kept slipping away as she struggled to remember. Smith had taken the books. Isn't that what they had said? And if the books were here, then where was Smith? She became aware of the blanket that covered her. Who . . . ? Smith? And if so, where was he now? In answer to her question her eyes fell on the small pool of blood drying on the floor at her feet. She stared at it as distant memory nudged her. There had been voices, an explosion of sound. Guns . . . Whose?

The books looked small and unimportant to her now. But her father had died for them, Charlie Forrester had been murdered because of them, and for the same reason she was here, trussed like an animal to a chair —for their secret story and secret names. Proof of the identity of the murderer of a young woman—and was that all? In the dim light of the chapel she had read Leah's letter. *Doctor Kurt Wallner . . . Remember him. . . . I was his mistress. . . .*

Her mind veered away from the quicksand of the words and settled on Brother Joseph. Was the Mass over? If she didn't meet him in the chapel after the services, would he come looking for her? Or would he just accept her absence unquestioningly and wait for her, telling his beads or playing Bach? Mariet and her grandfather—would they come when she didn't show up?

And after all, she thought numbly, could it possibly matter? She would be lost by then to the brutal hands, the searing pain. . . . *One offers one's body to the rack, keeping the spirit inviolate.* . . . How, Leah, when it is so easy to reduce a human being to animal responses?

She heard distant footsteps in the corridor, not soft and sandal-shod, but heavy-treaded. "Forgive me, Leah," she gasped aloud. "I'm not as strong as you were." Her heart hammered against her ribs, the blood pounded in her head. Pain and fear flashed through her body while thoughts and images tumbled through her head bringing her to this point of no return: her mother's kitchen table covered with the cheerful glitter of Christmas; the crowded streets of New York from the hotel-room window, Max's gentle mouth, his blue eyes; Dieter, like his young brother, slim and beautiful and alive. The piano at the hotel at Bad Godesberg . . . *It was the music I wanted. . . . There was a child. . . .* The key turned in the lock. *Tell them,* her mind screamed at her, *tell them!* But as someone approached and stood over her, she found she couldn't move. She remained with her head slumped on her chest, her eyes closed.

A hand touched her shoulder. The nasal voice: "Still out? I don't believe it." The blanket was ripped away. *Tell them now.* Her swollen lips started to form words.

"Untie her."

The brutal hand on her shoulder hesitated and the strange, hollow-sounding voice spoke again; one short, abrupt command in German and the hand was removed from her shoulder. In another moment she felt a fumbling with the wires at the back of the chair while someone released her wrists. She fell forward. Someone caught her before she struck the floor and carried her to the cot. Again the blanket, abrasive but warm, against the bruised flesh.

The strange voice said again, "Get out."

The door closed, leaving the room in a deep silence that seemed to last for a long time, while Judith, with her eyes shut, waited for what was to come. Every breath she drew was like a small convulsion, shuddering through her body.

Was this a part of the torture game or had she been reprieved? She opened her eyes just a little and peered from under the lids. A man leaned against the chair she had just been released from. The cruel, cutting wire lay coiled on the floor beneath it. The shaft of sunlight from the high, narrow window cast its light behind the man, leaving his face in shadow. She had only an impression of a square, broad-boned face, deep-set eyes, military-cut gray hair. The face seemed to waver in the dimness of the room as though she were seeing its reflection in an old, cracked mirror. A familiar-looking, tall, broad-shouldered man . . .

He moved his head and the light fell full on his face. A moan escaped through her swollen lips and Judith turned her face to the wall as though by that simple action she could avoid the consequences of the distorted image. It had to be a trick of the shadows, of her state of mind—a nightmare illusion.

After a long while the man broke the silence, saying in that strange, lifeless voice, "That's what she saw. That's why she turned to me."

"Turned to you . . ." Judith whispered each word in pain.

A chair scraped and Judith moved her head unwillingly to look at him. He had sat down, having pulled the chair next to the table where the books stood. Beside them now, as though they had appeared by magic, were a bottle of brandy and two glasses. He was filling the glasses.

Sunlight touched his face again. Her eyes told her that what she was seeing was not an illusion, while her mind in revulsion rejected it as impossible— . . . *how fate could have played such an ugly trick* . . . how her father, gentle and compassionate toward everyone except this man, should have a double in him, the man her father hated, who had destroyed his life. This was Wallner, of that she had no doubt. As to where he came from or why, that seemed of little consequence now.

"We could have been brothers."

"Never," she whispered, "never."

He came to her, holding out a glass of brandy, and if the devil himself had offered it to her, she couldn't have refused. She took a deep breath to prepare herhelf for the pain it would cause her to sit up. He put a hand out to help her.

"No," she gasped, shrinking away from him, and he dropped his hand and watched her slow, anguished movements as she pulled herself to a sitting position keeping the blanket close around her. Then she reached for the glass. Pain shot up her arms and she stared helplessly at the swollen, useless hands. She wanted to whimper and creep away like a wounded animal to some dark place and lick her wounds. Perhaps she would have done it if she could have, but the man was standing over her, waiting, so instead she held out both hands and with desperate determination clamped the glass between the wrist of one and the palm of the other. She lifted it clumsily and drank, ignoring the face close to hers. Some of the brandy spilled on the blanket, but she paid no attention. It stung her bruised lips and set fire to her throat, but in a moment she felt the warm, numbing effect.

She continued to drink from the precariously balanced glass as she watched him walk back to the chair, saying with a kind of weary scorn and waving at the books, "Judith . . . Did he send you for my head, Judith Weber?"

She had seen the resemblance in the newspaper picture, in the photo with the letter, but she simply hadn't allowed it to register, and her father . . . He had kept it secret for thirty years—this fantastic irony.

"Doctor Wallner," she murmured, staring across the room at him. Their eyes met, his deepset, dark and vacant, hers deepset, dark and burning with fever and hatred. He nodded, acknowledging with a thin-lipped smile the use of his name, as though there had been a formal introduction.

"How she must have hoped, until . . ."

"I admit she was exquisite when she came to the camp. One of the most exquisite creatures I've ever seen." He had sat down again beside the table, stretched out his legs, comfortably crossed at the ankles, holding his brandy glass in both hands. He might have been sitting before the fireplace in his study, casually discussing some meaningless subject. He stared straight ahead of him as he talked. "Like a delicately fashioned jewel—"

"A jewel out of Theresienstadt via a cattle car."

"Curiously that hadn't been enough to destroy her. It only honed her beauty, gave it a finer, more transparent quality. Her music, her body, her beauty gave me a great deal of pleasure, as you can imagine."

Breathing each word out in pain, Judith whispered hoarsely, "I can imagine. What of your laws forbidding the supermen from having intercourse with 'inferior' races? You were her lover—"

"You don't understand," he broke in, waving a weary hand at her stupidity. " 'Lover' implies equality. She was a servant in my house—less than that, really. I took her to bed when it suited me. And of course she was there for purposes other than my own pleasure. I was a scientist."

"History has called you other names."

"I can't be bothered with what people read in history books. It's what they do that's important and what they do—the mass of them—is pay lip service at anniversary times. Then they forget again and go back to their little lives filled with little things." He toyed with the brandy glass, the hollow voice low and heavy with boredom as he went on. "When the trucks took their comrades off to the gas chambers, don't you think the others didn't exult at their good fortune at being left behind? Of course they did. They may not have admitted it even to themselves, but it was there all the same. Victims make people uncomfortable. They turn away—"

"Did Leah make you uncomfortable?"

"Toward the end, yes. She changed, became quite ugly, really. It was—" He paused, took a sip of brandy and finished delicately, "—distasteful."

"Distasteful . . . !" Judith leaned forward, letting out a cry of pain for the effort it cost her. Her eyes were burning in her bruised face, the black hair, damp and tangled, clung to her forehead. "But you think of her sometimes, don't you? Doesn't she keep you awake at night? Is that why you've come to me now?"

For a long while the man didn't answer and Judith thought perhaps he hadn't heard. He bent his head to the brandy glass in his hand, picked up the bottle and refilled it, took a sip of it. Finally he looked over at her and smiled, a thin, ugly smile. The sun reflected light in his eyes like the last flare of a dying fire and for a moment Judith saw the young sadist in the bored old man as he straightened in the chair and spoke in a voice suddenly filled with passion.

"You'd like me to say that I spend tormented hours sometimes, wouldn't you? That some kind of atonement is exacted from me? Not true, Judith Weber. You must understand, I enjoyed my work. It was important, it had meaning and purpose for me. And do you think I'm the only one? Thousands of us who planned the experiments, who carried them out, who made the selections—even those who wielded the clubs and the whips—felt this dedication to our work. We don't sleep with guilt at night. On the contrary, we sleep peacefully in warm soft beds beside warm soft bodies. The goals we reached for were high. We believed in them enthusiastically. We still do. A few of you, like Leo Weber, may torture yourselves with guilt. You're a fool if you think *we* do."

Judith could only stare at the man as he sat stiff and straight in his chair, looking like some aging force of evil with the fading glow of passion on his gray skin. The cry rose silently in her throat—what can I do for you now, Leah? And for you, Father? If I could kill him? I want to kill him. . . . No shock at all came with the thought.

How could she have seen a resemblance to her father? How could there be between gentle Leo Weber and this man with his smile as corrupt and warped as his soul must be?

In pain, helpless and lost, Judith huddled under the blanket, watching him sip his brandy and waiting, waiting. . . . But when the question came, it was so quietly asked it caught her off guard.

"Aren't you curious, Judith Weber, why I left my comfortable home in Connecticut to come all this distance—" He waved a hand at the cold, stone walls of the bleak room. "—to this place to see you?"

She whispered, "Certainly not to save my life."

He turned his head to look at her, real surprise on his face. "But that's precisely why. Call it vanity—ego —curiosity—all of that and more." He was smiling at her because now they had arrived at the final question and it amused him. "But of course you don't know, do you? Leo Weber wouldn't have had the courage to tell you." He continued smiling while he looked at her, waiting for the question, willing her to ask it.

Judith looked away from him with an effort, her eyes seeking refuge in the sun's rays slanting in through the slitted window. No warmth there, no escape. She was trapped and her eyes were drawn back to his face while the question came whispering out of its own accord. "Did it die in the camp—the child?"

"Would you like me to tell you that it perished in the ovens?" His eyes glittered with enjoyment.

257

. . . Franz Halman . . . What he brought me . . . brought me . . . brought me . . . The words pounded in her head, sending pain radiating through her body. In a scarcely audible voice, she said, "Only if it's true," and watched him, feverishly hoping he would nod his head and admit to the one, small, casual murder.

From across the room the deepset eyes looked fixedly into hers, eyes that were so unlike the clear blue of Leo Weber's, the deeper blue of Sheila's. As he answered, each word fell separately and heavily on her ears.

"If the child had died, we wouldn't be speaking to each other now."

The glass slipped from Judith's clumsy hold, its contents spilling out onto the blanket. She paid no heed to it as she put her face in her hands and tried to close off the sound of the soft, malicious voice.

"Your hair is like hers. Raven-haired. And you have her white, translucent skin. Otherwise, I'm glad to say, you resemble—your father. Tall, big-boned—those strong, beautiful hands. You have her talent. Did you know I heard you play once?"

She had no strength left to fight the giddiness and nausea that were sweeping over her as she listened and tried not to listen to the hollow voice, gathering strength as it went on.

"An innocent and helpless infant—your future was in my hands. I had to make the choice and I think I made the right one. Partly I was influenced by vanity, I'll admit, but not dumb vanity. That's for animals. Your blood is hers, but mine as well, and tainted though hers was, there's good blood there. Franz Halman's mother and hers were sisters—of an old and noble family. Good Aryan breeding stock. You will marry your Max—a perfect Nordic type with a fine, keen mind. I followed his career with interest as well as yours. The purification process will begin with your children—and theirs—and so it will go on. Along with others, your children and grandchildren will hold the future of the Master race in their hands. Their province—culture and creativity. You must not be afraid to use your power. . . ."

What was he saying? Through the stupor that was overtaking her, she thought, he's mad—a sick, evil old man. *She* was sick, too, then. Madness and death were waiting in the shadows. . . .

"That, of course, is what it's all about. We made a good beginning. We must develop our Heroes only by ruthlessly upholding the Master race, by subjugating and exterminating the inferior races. Six million Jews, yes, and there were another five million as well. The Slavs, Gypsies, others—they had to go. Purification . . ." His voice dropped to a low monotone and he seemed to be talking more to himself than to Judith. The fire was fading. "Through war and extermination. Purification through biology, following the strictest rules of breeding. Constant purification to bring out the noblest and finest in the Aryan race . . ."

O judgment! thou art fled to brutish beasts,/And men have lost their reason. . . . lost their reason . . .

Judith felt herself slipping away, her thoughts tumbling through her head in a vague kind of rhythm. His voice came to her from a great distance. The life had gone from it, the fire had died.

"I'm old. I won't live to see it, but others will carry the process forward. There will be those who will try to hinder it, of course, like that silly newspaperman, Rosen. A story appears in the newspapers, there's a little scurrying around. But the questions stop. The matter is quietly dropped. Time, of course, is always on our side."

Judith, only half-conscious, leaned against the stone wall, her head whirling, her body burning with pain. She would have liked some more of the numbing

259

brandy. She could smell it where it had spilled onto the blanket, along with the other smells—the blood and sweat and bile. The cognac would give her courage for what was to follow.

"There are always those willing to help. You must have wondered how I got into the United States?"

He didn't wait for an answer. Judith had none to give.

"I paid for services and received them. He may have believed in our mission, our theories. I like to think that he did, but money made it a certainty. Money has a way of doing that."

The rhythmic beat in her head grew louder, like the beat of a waltz. *On Sunday the girls in their pretty dresses . . . Wiener Blut . . .*

"Babcock grew rich helping me and my friends. There were others besides Babcock. They must protect themselves now when the questions are asked. Heads rest uneasily on the pillow for a few nights until it's forgotten again. Because who really cares? Who really *believes*?"

She was far away, almost out of touch, deep in the alien, nightmare world. The blurred sound of his voice accompanied the rhythm in her head. She struggled to concentrate. That beat wasn't in her head. It couldn't be. The measured tread of feet in the corridor. It seemed to grow louder. She couldn't be sure. She heard a voice shout: "I can't! I can't bear anymore!" She swung her head, looking around, wild and terrified. Whose voice?

There was a clink of a glass, the rustle of cloth, a click. Through a kind of fog she could see the vacant face with the gray skin and dead eyes. His shoulders were bowed, his body seemed smaller, shrunken. In his lap a gun gleamed palely in the sunlight.

"I've done what I can. Others must take over. You can tell Max Halman I called off my dogs and you can have my head, Judith Weber, for what it's worth. Life has become an endlessly dull burden."

It was only an animal reflex that sent Judith's body twisting toward the wall, cringing, covering her face with aching hands. The beat had stopped. There were loud voices, the door crashed open, two shots echoed endlessly through the stone room, but Judith heard only one as something scorched her head and she tumbled over and over, breathless and lost, into a vast, dark silence.

Thirty-one

She floated up out of darkness to the edge of light, to distant, blurred faces, gentle hands, and soft voices. The sharp prick of a needle and she floated down again into the warm darkness.

She found her way to the light the next time without difficulty and discovered that she was lying in a wide, deep bed under a thick, old-fashioned feather comforter. Someone had removed her clothes and she was wearing a long, white nightgown of cotton flannel that smelled faintly of lavender.

She was content to lie perfectly still for a long time, eyes only partly open, to accept without question this bounty of safety and warmth and freedom from pain. There was only a vague headache and a twinge here and there to remind her of the recent horror. The day, the time, the place—none of it mattered. Her mind was dull and vacant and her body didn't seem to be a part of her at all.

Finally she moved her head and looked without concern around the unfamiliar room. It was long and low-ceilinged with a few heavy, old pieces of furniture. It had an unused look.

Light coming through the curtains of a window at the far side of the room was partially blocked by someone standing with his back to her. It was daytime then, she was thinking, as the tall, slim figure turned and she recognized him. The sunlight with motes of dust circling lazily in it illuminated the blond head and she accepted again without question, without surprise, that he should be here.

"It's all right now," he was saying softly as he moved toward her, as elegantly graceful as ever, though why shouldn't he be, why should he have changed?

"It's all right now," he repeated.

He stood beside the bed looking down at her and she could see that his face was thin and drawn. Lines pulled at the gentle mouth and the blue eyes were dull with fatigue. She smiled weakly at him with swollen lips while her eyes filled with tears which spilled slowly out and down her cheeks. She brought her hand out from under the cover to wipe them away and saw the heavy bandage that wrapped it, covering the wrists as well. The other hand was the same. She stared at them, wincing at the memory of the hammer fists and murmured helplessly, "I forgot, I forgot," while the tears continued to stream down her face.

"No, no, my darling," Max assured her swiftly. "They're not broken. The doctor is sure there's nothing—"

"How?"

"X-rays. You've been to the hospital and back." He held the bandaged hands lightly in his. "They'll be stiff and sore for a while. There's some therapy the doctor suggested—we can talk about it later—but you'll play again."

She accepted what he said with a nod and went on crying mindlessly while Max looked down at the white-bandaged head, the black-rimmed sunken eyes, and the purple-red bruises. He didn't care at all if she saw the tears that filled his own eyes. He sat down on the bed beside her, carefully, so as not to jar her, and took her in his arms and cradled her gently, her head on his shoulder, his cheek against the bandaged head. For a long while they sat like that without speaking.

"I was afraid I had lost you," he murmured finally and took his handkerchief and wiped her face with infinite tenderness. "At the hotel in New York, I was calling Ted Rosen, the journalist, you know. I had hoped he would persuade you—"

He felt her shaking her head on his shoulder but he went on speaking urgently. "Some things are better said. I was almost out of my mind when I found you had left, perhaps thinking I had betrayed you. Oh, Judith—" His arm tightened around her shoulders. "My only betrayal was in wanting to keep you safe. I can't ask you to forgive me for that."

Again Judith shook her head and said in a muffled voice, "There's no need. I don't think there was ever a need, really." She dabbed ineffectually at the wet cheek, remembering how she had lain, dry-eyed, on the couch in Max's hotel room wishing fiercely for the tears to come. There was no restraining them now. They poured out from some bottomless well where they had been stored for a long time. She whispered, "It's been such a long time," and touched his cheek.

He asked if she was in pain and she said, "Not really," and was surprised to be able to say it. "Stiff and a little sore and I seem to be one big bandage. Mostly I feel dopey."

Max smiled and brushed his lips against one of the bruises in the lightest of kisses. "That will make it well," he said and wished with a terrible longing that it could be that easy. "You *are* dopey. The doctor gave you a stiff shot of something late last night."

That accounted for the floating feeling, she supposed.

The tears finally slowed and stopped and the questions came.

"What time is it? What day?"

"It's Christmas morning. You're in Cornelius Steen's spare bedroom."

"I've been out a whole day."

"And Mariet is waiting to show you the Christmas tree which is there in your honor and Cornelius is preparing what looks like a massive breakfast feast.

He's been at it for hours, scolding and perspiring with creativity. It gives him great pleasure to do it, he told me, with you safe in his house. Brother Joseph has sent you a gift and I've sent for Tommy. He'll be landing at Bonn late this afternoon." Max continued talking with a kind of desperate gaiety as though telling her about these good people and what they were doing and holding her close could bridge their separation, wipe out the four bad days and what they had done to her. He knew it was hopeless but he went on anyway. "They are anxious for you to come down as soon as you are able. And there's someone else who wants to see you—to put it mildly."

"Someone else?"

"A very romantic young man who only puts up with me because he has to."

"Dieter?" She looked up at him, only a little surprised.

Max nodded. "We found you with his help."

"We?"

He hadn't really meant to start on the story. It seemed too soon, but from the look in her eyes he knew there was no avoiding it and he might just as well tell her as quickly as possible, get it over with and let the healing process begin.

"I say 'we.' It was Kemmler, of course, who did the work, who traced the Dutch customs official who passed you through. He had no trouble at all remembering you—and the two who followed you. He remembered your mentioning Steen's name and Kemmler phoned the police in Maastricht who located Cornelius. I had arrived at Bonn yesterday morning. Kemmler was the first person I saw." Kemmler with his sad eyes and red nose had taken him to the morgue where he had seen his tortured friend's body. Max drew in a deep breath and said in a low voice, "He told me about Charlie." Then he went on hurriedly. "Later, in the hotel at Bad Godesberg, Kemmler spotted Dieter. Someone told Kemmler they had seen you and Dieter together. It was only after considerable pressure that we were able to convince him to tell us what he knew. You had made him promise and he's the most honorable young man I've ever met—and stubborn, I might add. At any rate, he already knew something was very wrong and once he understood that you might be in danger, he never left my side. We must have mentioned Wallner's name in front of him though I don't remember doing it, and on the drive here he kept asking questions about him. I was too distracted to know what he was doing, where he was leading and, of course, I had no idea of his relationship to Wallner—damned young fool! He might have killed you—"

"I don't understand. Are you saying Dieter . . . ?"

"He had a gun. I didn't know he had it or how he got it until he pulled the damned thing out of his pocket and pointed it at Wallner, shouting something melodramatic like, 'You've brought dishonor on my family!' I don't think he'd ever handled a gun before and it had a kick to it which threw his aim off. The shot went wild and struck you—scraped you only, just above the temple, thank God. Wallner succeeded in shooting himself. Kemmler had asked the Maastricht police just to *be* there—we didn't want to go charging in, not knowing. . . ."

Not knowing . . . Max didn't tell her how endless the search had seemed—the drive from Bonn to Maastricht, the doubling back to the monastery, finding Brother Joseph. How the long minutes had dragged by as they searched the never-ending stone corridors, how the image of Charlie Forrester's body had stayed with him every agonizing step of the way.

"Dieter . . ." Judith murmured. "My dear, romantic young knight. The gun—will the police . . . ?"

"I don't know. That's up to them. Kemmler had a long talk with him afterward. He's already punished himself more than they can. And now—I think you should rest a bit and I'll find out about breakfast. We can talk some more later." He had managed to keep his voice level as he remembered Dieter's cry when he saw what he had done, remembered his own agony seeing her on the cot, not knowing whether she was alive or dead, remembered the raging madness he felt when they found Beeder and Ernst in a nearby room, casually drinking and smoking, still, outrageously, dressed in the monks' robes. Smith's unconscious form lay on the stone floor at their feet. Kemmler had restrained him with surprising strength from leaping at the two men, assuring him in his melancholy voice that he had plenty of evidence against them for Forrester's death and there was no way at all of their getting away with anything. Smith had been rushed to the hospital in the same ambulance that took Judith there.

With only the faintest touch of irony in his voice, Max said, "I have a message for you from our mutual friend, Smith."

"Smith . . . Yes." Judith frowned, struggling with some distant memory. "Blood," she whispered finally. "I remember seeing blood on the floor."

"He's in the hospital, weak, critical, but he'll be all right. He's tough, one of the toughest men I know. He said to tell you that it looks like the mouse turned on the cat, after all—or at least that's the way it came out. He's thinking seriously of retiring from the mouse-hunting racket." With surprise in his voice, Max added, "I think he means it."

"I'm glad he's all right," Judith said quietly.

A mistake to lock people into categories, Max thought, as he recalled Smith's bloodless face on the pillow when he had been allowed to see him for a few moments. He had been shocked at the man's appearance. As though he had been stripped of a protective covering, he lay exposed and powerless and alone in the narrow, white hospital bed. Max had felt stirrings of pity which he had tried not to show, knowing how the other man would hate it.

When Max, referring to an old joke between them, had asked "For a man with three pairs of eyes, how in hell did you ever get yourself into this spot?" Smith had hesitated for a moment, the gray eyes opaque. He said finally in a low voice, "Just a stupid miscalculation."

Max felt there was more he wanted to say but he didn't probe. He was thinking how glad he was that the man was alive and surprised at the same time by the strength of his feeling, considering the bitter antagonism of their last meeting. "One of your few," he told him.

"One of the few that counted."

Max didn't ask what he meant. He saw, without quite believing it, how the gray eyes lost all coldness when he gave Max the message for Judith. It might have been an illusion because they hardened again immediately when he asked, "It was Babcock all the way, wasn't it?"

Max nodded and Smith cursed softly under his breath for a moment, then said, "I should have known it. Stupid . . . ! I said I'd die in this racket and I've damned near done it twice. I'm getting out. Don't let me shock you. The truth is, I haven't any choice in the matter. This shoulder is pretty well shattered." With a flash of the old arrogance, he said, "Galling, though, to be brought down by a stupid little paid mercenary, isn't it? You can get too old for this game in more ways than one. Always wanted to go out in a blaze of glory." He grinned lopsidedly at Max and said, "Never mind. Everything has its compensations. I have a place in Vermont where I can watch the snow in the winter and the flowers in the summer and that's where I'll head as soon as they finish with me in Washington. Sounds weak minded, doesn't it? But there it is. Come on up. You'll find a well-stocked bar in the living room—and speaking of bars. . . . Can you get me something to drink, for God's sake? This damned place is as dry as the desert."

With a smile, Max reached into his pocket and pulled out the flask and handed it to Smith. "A slight dent from where it struck the floor. Beeder's head broke the fall. Your aim was pretty good."

"Not good enough. I never thought I'd use *this* as a weapon." He held it to his ear and shook it.

"Oh, it's full," Max said. "I figured it was the least I could do."

The man's voice had been growing weaker and Max could see that he was in pain. The nurse had come and told him it was time to go. At the door Max had tried, without his usual ease, the grateful words coming rather clumsily to his lips, to thank him for not turning his back on Judith and to apologize for his harshness in New York. The air in the room had become strained and they were suddenly back in New York in that cold, dismal courtyard, facing each other across a great distance.

"Forget it," Smith said harshly. "I was doing my job. Damned lot of good it did." His face was wet with perspiration as he added, "Thanks for the drink." He had twisted his head on the pillow, turning his face to the wall to hide a vulnerability that he couldn't handle.

Max had been silent too long and Judith moved restlessly in his arms. He tightened them around her, kissed her forehead, saying rather huskily, "My God, have you any idea how glad I am to hold you like this?"

She gave him a fleeting smile in response and said, "I must know the rest, Max."

"There isn't much more."

"Don't hedge. Whatever there is." With a trace of her old stubbornness returning, she said, "I'd like a cigarette and a cup of coffee, please, and then you can finish."

"You'll need something more nourishing than that," Max objected. "Cornelius's feast is waiting."

"Later." And as he still hesitated, she added, "Now, Max," with some of the fierceness he remembered from the hotel in New York returning briefly to her eyes and voice. "I want to know everything. Then I can put it away."

Put it away. . . . Pluck from the memory a rooted sorrow. . . . It won't be as easy as that, he thought with despair, but there was nothing else to do but give in.

While he was gone, Judith gazed idly around the room. Whatever sedative the doctor had given her was still partly in control and her reactions were slow, her memory still dull. She saw the suitcase standing in the corner of the room. Max must have brought it from the hotel. And the books were there, too, stacked on top of it. Judith felt the familiar cold touch her heart. What would she do with them now? A part of her was tempted to get out of bed and get them and read the rest but she couldn't bring herself to do it. Didn't she know almost all there was to know? Max could fill in the end bits and pieces. Perhaps later, she thought listlessly, she would read them and then file them under their proper headings in her father's library, where they would remain, concealing their private story of love and hate and horror. She couldn't discard them anymore than she could discard these past few days of her life.

She looked away from them to the window and suddenly the sun came flashing into the room, released from a prison of clouds. Like a spotlight, it illuminated everything—the suitcase, the books, the bed where she lay, the truth. The truth—that a part of the nightmare was finished, another beginning, that she was not the same and never could be. *A bad dream*, Sheila had said. *You'll carry it with you wherever you go.* When she said that, did she know?

When Max returned, he found her sitting stiff and straight against the pillows, gazing sightlessly down at her bandaged hands. He sensed the change in her, some terrible understanding she hadn't had a few moments earlier.

He put the tray on the little table beside the bed, helped her drink the tiny glass of Bols gin Cornelius had sent for medicinal purposes, helped her eat a crusty piece of bread hot from the oven with the butter melting on it. Neither spoke. Max lit her cigarette which she held awkwardly while he put the coffee cup to her lips. All the while he watched her warily.

Finally he asked, "Are you all right?"

"Yes," she said, and turned her battered face up to him and waited.

God! he thought, will I never see her smile again? Aloud he said, "You're not all right, Judith, my darling. I can see that." He set the cup rattling down on the table and turned his back on her, unable to bear the look in the feverish eyes.

He stood at the window and told her that it had been Babcock at the heart of it from the beginning—Babcock with his rage against the world and wanting all he could get—the power of money, of position. Never mind how he got it or who stood in his way. He was here at Steen's when Max's father had arrived. Probably he had eavesdropped on Leo's conversations with his father. He knew where to look for Wallner—in the same refugee camp Franz Halman had just come from. And knowing something about the loot the Nazis had stashed in various places, he set out on his own share-the-Nazi-wealth program. With the knowledge and connections he had from his wartime intelligence work, he set up an operation with Wallner as his partner for a while. When the doctor had left Auschwitz, he had some gold and jewels for ready cash but he had a supply of something else just as valuable, if not more so. He had documents—passports, work permits, identity papers. At the camp there had been a very select unit of prisoners who were experts in engraving and printing and the other techniques necessary for forging these documents. The prisoners were killed after their job was completed. Wallner made a nice bundle out of these documents, Babcock even more. Wallner and Babcock located SS criminals who wanted to escape from Germany, and after extracting as much money as they could, the man was given his false papers and fed into one of the displaced persons' camps. It must have galled these members of the 'Master' race to don the identity of one of the 'inferior' peoples—a Pole, a Czech, a Balt—but it saved their lives and that's what they were after. Ultimately, during the mass emigration program operated by the U. N.'s International Refugee Organization, they joined the legitimate D. P.'s on the ships that carried them to Canada, the U. S., Australia, wherever. . . . We don't know who the others were that Babcock helped, if any of them are alive. Not yet, but Kemmler has notified the police in New York—"

"Kemmler?"

"Of course. He has Beeder and Ernst in custody, but they are responsible for Leo's death as well."

"Yes, as well," she whispered.

"Babcock didn't know the letter and photograph existed then, in nineteen forty-five," Max went on. "That's something he only just found out. Leo might have let it slip in some conversation with him after he discovered Wallner was alive. Perhaps, when he first began to suspect Babcock, he simply confronted him with the evidence and asked him to explain. That would have been like Leo. Whether Babcock hedged or told him the truth—"

"On that night," Judith broke in, her voice harsh in the sunlit room, "Pete, the doorman, said there were three men. The third one wasn't Smith. . . ."

"No," Max said. "It was Babcock. Smith never knew until recently—but *I* should have known. Or is that just hindsight? I don't know. . . ." He expelled a long sighing breath as he turned back to Judith, thinking, Perhaps the worst is over now that she knows about Babcock. Perhaps we can come to terms together with that particular horror. Give her time and we can come to terms with all of it, "Together," he said aloud. "That's the key word." He smiled as he sat down beside her.

Judith seemed not to be listening. She was staring straight ahead of her, her bandaged hands making agitated movements on the blanket while she pursued the facts relentlessly.

"Babcock had to have the letter at all costs, yes, but if he had told me . . ." The hands became more agitated. "If—Father—" She stumbled over the word and went on harshly. "If he had had the courage to tell me the truth from the beginning—why didn't he? Why!" She loved him and hated him in the same breath as she looked around the quaint, old room seeking some kind of answer. With painful logic she said, "He never would have told me, would he? I never would have found out if he hadn't discovered that Wallner was alive. Then he could only think of Leah—and vengeance. He has it now—surely—he has it!"

"Judith—" Max put his hands on her restless ones. He couldn't pretend not to know what she was talking about. They had come to the basic fact and it had to be confronted. "He wouldn't have told you, no, what would have been the point?"

"Mother—Sheila—" Again her voice stumbled. She had become a stranger to old, familiar relationships. "Sheila knew?"

273

Max nodded.

"And you, Max?"

"Leo told me the story two years ago."

"Shortly after we met, you mean? So you would know who you were getting involved with? Who would be the mother of your children, if we had any?"

"My God, Judith!" He saw now where she was heading and he tried to forestall her. "There was nothing like that. You *must* know there wouldn't have been anything like that."

"Oh, yes! Surely you know why he saved my life— Wallner? Vanity, he said, but more than that. The taint in my blood could be bred out, purified, through both of us—"

"Judith—"

"Our children—" She plunged wildly on. "They would be purer than we are, he said, and *their* children . . . Ah—well on their way to being Heroes!"

"Enough, Judith, that's enough!" Max found himself shouting in his effort to reach her, to stop her.

She did stop and stared at him for a long time with blank eyes, scarcely seeing him, as though he were a stranger. After a while, in a dead-calm voice, stating it as a fact that he certainly must know already, she said, "You understand, Max—of course you understand why I can't marry you now."

"This isn't you talking, Judith. I can't believe it. You're stronger than this. You can put it in proper perspective. It takes getting used to, but you'll *have* to come to terms with it somehow."

Max felt that he was mouthing words that had no meaning for either of them.

"Come to terms with his heritage—yes," she said, still speaking in the cold, level voice. "He told me he enjoyed his work. Enjoyed it. He didn't even bother with the old saw about obeying orders from superiors."

The influence of the numbing drug the doctor had

given her had worn off and the pain was clawing at her. Not only the physical pain. That was small compared with the spiritual torture, the knowledge of Leo Weber's deception, the knowledge of who she was, how she had come to be. She wrapped her arms around herself and bowed her head, whispering, "I feel ugly, dirty. How am I going to live with it?"

Max watched her in fearful silence, watched it happening, and realized that she was moving toward a worse horror than the past few days had ever been, into a morass where there would be no firm footing at all. He had been careless in New York and had almost lost her. He wouldn't lose her again.

"You can't think clearly now, Judith. You shouldn't try. You've traveled through hell but you're no different now than you were four days ago." He leaned close to her, his voice low and filled with restrained passion. "You have always been Leo Weber's daughter from the moment my father brought you here to this house —who knows?—perhaps into this room. From the moment Leo held you in his arms, you were his, his and Leah's. He had to leave you with Cornelius and his wife for the few months the war was to last—he could scarcely bring himself to do that. How can you think back over the years with him and Sheila and doubt the place you held in their hearts? Doubt that you were, in *fact*, their child?"

"Doubt is easy now." The swollen lips twisted in a painful grimace.

It was a fresh, open wound and Max could only guess at what she was feeling and try to fight against it, with his back to the wall, against shadows in her mind that he couldn't lay his hands on.

"Doubt?" he asked, and added with the cruelty of desperation, "Or self-pity? Are you going to let yourself drown in self-pity?"

"He'll have won," she said in a flat voice. "There'll be no public trial, no retribution."

275

"Rosen will take care of that, I promise you. He'll write the story. I have Leah's letter. You can sit down with him—work it out any way you want to."

She didn't seem to hear him. "If I marry you, he'll have won the final victory."

Harshly, Max said, "He'll have won your way, too, won't he? With your reasoning he'll have won, no matter what! Isn't that right? You're going to let him win, bow your head like you're doing now, accept, retire from living altogether? You won't play again either, I suppose, because he loved music! Life's dealt you a blow—all right—you're not the first one. Leo deceived you, so did I—all right—we thought we were doing the best thing. Isn't there something you've forgotten? Something more important than any of this that we're talking about now? What's all the horror been about? Leah—your mother. You speak of his— Wallner's—heritage that makes you feel ugly, dirty. What about Leah's? Doesn't that count for a hell of a lot more?"

Max's passionate voice died off and there was silence in the room for a long time. He watched her anxiously, sensing her terrible struggle through a turmoil of emotion. But when she raised her head finally and looked at him, there was only simple astonishment in her eyes. In a faltering, husky voice, she said, "That counts—yes—that counts. I had forgotten."

Perhaps that was the first time she had thought of it in that way. Perhaps her identification with Leah had grown so strong toward the end that whatever shame, whatever degradation the young girl had felt all those years ago had been accepted by Judith for her to bear as well.

She was bowing her head again but Max put his hand under her chin gently and raised it, bringing it close to his. "That's the important thing, really, isn't it?—that she didn't die in the snow for nothing. Let it be finished, my darling. You can be free of it if you try. You've kept your promise to Leo—more than kept it. As for the other—you're not some fragile thing to break in the wind. You're a big, strong girl." He smiled at his sad attempt at humor. "Strong enough to come to terms with it. Let me help you," he pleaded, still holding the bruised chin in his hand. "Don't shut me out. Let me help."

Later they went down to Cornelius Steen's big, old-fashioned kitchen where the sun, its brilliance reflected from the purity of the new-fallen snow, poured through the windows, lighting every corner, where a fire blazed in the open fireplace and Cornelius's feast covered the long, polished boards of the table. The fragrance of baking bread mingled with the pine scent of the Christmas tree that stood in the corner of the room. This was the heart of the house. Life and love and warmth filled it and Judith sat in the center of it near the fire in a large, upholstered chair that Dieter and Cornelius had brought her from the parlor. She sat rather stiffly, trying, Max could see, to be a part of the placid love that surrounded her. Kees, that noble beast, as Cornelius called him, seemed to have adopted her. He lay sprawled at her feet, eyes closed, snoring softly, one paw placed protectively over her foot. Mariet was balancing precariously against her knees, holding a leg in the air, turning it to show to best advantage one of the new skates Cornelius had given her for Christmas. Dieter sat silently at the table, toying with a cup of coffee, his adoring eyes never leaving her face. The boy's own face looked pale and quite severe for he had grown a great deal older in the past twenty-four hours. He would never be quite so young nor so romantic again. The thought struck Max with a sudden shock that was not altogether pleasant: he's her cousin. He has a claim on her. And then, immediately: I, too, I have a claim on her. His eyes went back to Judith—his awkward, graceful, beautiful

Judith—made for music, not vengeance. He watched her with a kind of yearning, thinking how thin she had grown, her cheek bones, even under the swelling, looked sharp. The dark head seemed too heavy for the long, slender neck to support. Mariet had put her leg across Judith's knees and was unlacing the skate while Judith rested one bandaged hand lightly on the child's shoulder. She must have sensed his eyes on her for she lifted her head and they looked at each other across the room.

It's finished, he had told her, you're free. And they both had known he was lying. Max didn't deceive himself that they would ever be the same together again and only time would answer the question of whether she would be able to put it into some kind of perspective that she could live with. The haunted look was there in her eyes now. Leo Weber had, after all, sacrificed her to lay his own ghosts, to absolve his own guilt. Of course it wasn't as simple as that. Nothing ever was. He wondered sadly if Weber could have done it any other way or if Judith would have allowed him to had she known the whole truth from the beginning.

Her eyes held his for a long time until a faint smile touched her lips. It was very faint and perhaps it was his imagination, or his longing, that made him see something sunny in it, something positive. Whatever it was, it was there and it was for him. At least he wasn't a stranger anymore, and he smiled gladly back.

THE INTERNATIONAL BESTSELLER!

KG 200

J. D. GILMAN
AND
JOHN CLIVE

A Luftwaffe squadron that spoke perfect English.
If they'd succeeded, we'd all be speaking perfect German.

"This novel of aerial assassination, inspired
by actual historical events, booms right along to
an explosive finale."
Publishers Weekly

"Masterful ... the implications are spine-chilling."
The Denver Post

Selected by 2 Book Clubs

Avon ◆ 39115/$2.25

KG 9-78